always him

CORA ROSE

credits

Editor: Angela O'Connell

Cover photography by Michelle Lancaster @lanefotograf

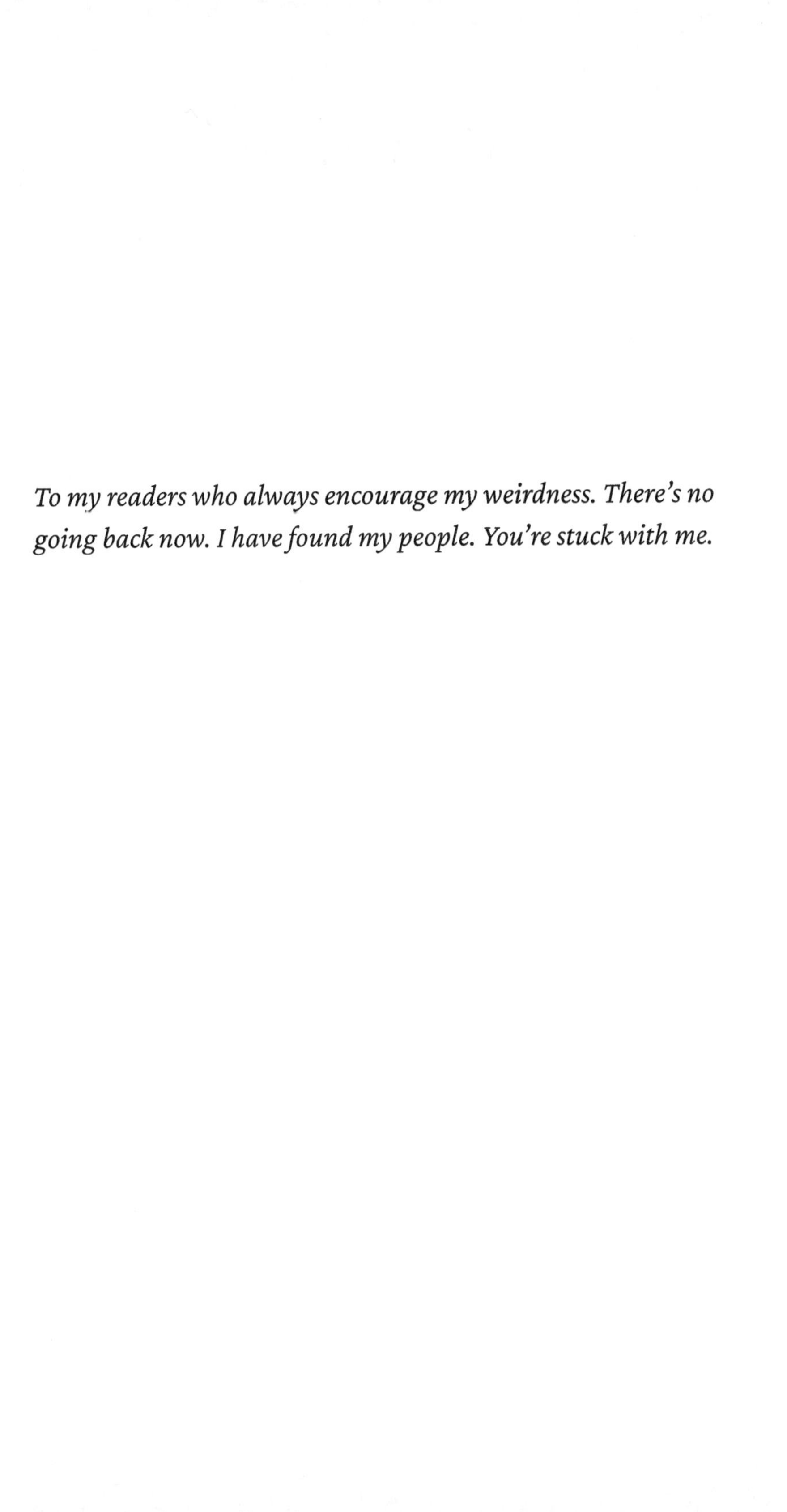

To my readers who always encourage my weirdness. There's no going back now. I have found my people. You're stuck with me.

preface

I am obsessed with these two. **Obsessed**. Their story flowed from me, just like Logan and Theo's did in *Until Him*.

I hope you love them just as much as I do.

Content warning: Landon is an amputee who struggles with mental health and internalized ableism regarding his disability.

one

LANDON

THE COLD WINTER air nips at my skin as I lean back against the hood of my car. In the distance, I can make out the twinkling lights of the Northern California city of Santa Cruz. It's a small town located at the northern tip of Monterey Bay. Just south of San Francisco. It's a beautiful place to live, right near the redwood forests, the Santa Cruz Mountains, and the Pacific Ocean.

It's nearly pitch-dark on this hilltop that Finn drove us up to. All I can see is the moon peeking out from behind the clouds and, of course, the light from my phone, counting down the minutes until the New Year.

"Four more minutes," I announce, glancing at my best friend sitting at my side. I've known him for countless years, the two of us inseparable from the day we met. My older brother, Logan, is also part of our trio of friends, but there is just something about Finn, something that's always drawn me to him.

For as long as I can remember it's been like this. I'm caught up in his orbit, never able to pull myself away. Even when we lived apart, I felt him pulling me, reaching for me.

Finn shifts next to me as one of his arms wraps around my waist, his hand landing on my hip, and I lean into his touch.

He's so warm, like a heated blanket. I just want to snuggle underneath him and never leave.

I love how he holds me and touches me every chance he gets. He's always been particularly affectionate with me, but he seems to have really latched on after my car accident.

I look down at my legs extended before me, one flesh and bone and the other a prosthetic from the knee down. I remember that terrible night over a year ago. The night that changed everything, some things for the worse, but mostly for the better. I have to focus on the positive, the silver lining, or else I'll break down.

Looking at Finn, I know he's it. The ray of sunshine in an otherwise terrible memory.

I glance down at my phone again.

Three more minutes.

"So, who are we gonna kiss when the clock strikes twelve?" I tease, smiling and nudging Finn lightly. His large body barely moves an inch, though. He's so strong, his broad shoulders bigger than mine, his legs thick with muscle. You can tell he works out just by looking at him. He's a swimmer and a water polo player at his college. I've seen him play countless times, the way his abdomen flexes as he shoots out of the water, his biceps bulging as he launches the ball across the pool. It's impressive, really. I don't think I could ever do that. By nature, I'm a runner.

I glance down at my leg again. Well, I was a runner. I have to wait to be fitted for a new prosthetic before I'm able to move like that again.

Finn goes still; I'm not sure he's even breathing as my words linger between us.

Kiss. Who are we going to kiss?

I glance up at him and reach out, running a hand through his dark-brown hair, cropped close to the sides of his head. It used to be longer, but he cut it before winter break.

He looks good all the time and I can't help but feel a little jealous. With those dark eyes, those high cheekbones, and those lips. So fucking handsome. Yeah, I can be straight and still think these things objectively. I have eyes. Sue me.

And to be honest, it wouldn't be a hardship to kiss him.

Yeah, we're both straight, and we've never done anything sexual before. But really, what's a friendly kiss between buddies? We already cuddle all the time so a peck on the lips doesn't seem that strange.

"Who says a kiss is mandatory?" he asks softly.

I roll my eyes and nestle in closer to him. He's always so serious, always overthinking.

"It's not a new year if we don't kiss someone. My dad says it's bad luck not to."

He turns his head toward me and his dark eyes, which I can't see clearly at the moment, are watching me intently. I lean over and nuzzle my face against his jaw, the stubble there abrading my skin.

Yes, I realize this isn't typical for straight dudes, but I do it anyways. Fuck everyone else. I like being affectionate with Finn.

I crave it.

"We'll kiss," I say, pulling away slightly. "You and me. My family has enough bad luck without throwing this into the mix."

He swallows loudly. "I don't think that's a good idea."

I cock my head and watch him. "Why not? Does it gross you out, thinking of your lips on mine?"

He runs his free hand over his mouth, his fingers digging into my hip. "No."

"Good. Then we'll do it."

For some reason, I didn't want him to turn me down. It would hurt my feelings a little bit. I mean, we do almost everything else, what's one itty bitty kiss between friends?

He's silent for a long minute. The sound of the wind moving through the trees is the only thing I can hear, and then suddenly he whispers, "How many more minutes till midnight?"

I click my phone on. "Seconds," I say softly.

His hand tightens on me, and I keep my eyes on the phone, excited for the year to come. For what could be.

When the ticker reaches ten, I start counting down, and when I get to one, our heads turn. His lips are just centimeters from mine, and I feel his soft exhale on my skin.

Without a second thought, I close the distance, leaning forward and pressing my lips to his. They're smooth and warm, and like everything else having to do with Finn, so comforting.

At the touch of our mouths, Finn's body stiffens, his tense hand locking me in place, holding me against him.

After a few moments, we pull away and stare at each other. Energy crackles between us and I let out a shaky breath.

"That wasn't so bad, was it?" I murmur, my words nearly floating away with the breeze.

His tongue darts out and swipes at his lips, his hand still clenched on my waist.

"No," he breathes.

Huh, is he okay? He seems nervous. Maybe he hated it—kissing another dude. Kissing *me*. But he'd never tell me, not wanting to hurt my feelings.

Don't hurt my feelings, Finn.

"You sure? You don't look like it was okay," I ask, reaching out and running my hand across the line of his jaw.

"It was fine," he says and then faces forward again, pulling me even further into him. I'm so close that I'm nearly on top of his lap at this point.

"I mean, it had to be better than *fine*, right?" I huff out a laugh. "I've been told I have a way with my mouth."

He digs his fingers into my side and I chuckle.

"You're such a smart ass," he mutters.

"You love my ass," I reply, and Finn pinches my side lightly.

"Shut up."

"You said it in your sleep one night," I say, laughing. "It's forever burned into my brain. I can't forget that shit."

He grumbles a little under his breath and I lean into him, my lips brushing his stubbly jaw.

"You dream about it. You dream about me. Admit it." I love teasing him. It's just about my favorite thing, getting him all riled.

He shifts and then I'm suddenly on my back, Finn's large body on top of mine. He cradles the back of my head with both hands, so I don't knock it against the hood as he stares down at me.

"I told you already," he says gruffly, his heavy leg pinning mine down. "Dreams don't mean anything. They're just dreams. Nonsensical nonsense."

I smile widely at him and run my hands up his arms. "That's okay, boo. I know I'm irresistible."

I can't see his eyes clearly, but I know he's rolling them.

He always says I'm too ridiculous. Yes, well, so is he. Dreaming about my ass and then pretending like he didn't.

No takesie-backsies, Finn.

"You going to keep being an asshole or can I let you up?" he asks, his thumb brushing against my temple.

I lean into the touch a little, loving his hands on me.

"No, I'm done. I've learned my lesson, Daddy; let me up."

He huffs a laugh and moves off of me. "Jesus, you're getting worse and worse. I can't imagine you in fifty years."

I snort a laugh. "Yeah, well you love me just as I am. I have no incentive to change."

He helps me sit up and tugs me into his side once more. I lean my head against his shoulder, and we just sit there for ages, my eyelids growing heavy with sleep. There is only one place I feel safe these days. And it's wherever Finn is.

"Alright, Landon, time to go. You need to get to bed," Finn says, his mouth muffled by my hair.

I sit upright slowly, blinking at him. Without thought or planning, I press my lips to his once more. Everything with Finn just feels so natural. It doesn't feel wrong or weird at all. It feels absolutely right.

Of course, he lets me do it. He never says no to me.

I pull back, our mouths parting, and I scoot to the edge of the hood.

"Alright, drive me home, Finn," I say because I'm still not comfortable behind a wheel with my prosthetic. It will take a while to get there. In the meantime, I have Uber and Finn.

Always Finn.

Always him.

"Yeah," he breathes, clearing his throat and walking me to the passenger side of the car.

He pulls the door to his car open, helping me inside, and when we drive down the dirt road back to civilization, I just turn my head and watch him until I fall asleep.

* * *

We enter my apartment, my body leaning against his as we stumble to my bedroom. I feel his hands on me, pulling my shirt over my head, tugging my pants down my legs, and gently removing my prosthetic right before I flop down on the bed clad in only my underwear.

"Always trying to get me naked," I mutter with a laugh.

"You wish," he grumbles. "Can you scoot over?"

I'm sideways on the bed, sprawled out like a starfish, taking up the whole mattress. But I don't even bother moving because I know he'll get in beside me and move me just where he wants me.

He makes everything right. All the crooked parts even out when he's around.

"Don't even know why I bother asking," he mutters, and then I feel the bed dip. He's crawling up next to me, pulling me up against his warm, hard body and I become putty in his hands.

We started doing this months ago—sharing a bed, cuddling against each other all night.

I don't hate it.

I fucking need it.

My best friend in all the world curled up next to me, feels like home.

I turn over and fling my arm over his bare chest, burrowing my head right into his shoulder, smelling the scent of his deodorant. A contented sigh escapes me.

"Happy New Year, Finn," I mumble into his skin.

"Happy New Year, Landon," he says softly, his lips pressing onto the top of my head.

And that is how we fall asleep.

* * *

I wake up pressed against him, almost on top of him. I never really move far, and he doesn't seem to mind. His hand is splayed across my lower back, the tips of his fingers tucked into the waistband of my boxers. My hand is resting right over his heart.

I can feel it thumping against my palm and my lips turn up at the corners.

This routine of falling asleep in each other's arms happened organically. It was just the natural progression of our close relationship.

My family is what you might call "overly affectionate". My parents are big huggers and cuddlers. So, Finn and I grew up together, hugging and holding hands. I remember sleepovers with my head in his lap, just talking or playing video games for hours, his hands in my hair, his fingers grazing my cheek or the shell of my ear. Finn's dad isn't affectionate like mine though, so it took a while to drag him over to the dark side. But once he saw how awesome it was, he just opened himself up to me.

After the accident, however, that's when things evolved.

He was with me every step of the way through my recovery, holding me, comforting me.

I needed Finn in those moments more than I needed air.

When I finally moved into my apartment near my college campus eight months after the accident—a move made to offer me more independence—Finn would drive out and visit me on the weekends.

In the living area of my place is a small pull-out sofa but the mattress is lumpy and uncomfortable and every night that he slipped out of my bed and moved onto it, my heart withered. So, after a few weekends of guilt, I just invited him to stay in my bed, all night.

And fuck, I'm glad I did.

We had started on opposite sides of the mattress but always woke up in the middle of the night or the morning plastered against each other. I wasn't surprised this happened. I'd always been snuggly with Finn, and after the accident, with him holding me constantly, touching me, soothing me, I just grew used to it.

My body craved it.

So after the first few nights, I stopped pretending like I didn't want it, like I didn't want to fall asleep in his arms.

From there on out, we just started the night wrapped around each other. We stopped pretending like we didn't need it.

We have fully accepted it now.

I feel my cock hard against his thigh and I press it against him to relieve some of the ache.

Yes, I admit this is a little odd, but it happens, and there's nothing I can do about it.

The first time we'd woken up with our cocks pressed together, we laughed about it and then joked about it over coffee. Well, I joked about it, mostly. Finn just had that crease in-between his eyebrows until I made him crack a smile.

It's not a big deal, Finn. It means nothing. We're both straight. Just friends with dicks and morning wood. It doesn't have to be weird.

"Mmm, morning," Finn says, his hand flexing against my back, his body turning slightly to pull me right up onto him.

I go willingly, pressing my cheek against his chest, my ear right over the thumping of his heart.

His hands slide up and down my back and I just sigh against him.

I am dreading the end of winter break when he has to

leave me again. I want him here with me all the time. I'm hoping once he finishes college next semester, he'll move in with me. I want to be roommates with him, want him near me all the time.

As it is, his clothes are in my closet and dresser drawers, and his toiletries are in the bathroom. He's all but moved in. I'm going to be so sad when he packs up his stuff and leaves.

I can't think about it too hard or my chest pinches painfully.

"What do you want to do today?" he grunts from beneath me, not realizing where my mind has gone.

What do I want to do? Stay in bed with him all day and snooze. Just use his body like a La-Z-Boy recliner.

"Coffee," I mutter and then lean up a little and stare down at him.

His dark chocolate-brown eyes meet mine and he smirks.

And just because I can—because why the fuck not? —I press my lips to his. It's a short, gentle peck and then I pull back.

Finn's body tenses under me, his eyes widening slightly, and my eyebrows meet in question.

"Do you hate it? Kissing me?" I ask, trying to read the look in his eyes.

His gaze moves away from mine, focusing on the ceiling, and he sighs, his body deflating and relaxing a bit.

"No. It's...fine."

"Are you sure?"

"Yeah, Landon. I'm sure."

I smile widely and then roll off of him.

"Good, because I'll be doing it all the time now probably."

Finn throws an arm across his eyes and huffs a little, shaking his head. "God help me."

"No one can help you now. You know how it is with this family. Once we claim you, you're ours," I reply as I reach for my prosthetic, but before I can put it on, Finn is in front of me, squatting down a little.

"Hell no," he says, his arms spreading wide.

I know exactly what he wants. I wrap my arms and leg around him and he picks me up, his hands on my ass, jostling me slightly as he gets me situated against him.

Look, he doesn't need to do this, but I let him anyways. It reminds me of how he would carry me around during my recovery, how gentle he was with me. Through the trauma of losing my leg, I craved his touch, those moments he'd cradle me in his arms.

We move into the bathroom and he sets me on the cool countertop as I reach for my toothbrush.

He stays beside me, my thigh hitting his hip as we brush our teeth, and when we're done, Finn helps me stand. With my hands clasped onto the counter behind me, he tugs my boxers down.

"Shower and then coffee?" he asks, helping me hop to the tub. Inside is a shower chair that has saved me on multiple occasions. Who knew these things existed until I needed one?

Not me, that's who.

"Yeah, and food. Feed me, Finn. I'm getting hangry," I say, and he smirks at me.

I lean against his chest as he turns on the shower, testing the water with his hand until it runs warm. My palm moves across his bare stomach, and I feel the muscles ripple and tighten under my touch.

I love it, how smooth and strong he is.

"Alright, in you go," he says, helping me onto the shower chair. "I'll get your prosthetic."

"No need, you can just carry me everywhere, Finn. Wear me like a backpack," I say with a wink.

He rolls his eyes and then without another word, he slides the shower curtain in place, leaving me to wash alone.

For a moment, I just sit there, remembering the days he'd shower with me. He was never fully naked, but he'd hold me from behind, his hands sliding the soap along the planes of my body.

I wish he'd come back in and do it again, but I know that would probably be too much to ask. I'm capable of doing all of this stuff myself now. I live here by myself most of the time, after all. Finn just seems to enjoy helping me, and I'll be honest, I love all the attention. I'm a slut for it, as you can tell.

But I don't want to push my luck, so I quickly wash myself and get out of the shower on my own. I use the counter to balance myself as I dry off and hop to the door. When I fling it open and see Finn standing on the other side, his arms folded across his chest and his eyebrow arched at me, I just roll my eyes.

"I don't need you to cart me around like an invalid. This is the twenty-first century. I have a very high-tech and expensive prosthetic I can wear."

"Yes, well, you told me not to bring your prosthetic and I didn't want you to slip and die trying to hop around on one fucking leg."

I snort at the thought. Because that has happened before. Learning to move around on one leg is no joke. I have had many bumps and bruises from trying to learn to move around while missing a limb.

Finn mutters under his breath and then leans down and pulls me into his arms despite my weak and not very convincing protests. The towel drops away from my waist as he does so and puddles on the ground, forgotten.

I press my naked body against him, wishing he wasn't wearing a shirt so I could rub myself all over him. For the short five-step walk to my room, I just nuzzle my face against his neck and inhale him.

Even before a shower, he has a unique scent—earth, evergreen tree, and chlorine. He even smells like home.

He sets me gently on the bed and I don't even bother covering my dick up. It just hangs limply between my legs as he walks over to the dresser and tosses me my boxers, a pair of pants, and a shirt.

"I'll be back," he says and then disappears.

I hear the shower turn on as I pull the t-shirt over my head and then work my pants on. Let me tell you, this missing leg thing was a learning process. Who knew that putting pants on with a prosthetic could be so hard?

I figured it out though. First, I put the pants on over the prosthetic, then attach the prosthetic to the end of my leg, and lastly, pull the jeans the rest of the way up.

It took a lot of frustration and tears to figure this shit out. Plus a lot of YouTube videos. Thank god for the internet.

When Finn reemerges with a towel around his tapered waist, he grabs his clothes from the dresser and drops the towel.

I sit and watch him dress, taking comfort in the familiarity of it—the lines of his body and the way his muscles bunch beneath his skin, how fluidly he moves.

When he's done, he turns around and startles a little.

Yes, Finn, I'm staring at you creepily.

"What?" he asks, reaching out for my hands and pulling me up.

"I was just admiring your hot ass."

"Jesus, you can't say shit like that to me."

"Try and stop me, Finn," I reply and he just sighs in resignation.

"Yeah, alright, smartass. Ready to go?" he asks, his arm moving around my waist.

I lean against him, my hand sliding across his back. "Yeah, let's go. You don't want to see me hangry, Finn."

"Yeah, too late for that."

two

LANDON

"DO YOU FEEL MORE HUMAN NOW?" Finn asks as I stare at him over the mug filled with coffee.

We are tucked into an oversized chair in the local coffee shop, my leg thrown over his.

He's leaned back, his large hand cradling a mug as he watches me with a smirk.

"Slightly," I say, taking a long, indulgent sip. "I probably need another cup to be fully functioning."

"There's barely any coffee in there. It's just sugar and milk."

"God, but who cares, it's so damn good," I say, my tongue running across my upper lip, removing the foam I'm sure is stuck there. Finn's eyes track the movement before shifting away, looking intently at the people milling around the pickup counter.

"Got any more of that scone left for me?" I ask, drawing his attention back to me.

Finn breaks a piece off of his blueberry scone, and instead of letting go of my mug, I just open my mouth and let him slide the piece right inside. His fingers brush against my tongue and I close my lips around them.

Yes, we've been mistaken for a couple before. I just laughed it off because what? Men can't show affection without being a couple? I hate that shit. I just want to be held and fed.

I want to be cared for.

Finn does that for me. He always has, and hopefully always will.

I could give two shits about people and their assumptions. All that matters is that I'm happy and he's happy.

"God, they make the best scones here," I say around my bite. "Like, how are they so delicious?"

Finn pops a piece into his mouth and rests his hand on my thigh, massaging it lightly.

"No idea. But you won't be finding out."

"They should really share their recipe," I grumble, glancing at the counter where a cute blonde girl is serving customers. "Maybe that new chick will hand it over if I ask nicely enough." I waggle my eyebrows.

Finn's hand tightens on my leg slightly and I laugh softly. "Hey, I gotta put what God gave me to good use."

I gesture to my body and Finn's eyes slide across it. I mean I'm not as hot as Finn, but I got stuff to work with. I'm a bit taller than average with lean musculature, and even though I'm not as wide or as strong as Finn and my brother,

Logan, I used to run track so I have some definition. Even if some of it slipped away while I was healing. But I've always been active, and I've been slowly building it back up.

Plus, my face is nice, I think.

I never had any complaints at least.

The only thing I've struggled with confidence-wise is losing my leg. I joke about my disability a lot; making light of the situation helps me to cope. But honestly, sometimes, I just don't feel whole anymore. It makes me sad that I can't do some of the things I used to do and I worry that people will think I'm a burden. I'm working on that in therapy though, and I know one day I'll meet someone who will love me as I am, missing limb and all.

Maybe soon I'll start dating.

But then again, it doesn't really appeal to me. I haven't really looked at someone like that in a while. Not since the accident really. I know that the trauma of losing my leg, of accepting that it happened, is part of the reason I've been so reluctant to put myself back out there. The other reason is... huh, I'm not really sure what else is holding me back. But to be honest, I don't really care enough to analyze it at the moment. I'm happy enough with how things are now.

Finn removes his hand and gestures toward the counter.

"You're welcome to try and pry it out of her, but you know how they are. They don't share their recipes. You can flutter your pretty eyes at them all day long, but it won't help."

"Oh, you think I have pretty eyes?" I ask, fluttering my eyelids at him dramatically.

He huffs a small laugh and then gestures toward the girl behind the counter again. "Go ahead. Do it."

Meh. I have no desire to get up and flirt with someone right now. It sounds exhausting. So I just scoot a little closer to Finn, practically on top of him now.

"Later," I say, sipping at my drink again. "Anyways, did you know Logan and Theo are going to be at my parents' house for a week? They're bringing Curie."

Finn throws back the rest of his drink—this man does not savor coffee like I do—and says, "Yeah, we should hang with them when they're here. I know Logan has been bugging me about it. Wants us to get to know Theo better or some shit."

"Yeah, and man, they are so cute together, right? Ugh, the way they look at each other," I say and Finn shrugs.

"Yeah, I guess."

"I mean, it was kind of a weird start, but I like Theo. He's quiet, but nice. I think he's good for Logan."

Finn doesn't say anything and I let him stew for a few moments. I know he struggled with the two of them being together. I was there while he was processing all of it. He felt like Logan was being used and hadn't liked Theo in the beginning, but now, I think he realizes how much they need each other. How well they complement each other.

I finish off my latte and then let Finn feed me the last of the scone, his fingers lingering against my lips as I chew.

I purse them a little, kissing his fingertips lightly, and let out a sharp laugh. Because his eyes narrow in annoyance and something else I can't quite make out.

Well, too bad, Finn. I'm kissing you now. Try and stop me.

"Alright." I sit up a little and pat my stomach. "I'm going to order a cup to go and then we can go to my parents'. Dad has been bugging us to stop by."

Finn moves to stand, but I press a hand to his chest.

"I can do it, Finn."

He rolls his lips between his teeth and nods. It's a delicate balance with him. He wants me to be independent, but he struggles with letting me go. I get it. I do. I want him with me every step of the way, but I know he won't always be there. One day, he'll find someone else, and I'll be left to fend for myself.

That thought makes my chest ache, so I shove it aside.

I do that really well. I love sweeping things under rugs. I have an extensive collection of brooms.

I push up and walk toward the counter, only vaguely realizing I'm walking on my prosthetic. Learning to use it was a fucking chore, but I'm glad I persevered.

"Hey," I say offering the girl behind the counter a small smile. "Can I get a peppermint mocha to go?"

Her cheeks flush and I feel a little flutter in my chest. It's been ages since I've had sex and she's cute.

Still, I'm not sure I'm ready for anything yet. Not sure I'm ready to put myself out there.

I scan my phone to pay for it and then lean in a little. "And hey, any way I can grab the recipe for those scones?"

Can you really blame me for trying?

She bats her lashes at me but before she can tell me anything, I feel Finn's hand around my waist. Instinctively,

I lean into him, and her eyes fall to where our bodies connect.

"Oh," she says, clearing her throat. "Right. You guys make a cute couple."

I don't even bother correcting her. I just send her a wink, and Finn and I move to the pick-up counter.

"You shouldn't let people think we're together," Finn says, his arm still around me. Yeah, well, if he doesn't want people to think we're together maybe he should be the first to step away.

Not that I want him to. I want him to stay right here, next to me. I don't even know what I'd do if he pulled away from me.

I glance up at him and meet his serious stare.

"It's too hard to explain. Let them have their assumptions. I'll probably never see her again anyway."

"We can just say we're best friends. It's the truth, right?"

"Yeah, sure," I say and then, because I feel like it, I lean into him and press my lips to his slightly open mouth. He tastes like cinnamon and vanilla.

"Landon," Finn scolds softly, his hand tightening against me. "You.... Fuck. You can't keep doing that."

My eyebrows slam together. "Why not?"

Finn swallows and looks away right as my drink is placed on the counter. He grabs it and hands it to me.

"Never mind. Doesn't matter," he mutters and then we walk outside. The cold air nips at my exposed skin and I pull my sweatshirt sleeves down over my hands, carefully cradling my coffee between them.

When we make it to Finn's car, he opens the passenger

side door for me, but before I slide inside, I ask, "If you want me to stop, I will. I never want to make you feel uncomfortable."

His jaw works back and forth as he eyes me, and he shakes his head. "I'm not uncomfortable. Forget I said anything. It's fine."

"You sure?"

"Yeah, Landon. I'm good."

I offer him a small smile and sink into the car. Yeah, maybe best friends don't kiss like that, but I fucking like it. I don't know why I do, but I don't want to stop. Just like everything else Finn and I do, we do it because we want to.

I like kissing him. It feels nice and it's just one more way I feel close to him.

I don't know if I'll ever feel this way about another person for as long as I live.

three

LANDON

"YOU'RE HOME!" my dad, Basil, exclaims as if we hadn't just seen him a week ago for Christmas. "My boys."

He pulls me in for a bear hug and then lunges for Finn. He lifts him up, which is no small feat and Finn's feet dangle above the ground for a moment.

"Dad, are you high again?" I ask, taking note of his red-rimmed eyes. He's either smoked a bowl or he's been crying. Knowing him, it could go either way, really.

Or maybe he did both. He gets very emotional when he disappears into his shed for some quality weed time.

"Mom and I did smoke a bit and then we got to looking at pictures of you and Logan when you were babies and we both got a little teary-eyed."

I roll my eyes and watch Finn move into the kitchen just

23

as my mom walks in from outside, their baby goat, Vincent, trailing behind her.

I see my mom's red eyes and bite back a laugh.

Yeah, the two of them are wasted. It's ridiculous. Sometimes, I swear to god, they're just oversized teenagers with a vegetable patch and farm animals.

"My babies," she says, wrapping me in a long-drawn-out hug, the goat bleating in the background, before smothering Finn. "How are my boys?"

Finn eyes me and then arches an eyebrow.

"We're fine," he says, leaning back against the counter and eyeing the cat tree my dad has been working on lately. It keeps getting bigger and bigger. Pretty soon it's going to take up the entire living room. My dad calls it the kitty mansion. Theo's cat, who visits from time to time, has it made.

Only the best for the sweet girl.

She's not all that sweet if you ask me. She stole my keys the last time we were all here. I still haven't found them; had to have a new set made.

"And how was New Year's? What did you do?" my mom asks.

"We went to the overlook," I say, resting my head on Finn's shoulder.

My mom clasps her hands in front of her, smiling crookedly. Yeah, she had more than a smoke. She must have been in there for a few hours. Maybe ate an edible or two, as well.

"That sounds lovely," she says, and my dad sniffles a little, his eyes on the two of us.

"And who did you kiss when the clock struck midnight? It's bad luck to not kiss on New Year's, you know."

"I kissed Finn," I say, and Finn slaps a hand onto his forehead, his cheeks flushing red.

"Don't tell them that," he grumbles, and I smirk at him.

"Why not?"

"*Because.*"

"Um, that is not an answer. We both know this."

"Because we will never let either of you live it down!" my dad nearly squeals. "I am so happy for you two. *Finally!*"

My eyebrows slam together and my cheeks flush. "What?" Now I'm a little confused. Because what the fuck is he talking about?

My dad waves a hand between us. "You two are finally together. After all this time!"

I shake my head. "No, um, we're just friends. Friends who kissed on New Year's. I didn't want any bad luck to come my way if we didn't."

Finn sighs loudly next to me and I nudge him with my elbow.

"Back me up on this," I hiss, but he just stares blankly at me.

"Oh my god," I say and then lean forward and smack my lips against his. "See? It's not a big deal."

My parents just stare at me, perplexed, and Finn closes his eyes, slowly shaking his head.

"It's not normal, Landon," he murmurs. "Kissing me like that."

"Well, who said we were normal?" I reply, throwing my hands in the air. "Normal is boring and I mean, look around us. Take a good look. Does any of this look fucking normal to you?"

Vincent bleats again loudly as if in agreement.

Thank you, Vincent. You get me.

My parents blink and blink, too high for this conversation. So, I just link my hand with Finn's and say, "We will be outside. When you're sober, come join us."

I pull my best friend out the backdoor and he chuckles as the cold winter air bites into our exposed skin. My lips turn up in a smile. Fucking ridiculous family.

"You shouldn't have done that. Their brains are mush right now. They will think they conjured it up. It's going to fuck with their minds and with how you guys never actually talk about things..." he snorts. "They're going to be so confused."

"Well, maybe we should make out and really throw them for a loop. That could be fun."

He sighs and pulls me into him, threading his hands through my shoulder-length hair and pressing his cheek to the top of my head.

"That sounds like a terrible idea."

"Even if it were to fuck with their minds?" I ask, peeking up at him.

His eyes meet mine and he wets his lips. "Yes, even to fuck with them. It's a terrible, awful idea."

"Hmm," I say and then press my cheek to his chest. "I'll think about it. I think I can convince you to do what I want."

He huffs. "You always do. I don't know why I even bother fighting it."

I turn my head to glance at the shed. Speaking of...

"Want to smoke too? I mean, what else is there to do? If we go inside, my dad might rope us into a project."

"Yeah, but being high when your parents are high is never a good idea."

"Yes, but when has that ever stopped us?"

Without even waiting for his refusal, I pull him to the shed on the far end of the property.

When we enter, the scent of weed and soil permeates the air and I push Finn down into one of the camping chairs before moving to grab a joint from the cabinet.

I light it up and take a deep inhale, ignoring the other chair across from him and plopping down in Finn's lap. I hold the smoke in my lungs while gently cupping his jaw in my hand, pressing my lips to his, and exhaling slowly.

Our lips brush softly as I let the smoke pass from my mouth into his.

He inhales it, our eyes locked, and I watch as his pupils dilate in the dim light.

One of his hands slides around my waist, his pinkie slipping under the hem to caress the skin of my stomach and I lean further into him.

I offer up the joint and he takes it from me, placing it between his lips and inhaling deeply. He leans forward and presses his lips against mine.

The smoke shifts into my mouth and I move against him to get a better angle, threading my hands through his hair, holding his open mouth against mine.

We just breathe into each other, my mind growing foggy like the cold mornings in winter up here when the ocean pulls the clouds over the bay.

Finn's hands slip under my shirt and brush up my back and I shudder under the touch, just loving the feel of him against me.

The joint falls to the ground, snuffing itself out, and still, we don't move, our lips pressed together. Everything else just fades away.

It's just him and me.

My eyes flutter closed and I inhale *him.*

A sudden loud bleating has my eyes popping open and I turn toward the door to see Vincent standing on the threshold, his little rectangle-shaped goat pupils watching us.

I can't help but grin at him as I lay my head against Finn's shoulder.

"My parents are neglecting him," I say.

"He's a fucking goat. He could survive on grass and trash."

I let out a loud chuckle.

"They're never just animals with my dad. They're like children to him." I push myself up, moving to where Vincent is standing. I scoop him up and cradle him to my chest.

"Let's go find Dad," I tell the tiny goat.

I don't even need to glance behind me to know that Finn is following me. I just know he is.

A hand slips around my waist and my heart flutters in my chest.

See?

He's always right there.

We make our way through the backyard, past the greenhouse and chicken coop, and toward the backdoor when I hear it. A loud rhythmic thumping vibrates through the windows.

"Oh, Jesus, for real?" I mutter, and Finn lets out a dark laugh. "They couldn't wait until later?"

The notorious sex playlist—90s R&B—is blaring from the speakers inside the house and immediately I know exactly what my parents are doing right now.

I shudder.

There are things my ears cannot unhear. There are things my eyes cannot unsee.

"Let's just go for a walk while they get it out of their system," Finn says. "You want to grab the leash for this guy?"

He looks at Vincent and I shake my head. "I'm not going in there. No fucking way."

"Fine. If you insist, but if I see something nasty, I won't be coming back here with you ever again."

"Like they'd let you avoid them. You're like a son to them," I say as he disappears inside.

A moment later he reappears with Vincent's leash. He clips it onto the goat's collar, and I set him on the ground, the three of us making our way to the side gate and out to the road.

My parents live outside the suburbs in an unincorporated part of the city. Mainly they chose the boonies so that my dad could raise his chickens without complaint and have enough land to grow his vegetables. And it's a good thing because Vincent is a loud asshole when he wants to be.

"How long do you think we'll be out here?" he asks as we step over a large crack in the pavement

I side-eye Finn. "God, I hope they're quick about it.

Sometimes they go through the entire playlist. That's a lot of TLC and Color Me Badd."

He shoves his hands into the front pocket of his hoodie, and I frown a little. Reaching out, I tug one of them out and link my hand with his. Pfft. Trying to hide it from me.

He squeezes it a little and then pulls me against him, his hand sliding around my hip. Where it belongs.

We walk down the road, letting Vincent graze on the weeds growing from the pavement, and then we turn around and make our way back home. Thankfully, when we arrive, the playlist is off and my parents are in the kitchen, snacking on chips.

I let Vincent off his leash, and he prances around the house, bleating happily.

He's probably glad they're done too. His poor little goat eyes. The things he must have seen.

"Oh, you took your time," my mom says with a smile, and I waggle a finger at her. "We couldn't find you."

"I wanted to make sure we didn't see anything horrifying. So, we left."

My dad chews loudly and shrugs, "No need to be snarky. You know how we get."

I tilt my head at him and sigh. "Don't remind me. It's disgusting. So, what's the plan?"

"We ordered pizza, wings, garlic rolls, one of those giant chocolate chip cookies, and a gallon of soda," Dad says. "It should be here soon. Want to watch a movie while we pig out?"

I glance up at Finn and he shrugs. "Sure."

So, we all settle on the couch, and when the food arrives,

we dig in. As I scoot between Finn's legs and rest my head against his chest, his hands settle around my waist and I let my eyes sink closed, feeling warm and safe in his arms.

When we arrive back at my apartment, I'm almost dead to the world. It's later than I thought. My parents had a hard time letting us leave. My dad kept showing me the additions to the cat tree and then spent a bunch of time showing us all the tricks Vincent can do. Spoiler alert: he can do zero tricks. Unless blinking and cocking his head in confusion is considered a trick.

Now it's almost midnight and my eyes are heavy. Every day, I wake with so much energy, ready to conquer shit, but by nighttime, I'm pooped. Dead to the world. Lights fucking out.

I flop back onto the bed and immediately Finn starts to undress me, pulling down my pants and removing my prosthetic before tugging my shirt off.

"Boxers too," I grumble because I just want to sleep naked tonight. I want to feel the cool sheets against my skin, want to feel free. Feel Finn everywhere.

My best friend hesitates a moment before his fingers slowly tug them off, leaving me blessedly naked.

"God," I mutter, letting my hands travel across the sheets. "Sleeping naked is like the best thing ever."

Finn huffs a laugh and I watch as he undresses, tossing his shirt and pants into the hamper.

"You can sleep naked too," I tell him.

He shakes his head, running a hand through his hair. "Not a good idea. What if there's an earthquake? Do you want to be running around bare-assed?"

I try to roll my eyes but they're too tired. Finn crawls in next to me and pulls me into his arms. I wrap myself around him, throwing my leg over his, and tuck my face right into his armpit before letting sleep pull me under.

* * *

I wake up suddenly, my body thrumming with need. My eyes take in the still-dark room and I can hear heavy rain pounding against the window.

Fuck, it's been a while since I've gotten off. Don't even get me started on sex. The last girl I fucked was right before my accident. I haven't been with anyone since.

I shift against Finn, my ass brushing against his hard dick and his arm tightens around me.

"You awake?" he whispers, his voice thick with sleep.

"Yeah."

"You okay?" he asks.

"Yeah, just.... Fuck, I'm horny. It's been a while. Too long. My dick needs a little attention, I guess."

Finn stiffens behind me, and I stretch out against him, my cock brushing against the sheets. A zing slips up my spine and a soft moan escapes my mouth.

"Would you mind if I just got myself off real quick?" I murmur.

Finn doesn't answer right away, just lets silence permeate the room. I don't think he's even breathing.

It shouldn't be a big deal. We've engaged in mutual jack-off sessions, he and I. Multiple times in high school, actually. It was never a big deal then and it shouldn't be one now. Besides, getting up and putting on my prosthetic and then walking to the bathroom is such a chore. I'd rather just lie here and get it over with.

"Yeah, that's cool," he says and then I feel him reach back. A moment later, a wad of tissues is pressed into my hand.

I wiggle against him and he grunts, moving his lower half away from me.

"You can get off too, if you want."

"Not happening," he says, and I smile at the irritation in his voice.

"Whatever works," I say, and shift in his arms, my hand brushing against Finn's as I reach down and grasp onto my dick.

The minute my hand wraps around it, I gasp. God, I need to do this more often. It's been way too long.

My hand slowly starts to pump my cock as Finn presses against me, his hand sliding against my stomach.

Fuck, I like that. I like being touched while I'm getting off. We've never done this before, but I really like it.

I lean my head back a little and Finn's lips brush against the side of my neck. The tissues have been discarded in front of me. I don't even care if I mess up the sheets. Don't fucking care. All I care about is this...this....

A low groan is ripped out of me as I stroke myself faster. Finn's fingers trace a trail from my stomach to my hip and then splay across my thigh. His breath is hot and heavy against my skin and my nerves are on fire.

"God, Finn," I groan as his hand squeezes me tightly. "Fuck. I'm close."

His body trembles a little behind me and I feel my body start to tighten, my balls drawing up against me and then I feel his hand against the tip of my cock, the tissues pressed against it, the skin of his palm pressed against a sliver of me.

And that's all I need to unload.

My body shudders and convulses as stream after stream of my release is emptied into the tissues in Finn's hand, and when it's done and my body is liquid, Finn gently wipes me up and slips out of bed.

I turn to watch him go and let my eyelids flutter closed when he's no longer in my line of vision.

Sometime later he returns to bed, pulling me back against him.

And I sleep like the dead.

four

LANDON

"MORNING," Finn's deep voice says above me. I arch into him, last night coming back in vivid replay, and sigh. I kind of want to do it again. I liked the feel of someone behind me, of the warmth of naked skin against mine as I was coming. Hmm, or maybe I just want Finn touching me again. I always like him touching me, anyhow.

"Morning," I croak.

His hand threads through my hair and tugs on it lightly, causing pleasure to ripple through my body. Goosebumps erupt on my skin and I bite back a groan.

"Coffee?" he asks and I let my hand slide up his chest, reveling in how his muscles ripple and bunch beneath my touch. He has so many of them. I want to spend the morning counting them.

"Hell yes."

He chuckles. "Well, then we should get up then."

"In a minute," I say, burrowing further into him. I'm not ready to leave him yet, and, of course, he lets me tuck myself into his side.

"Thanks for last night," I say, my lips against the skin of his side, my nose tucked near his armpit. I inhale his scent and feel my body reflexively relax.

"Yeah, sure," he says, and I peek up at him.

His cheeks are flushed red, and I trace my thumb over his jaw

"Did it bother you?"

He swallows and shakes his head slightly. "No."

"Good because I think I need to do that more often. My dick has been neglected for far too long."

"You probably need to get laid," Finn says, and I roll on top of him, our hard cocks sliding against each other and another zing of pleasure shoots through me. I ignore it and push myself up on my hands, staring down at him.

He has a light stubble on his jaw and his eyes are hooded from sleep. There is a slight pillow crease on his cheek.

God, he's handsome. I just love looking at him. Yes, I have eyeballs. I may be straight, but I know when a dude looks nice. And Finn looks hella nice, especially in the morning all rumpled and shit.

"I'll get out there eventually. In the meantime, I have my trusty hand and your adept ability to catch my cum."

He shakes his head in disbelief and I laugh loudly.

"I am never doing that again," he tells me, and I roll my eyes.

"I bet you will."

"Jesus fucking Christ," he mutters, and then suddenly I'm on my back, Finn pressed against me.

He arches into me once and my dick takes notice of the sensation. It throbs painfully between us and I let out a lengthy exhale.

Fuck.

But before I can do anything, he pushes up and off of me and turns away, adjusting himself.

"Let's go get coffee and maybe then you'll start thinking more clearly," he says, moving toward me and flinging the sheets off, exposing my hard cock.

His eyes glance at it briefly before he crouches down and opens up his arms.

I scoot toward him, linking my legs behind him as he lifts me up and brings me to the bathroom.

I'll just have to get off in the shower.

Obviously, my dick is a little confused. I may be a little confused too. Not sure what all of this means, but like usual, I don't examine it too hard. I just brush it under the rug and bury it there. I'll come back to it later. Maybe. Probably not.

The two of us go through our routine, brushing our teeth and Finn turning the shower on, and as soon as I'm settled in my chair with the curtain closed, I wrap my hand around my cock to try to stroke it into submission.

But the whole thing takes a lot longer than I expected. Minutes later, a worried Finn yanks the shower curtain back and I gasp, my hand gripping my still-hard dick.

"You've got to be kidding me," he mutters, and a laugh bubbles out of me.

"It's taking longer than I thought," I say and he sighs.

"I thought you'd fallen or some shit, and here you are just jacking off. Have you even washed yet?"

"No," I say and then lean back in the chair. "Wash me, Finn, while I come."

"You are fucking ridiculous. No way."

"But it will be faster and my dick is giving me trouble."

He is seriously debating it. I can see it in the twitch of his bottom lip. I can read this guy like a fucking magazine.

"Pretty please, Finn," I say batting my eyelashes at him. "I need you."

"Not today, Satan," he says and then jerks the shower curtain closed. I sigh and stare down at my dick and pump it a few more times before I give up.

"I'm not Satan," I mutter as I quickly wash and rinse. When I pull the shower curtain open, I see Finn leaning against the wall, my towel in his hand.

"My dick is neglected and upset at you."

Finn rolls his eyes, tossing the towel toward me. It hits my chest and I use it to quickly dry off.

"Yeah, well, it's not that neglected. You got off just last night."

I stare at him and then down at my dick. It twitches, half-hard between my legs.

"Ugh, you're literally a boner killer."

He moves toward me and scoops me up. I press my face into his neck and let him tote me to the bedroom.

"We're meeting your parents at the farmer's market soon so get dressed."

He tosses me onto the bed and I pout dramatically. "Dress me, Finn."

"For fuck's sake," he grumbles, but there's a slight smile on his lips, a small upturn at the corners and it makes my heart flutter.

"Dress me up like a doll."

Finn's eyes narrow and I can't help but laugh because he's so annoyed, his head shaking slightly.

"You're too fucking much," he says as he tackles me back onto the bed, a yelp escaping my mouth as he presses his strong body into mine.

Our hips grind against each other and I feel my cock perk up and take notice.

Oh my god, my dick has issues.

"You're making me hard," I tell him as I lean up and press a kiss to his lips. He rears back a little.

"Stop it," he growls and then pushes himself up as if trying to leave me. I cling to him, my leg wrapping around his waist, my arms around his neck, and he stumbles slightly.

"Get the fuck off of me," he chuckles, and I bite down on his neck lightly.

"Jesus fucking Christ, Landon," he says, narrowing his eyes.

But I don't let go; I just hang on, like some kind of sloth swinging from a tree, unwilling to move from my branch. I have a home now. Like hell I'm giving it up.

And instead of fighting, Finn gives up much too easily. He swiftly flops down on top of me and smothers me with his large body.

"Oof, oh my god, get off," I say, his hair getting into my mouth.

I sputter and try to push him off, but he only sinks down a little further.

"Finn," I wheeze, and he laughs. "You're such an ass. You're crushing me."

I pinch his sides as he bites down on my ear, his teeth tugging on my lobe. My arms break out in goosebumps at the sensation and then I gasp when I feel his tongue slide inside.

I groan in half-disgust and half-excitement as I buck my hips, my lonely dick getting all sorts of ideas. Which is ridiculous. Because this is Finn.

I seriously need to get out and have sex. Like yesterday.

"Say you're sorry," he says, his voice low and rough.

"Make me."

He grunts and then sits up, his cheeks flushed and his hair mussed. I want to run my hands through it, tug on the strands and pull him closer, but I can't. He's grabbed onto both of my hands, holding them tightly above my head.

"We're going to be late," he says. "And you know how your dad gets when we're late to the farmer's market."

I blink up at him and our gazes lock. For a few seconds, we just stare at each other and I feel my chest constrict.

"It's your fault. You wanted to wrestle instead of shower. I'll just blame you," I manage to say.

"You were the one spending hours getting off."

I snort and Finn smiles down at me. "Correction. I didn't get off. It was an attempt and a poor one at that. Very disappointing."

Finn lets go of my hands and they flop to my sides, curling into the sheets beneath.

"I'm going to shower and then we're going to go, and if you're lucky, we'll have time to stop for coffee."

I flutter my lashes at him and run a finger up his arm. "Like you wouldn't stop for me anyways."

He huffs and begins to extricate himself from me, but I lean forward and grasp the back of his head, pulling his lips to mine.

It's a quick smack and Finn sighs loudly.

"Done now?" he asks, and I flop down on the bed once more, staring at the ceiling.

"Yeah, I'll be ready by the time you're done."

"Not fucking likely."

"You're late!" Dad says, rounding his table piled high with baskets of vegetables. He's an older version of my big brother, all wide shoulders and thick arms. And a fucking goof to the core. My dad stumbles a little on the leg of the table and jostles my cup of coffee as he crushes me to his large chest in a hug. I mutter "careful" under my breath because as much as Finn threatened to not stop and get me coffee—to try and punish me for just lounging about naked after he got out of the shower—he stopped and got me fucking coffee. Do I know him, or do I know him?

"Sorry, sorry," my dad mutters and then moves to hug Finn. "I thought you were bailing."

My mom eyes the two of us and smirks. "He kept going on and on about it. Practically wrote you out of the will."

Dad glances over at Mom and waggles his finger at her.

"I wasn't that dramatic and you were going on about it too. You were doubting their love for us. You know how I feel about the farmer's market."

"Yeah, yeah, it's some kind of religious experience for you. But we're here so stop being so ridiculous," I say, leaning into Finn. "Plus if it's anyone's fault that we're late, it's Finn's. He took for-fucking-ever getting ready."

Finn's hand tightens on my waist and I grin up at him.

"Somehow I don't believe that," my dad says and then shakes his head. "Never mind, no time for chatting right now. I have customers! And I need you to watch Vincent. He keeps eating the vegetables."

"Seriously?" I look down at the goat and notice he does look a little rounder. He just blinks those weird goat eyes up at me, innocent as a fucking baby.

I don't trust this one. He's nefarious. Has all sorts of secret plans.

"Yes, he has no manners." My dad leans down a little and his words come out a little higher. "You're a hungry bug, huh? Just so fucking hungry...."

Finn arches an eyebrow at me and I bite back a laugh. We've both heard my dad talking to the animals on numerous occasions. They're his best friends. "Anyway, he ate like the entire basket of zucchini, and they're my best sellers this time of year. So I need you to occupy him before he makes off with my asparagus."

I grab the leash from my dad and the goat bleats loudly as an older couple makes their way up to the table.

"Go shop and then bring me one of those pastries I love. Actually, two. One for your mom."

"So glad you remembered me," my mom says with a smile, but my dad is too busy chatting with the customers to notice her.

She rolls her eyes and sighs. "It's a good thing I love that man."

I snort a laugh as I press a kiss to her cheek, grabbing onto Vincent's leash and tugging him gently into the slowly growing throng of people milling about. All around us, popup stands line the street of downtown Santa Cruz, each booth featuring different items for sale. You can find anything from fresh fruit and veggies to homemade soap and lotion. I fucking love coming down here. You can find the weirdest stuff.

"Where are those pastries again?" Finn asks.

"They're usually all the way in the back," I tell him as we make our way slowly through the crowd. "And you have the bag, right? Because I'm leaving here with a ton of shit, Finn. You're not holding me back this time."

Finn holds out a hemp bag and ruffles my hair. He tries to reel me in when we come here but is mostly unsuccessful. I have my ways of convincing him to let me go wild.

"Good, because look, I'm getting the fucking Llama Lotion this time," I say, my eyes wandering the stands, looking for the booth with the two older ladies hunched over behind it. They look a million years old, but their skin is so shiny.

"Jesus, not again," Finn mutters, his pinkie slipping beneath my shirt and stroking the skin of my hip.

"I want the fucking lotion, Finn. You saying no to it only makes me want it more."

"It looks shady. You'll probably break out in a rash if you use it."

"You're so judgmental. Those ladies have very soft skin."

"They have oily skin."

"Pfft. I'm going to buy it and you're going to rub it all over me."

Finn shakes his head as Vincent nibbles on someone's skirt. I apologize profusely and then lean down a little, Finn's hands encircling my waist as I do so.

"Don't do that, little dude. You're going to get us kicked out of this place and my dad would be heartbroken."

Vincent just stares up at me, his ears twitching, and then bleats loudly.

Apparently, he's not keen on listening to me.

"You do know he can't understand you, right?" Finn says when I straighten back up.

I shrug and then smirk. "I don't know why you grumble so much. You've been in this family for how many years...?"

"Eight years."

"And you're still surprised we talk to goats?"

Finn smiles at me softly and I lean in, pressing a gentle kiss to his lips.

He sighs and then says, "Let's go get your fucking lotion, but don't blame me when you end up in the emergency room needing a skin graft."

We meander the stalls for about an hour and I purchase my lotion, a handful of exotic vegetables my dad doesn't grow, a succulent, and a small bushel of sage and oregano.

"You're not going to burn that shit in your apartment, are

you?" Finn asks me as I bring the herbs up to my nose and inhale.

"You bet I am. She said it wards off evil spirits."

He stares at me and I laugh. Fuck, I cannot wait to light this up in front of him and watch him grumble and moan.

"My cousin, Aspen, swears by it," I say.

"Your cousin is insane."

"No, he's not. He's just eccentric."

"He plays the flute to his pumpkin patch and covers himself in bees."

"Yes," I say with a sniff. "So?"

Finn shakes his head, grabbing onto the bag and stuffing the herb bundle into it, and then pulls me back into his side.

"Jesus, Landon. Sometimes I don't know if you're fucking with me or what. I swear to god."

I lean my head against his shoulder and smile up at him. "When we're eighty years old, you'll finally come to terms with the fact that I am positively serious about everything."

His hand tightens against me as he clears his throat. "Alright, let's get those pastries for your parents and then head back."

"You're ready to rub that lotion on me, aren't you? You're dying to smooth it into my skin."

"Not fucking likely. I'm not touching that shit."

"Oh, but you so are."

He gently nudges me forward and we end up in front of the stand that sells pastries. Vincent starts nibbling on the tablecloth and I bend down to try and extricate it from his teeth.

"Sorry about him," Finn tells the brunette girl behind the table.

I glance up and see her face slowly turn beet red as she fiddles with a lock of her hair. She's obviously noticed how hot Finn is. I mean, it's impossible not to notice. He's like the twinkling lights of Vegas in the vast barren desert. He's gorgeous.

Finn is seemingly oblivious to her simpering, though. He just points to the display case and asks for two raspberry cheese Danishes.

She fumbles with the tongs and drops the bag, but Finn doesn't even seem to notice her bungling. He's intently watching me, still unsuccessfully trying to get Vincent to stop eating the tablecloth. There's now a large gaping hole in the fabric.

"Here," Finn says and then bends and picks up Vincent, who goes willingly and happily. I don't blame him; they're nice arms to be wrapped up in. I'm mildly jealous of the goat now.

The sight of Finn holding the tiny goat only makes the girl behind the table sputter and practically drool, her eyes shooting heart emojis. For a moment, I'm annoyed because really, have some decorum and stop ogling him. We could be a couple. We're not, obviously, but she doesn't know that. Just plain rude.

I snatch the bag of pastries from her and wrap my arm around Finn's waist.

Her eyes swivel down to where we connect and then dart away.

Yes, well, good. Finn doesn't like people staring.

"Ready?" I ask and as Finn glances down at me, I can't help myself. I lean up and kiss his cheek.

Vincent takes this opportunity to latch onto and nibble the hemp necklace around my throat, and I gently swat him away.

My god, this goat needs a hobby. Maybe I should buy him a pacifier.

"Yeah, let's go before he starts eating shit he shouldn't," Finn says, setting Vincent down away from the table, and handing me the leash.

"Where have you been? That ship has sailed."

"Smart ass," he says and then leads us back into the crowd.

"You love me."

He glances down at me, biting on the inside of his cheek, repressing a smile.

"Yeah, Landon. I do."

five

FINN

"MY BABY BROTHER should be here soon," my new friend, Logan, says. He smiles at me, a goofy crooked smile, and runs a hand through his curly hair. He's big for an eighth grader, bigger than me, although not by much. He told me he's on the swim team and I wonder for a moment if I should join. I don't really know the different strokes all that well, but we live in a neighborhood that has a community pool. I could learn. "We can't leave until he shows up. He'd kill us if he had to walk home alone."

I lean back against the wall of the school and glance around. New school. New friends. Thank god my dad finally landed a good job here. It's one I hope he keeps. I'm so tired of moving from place to place. I'm only fourteen and I'm fucking tired.

"Ah, there he is," Logan says and pushes away from the wall. My eyes travel across the lawn to where a slender kid makes his way toward us. He's wearing skinny jeans and a black t-shirt a couple sizes too big for him.

"That's Landon," Logan says and waves at me to follow him. I just met Logan today, but he's already told me his brother is a year younger than me and in the grade below us. I know that he and Logan are very close; I can tell by how Logan talks about him.

I follow tentatively, watching as Logan's brother approaches us. I've always hated meeting new people—having to make new friends—but with a dad that moves around as much as mine, it's an inevitable and inescapable part of my life.

"Hey, little bro!" Logan shouts and Landon smiles widely as we come to a stop in front of him. "You took your damn time."

Landon laughs a little and my entire body thrums as I take him in. He's a couple inches shorter than me, and has a slender torso and shoulder-length light brown hair. It's not as curly as his brothers, but wavy. And then my eyes move to his face, and butterflies erupt in my stomach.

Fuck.

"I want you to meet my new friend. Landon, this is Finn Ledger. Finn, my brother Landon."

Landon's smile widens as he turns to me and my heart thumps awkwardly in my chest, my breath coming out a little stuttered. What the fuck is wrong with me?

"Hi, Finn. Great to meet you," Landon says and gives me a small wave.

The way he says my name makes goosebumps break out on my skin and I feel my cheeks start to warm.

"Hi," I manage to say, realizing I need to appear normal. I'm not going to be fucking weird about this. I've just made some new friends. I don't need to scare them away by being the weirdo new kid. I mean, I *am* the weirdo new kid, but no one else needs to know that.

"You new here?" Landon asks, adjusting his backpack on his slim shoulders.

"Yeah," I croak out.

"Cool, you walking home with us?"

"Yeah, he lives just a block over," Logan answers for me. Thank god. I've lost the ability to make conversation.

"Nice. Let's go. I'm starving."

Logan wraps his arm around Landon's shoulders and I just eye the way they lean into each other. I've never had siblings. It's always been just me and my dad, a distant man who mainly keeps to himself. I can't even remember the last time he gave me a hug. So this open affection Landon and Logan are showing is so foreign to me.

"You coming?" Landon asks, peering over his shoulder at me. And that's when I realize I haven't moved. I'm just standing awkwardly, watching as they walk away.

Landon holds out his hand toward me and I stare at it.

Shaking myself into action, I take a few steps toward him and slip my hand into his.

Landon's eyes widen, probably because he didn't expect me to do this, and for a moment I'm mortified because of course he doesn't want to hold another dude's hand. We're in middle school. That's not something we do.

My cheeks flame as I attempt to pull my hand away, but his grip on me tightens and I feel my chest constrict again.

"It's okay. It doesn't have to be weird," he tells me softly. I stare down at our interlocked hands, his so much smaller than mine, and then I meet his eyes. They're so fucking pretty. Hazel with flecks of green. His freckled nose scrunches and my knees grow weak.

"Okay," I say, clearing my throat.

"We're very affectionate in this family. Tons of hugs," he explains. "Just wait till you meet our dad."

Logan musses his brother's hair and smacks a kiss on his cheek. "Hell yeah. Nothing wrong with it. It's a natural way to show you care."

"Yeah, that's *not* how we do things in my family," I mutter.

Landon squeezes my hand and then leans his head on my shoulder. "Oh, well, that's okay. We'll just have to give you extra hugs to make up for it."

And when he looks up at me with that warm smile and those fucking eyes, my heart melts.

Oh. Shit.

six

LANDON

I FLOP ONTO THE BED, full and exhausted from our outing earlier. My dad, like usual, wrangled us into helping him load all of his shit into his van once the market was over. I managed to persuade Finn to take me out to lunch after. I was hungry and ate way too much. Now I'm stuffed and tired, and my leg kind of aches, if I'm honest. Not that I'll tell Finn that because he'll just worry.

"Your leg hurts, huh?" Finn says and I lean up a little so he can see my full eye roll. I really want him to get a good look.

"Stop reading my mind, Finn. That shit is creepy."

He leans forward and starts to unbutton my pants, and I just flop back down and let him undress me.

He probably wants to examine my residual limb and make sure it's not bruised—like he could do anything about it if it was. But he just likes to worry about me. He has a crease between his eyes that's only gotten deeper since the accident. Sometimes I press my finger against it, willing it to go away.

"Grab that lotion I got and rub it on me," I tease as he gently removes my prosthetic and lifts my leg a little, his eyes focused on the end.

"It's a little red. You overdid it today."

"I'm *fine*," I say as he rubs his fingers gently over it and my nerve endings light up from his touch.

He gently sets my leg back down as I say, "That lotion is supposed to help with inflammation. Do it, Finn. Make me all better. I know you want to."

He grumbles a little under his breath. "You're a little shit, you know that?"

I smirk when I hear the rustle of the bag and then Finn tosses the bottle of lotion on the bed next to me.

"If I do this, you don't tell anyone. And I'm only putting this on your legs. Got it?"

I snort and then lean up and tug off my shirt, leaving me in only my blue boxers. Life is so much better when you're naked.

"Boxers off," I say, and arch my hips up.

"Hell no."

I chuckle and then just starfish myself across the mattress.

"You're not supposed to say no to me. Need I remind you? I only have one leg. Feel sorry for me, Finn."

"Feel sorry, my ass," he grumps and then squirts a liberal amount of lotion into his hand, rubbing it together with his palms, and then presses his big hands into the muscles of my thigh.

I sigh emphatically as he works it into my skin, massaging my sore muscles. God, I love when he touches me like this. Like he owns me.

I groan as he works up my inner thighs and my dick thickens a little from the sensation. His fingers glide up under the hem of my boxers as he massages my groin and damn, that feels *good*. He's never done that before and I fucking like it.

"Ugh. Just take my boxers off and rub that shit on my dick. It's still upset about earlier," I tease, and Finn's hands freeze.

"Like hell," he mutters, removing his hands, and I feel the absence acutely. Shouldn't have teased him about that, I guess. I could be having my groin massaged if I'd kept my mouth shut.

My eyes pop open and I stare at my best friend who is watching me with flushed cheeks and a scowl.

"Please. Don't stop," I say, feeling like a puddle of goo and wanting this to continue for a little longer. A few more hours should be enough.

Don't stop, Finn. Make me feel good.

Finn wets his lips and swallows. "You're a manipulative asshole."

"You love me," I say, reaching up and grabbing onto his hands and placing them on my stomach. "And my skin feels amazing. This lotion is working miracles. My leg doesn't even hurt anymore."

"Liar."

I mean, I kind of am. My leg still aches, but it's overshadowed now by how good Finn's hands feel on me.

His fingers flex on me and then he shifts up the bed so he's kneeling next to me, his hands moving in slow circles across my abdomen as I close my eyes once more and just sink into the mattress.

"God, you touch me so good," I moan, my words a little slurred.

"I can tell. Your dick is hard," Finn grits out, and I peek an eye open and yep, there it is. Just tenting my boxers like it's gone camping.

I sigh and press a hand against it. It doesn't help and I resign myself to my fate. Finn is giving me hard-dick syndrome. I will shove this under the rug along with all of the other things there. It's a mountain-sized pile now.

"You've seen it before. Doesn't mean anything."

He's silent for a moment, his breath coming out a little heavier as he works his way up to my shoulders, and then his fingers are brushing across my jaw and over my cheeks.

One of his fingers softly caresses my upper lip.

"You want to kiss me again, huh?" I say with a smile, my eyes still blessedly closed. "I have very kissable lips."

Finn doesn't answer, just reaches under me and roughly flips me over.

"Oof."

"Not fucking likely," he responds and then he's straddling my lower back with his thick thighs, leaning into my shoulder blades, and roughly kneading me with his strong hands. The pressure is almost painful and I grunt and moan as he presses into the sore muscles.

My hard dick presses agonizingly into the mattress, the friction of him against my back doing things to my libido.

"God, Finn," I gasp as he works his hands down my spine to my ass. "Don't stop."

"Jesus," he says softly, and then he shifts, and his palms are on the globes of my ass, kneading them roughly. The movement rocks my body against the mattress causing friction on my oversensitive dick. Over and over, he does it, just grinds me into the bed and I can't fucking help it. There's nothing I can do to stop it.

A low moan slips out of me as my balls draw up and I shudder, coming in my boxers and onto the sheets. My body trembles as my orgasm pulses through me and then, when it's over, I lie there, still as a fucking corpse.

"Are you...are you for real?" Finn asks, his body stiff behind me.

"Evidently I like my ass touched," I mutter as a mortified laugh escapes me. Because Finn has given me plenty of massages and I've never had an orgasm while he did it.

Shit, if I think about this too hard, it's kind of embarrassing.

Finn climbs off of me, and I can't help but add, "You just gave me a happy ending."

"Shut up," he says and then is striding out of the room. I don't even know how long he's gone because I doze off. I guess I'm not *that* embarrassed about what just happened. I have no shame apparently. Finn has seen me at my literal worst. I don't think there is anything I could do that would drive him away.

"Turn over," Finn says and my eyes slowly open. He's

leaning over me, a washrag in his hand. When I don't move fast enough, he reaches down to move me himself, but his hands can't get a grip on my slippery skin. I can't help the giggle that erupts from me.

"You're greasy," he mutters and my laugh grows louder.

"I'm glowing."

"You're oily and you smell like an orgy in the aromatherapy aisle at Whole Foods. You need a shower."

I arch into his touch. "Yes. I do. Wash me, Finn."

"You're filthy."

My eyes water from laughing so hard as Finn tugs my boxers off and cleans me up.

"You're a fucking mess. Have you always been like this?"

"Yes, I have. It seems I need to get laid."

Finn's dark eyes meet mine, his thumb brushing against my hip.

"And so do you," I add.

He chews on his lip and I smile softly at him.

"I think this was a wake-up call."

His throat clicks loudly as he swallows, his Adam's apple bobbing in his throat. "Yeah."

I reach up and brush his cheek gently. "I think I need to set up a Tinder profile. Will you help me, Finn?"

His eyes shutter and he tilts his head down, exhaling softly. "Yeah, sure."

My hand flops down on the mattress next to me and I sigh.

"But not now. Maybe later. When I'm feeling more motivated."

Finn runs a hand down his face and looks tired. The man

is really a saint for putting up with my shit. I don't know how I got so lucky finding such a great best friend.

"Come here," he says, extending his arms toward me. "I'm going to wash the sheets."

I scoot over to him and let him cradle me in his arms as he carries me to the couch in the living room. He tucks me underneath a blanket and the warmth of it coupled with the residual fatigue from my orgasm lulls me into a nap.

Neither of us mentions what happened for the rest of the day. After dozing for some of the afternoon, we get up and lounge around the apartment, ordering Uber Eats and watching a movie until Finn carries me to bed.

I fall asleep on his chest, his heartbeat gently pulsing against my cheek.

It's dark when I suddenly wake, the wind outside rattling the windowpane, and the bed is empty and cold. My hand runs along the space where Finn usually is, and I feel his absence intensely. I grab his pillow and inhale the scent of him before turning over onto my back.

Ugh, where is he? I can't sleep without him. You should see me during the semester, when he's ten light-years away. I'm a zombie. I cannot wait until he's graduated and can move in with me. Then I can finally have some mother-fucking peace. I mean, we haven't discussed this, but I know he'll do it.

He needs me as much as I need him.

My eyes take in the dark room and then they catch on a sliver of light from under the bathroom door.

I sit up, pull on my prosthetic and move toward the closed door. What the hell is he doing in there at four in the morning?

My mouth opens to call his name but I freeze when I hear it—a muffled *"fuck"* and the sound of something hitting the wall.

Taking a step forward, I press my hand to the doorframe and lean in, listening.

"Fuck! Fuck this," I hear him mutter and then a low, almost painful, groan.

"Finn?" I ask softly, hoping he's okay. What the hell is he doing in there? My hand moves to the door handle, but it's locked.

Shit, when has he ever locked a door? It must be serious. He never keeps me out; he never keeps secrets from me.

For a moment, there's just silence from the bathroom and I wonder if he's going to answer me. Worry starts to gnaw at my stomach, but then I hear, "Yeah, Landon, I'll be out in a minute."

"Are you okay?" I ask, rubbing at my tired eyes.

He clears his throat. "Yeah. I'm fine. Go back to bed. I'll be there in a bit."

But I don't move. I just stand there, hovering on the other side of the door, listening as the sink faucet turns on and he moves about the bathroom. When the door finally swings open, he nearly mows me over.

He clutches onto my hips, steadying me. "Jesus, Landon. Why are you hovering in the dark?"

"I wanted to make sure you were okay."

He runs a hand through his hair and eyes me. "Yeah. Yeah, I'm good."

I fiddle with the waistband of his boxers as I stare up at him. "You locked the door."

"Yeah, well, I wanted some privacy," he tells me before sweeping me up into his arms and carrying me back to the bedroom.

He sets me on the edge of the bed, carefully takes my prosthetic off, and then tucks me beneath the sheets. He crawls over to me, a sigh escaping him as he pulls me against his chest.

But I'm not ready for this conversation to be over. Something was wrong in there. I could tell. I could feel it.

"What did you want privacy for? I mean, you've literally helped me wipe my ass before...."

He doesn't answer and I lean up on my elbow, glancing down at him. His hand automatically sweeps into my hair, tugging on it gently.

"What are the chances of you letting this go?"

"Um, I'd say slim to none, but that would be a lie. I'm holding on for dear life."

"Fuck. Fine. I have needs, okay? I just needed to...get off. It's been a while."

I blink and then blink some more because...I didn't even think of that.

"Oh."

"Yeah. *Oh*," Finn repeats and then tries to push my head back onto his chest, but I'm stronger than I look. I keep my neck straight and my arms locked. I'm a motherfucking giraffe.

"When's the last time you had sex?" I ask, my finger running along the edge of his nipple. It hardens beneath my touch.

"Not telling you that."

"But we tell each other everything," I say as I run my finger up his neck and across his jaw. It's a little stubbly. He hasn't shaved in a few days. I love that look on him. He's so fucking handsome.

"Yeah, well, it's irrelevant."

"But I want to know."

"I know you do. You're insatiable. But I'm not disclosing that shit, Landon. Some things have to remain private and that's my business."

Fuck, that kind of hurts my feelings a little. Because since when is *his* shit not *my* shit?

"Well, I haven't had sex since before the accident," I reveal, hoping he'll give me something. But he doesn't. He just stares at me, his hand massaging my scalp.

I brush my finger over his bottom lip and press against it. It's soft and warm and I want to lean down and press my lips to his.

"We both really need to find someone to fuck around with."

He lets out a breath and his hand slips from my hair, falling onto the bed beside me.

"Yeah, Landon. We can do that. But can we fucking sleep first? I'm tired."

I slide my finger across his bottom lip once more and then tuck myself into his side.

"Yeah. Okay, but I know you'll tell me your secrets eventually. I have my ways."

"Yeah, fucking try me," he mutters.

I fling my leg over his and my arm snakes around his waist.

"I'll try you, Finn. I'll try you so fucking hard."

He mutters a curse as my eyes close and a small smirk lifts up the corner of my mouth as I drift off to sleep.

seven

EIGHT YEARS AGO

FINN

I PULL myself out of the pool and sit on the edge of it, my legs dangling in the water, my chest heaving from exertion. Swimming like this is harder than it looks. Logan is helping me perfect the strokes I need to be able to join the swim team this year and he's also helping me improve my time. The school's coach is allowing me to try out for the team and I think I have a shot. Maybe.

Actually, I don't really know if I do or not.

Fuck.

"You're doing good, dude," Logan says as he pulls himself out of the pool. He shakes his hair out and then glances back at me. "Gotta pee though. You want a drink or something?"

"Sure. Water."

"Cool. Be back," Logan says, grabbing a towel and slinging it over his shoulders before moving toward the bathrooms.

I glance around the public pool and note a few people lingering. There aren't many though, which makes it easier for me. Fewer people in my way when I'm flying across the pool. I lean back on my hands and tilt my head back, soaking up the rays. It's September and still a little warm out. Gotta catch the sun while it's still shining.

"Hey, Finn," a familiar voice says to my right, and I squint up at Landon who is standing next to me in only his swim trunks.

I immediately divert my eyes because he has no shirt on and it's making me feel funny.

"Logan texted and told me you guys were here practicing for your tryouts. Can I join?"

I shrug, trying my best to ignore him. But it's impossible. I can't keep my eyes off him. It's been two weeks and these feelings haven't disappeared. They've only grown. I don't know what to do about them.

I am trying like hell to do what my dad does with pretty much everything—ignore it until it disappears.

Doesn't seem to be working well though.

A splash has me opening my eyes and peering into the pool. I see Landon emerge, a crooked smile on his face, his hand pushing his wet hair off his forehead.

"Come back in, Finn. Swim with me."

I pull my bottom lip between my teeth and debate it

because these feelings only seem to grow when I'm near him. Like I said, if I can avoid him, I can push them aside.

Kind of.

Landon swims over to me, right between my legs, and tugs on them. The feel of his hands on me gets me every time. And they're always on me.

"Come on. Come in with me."

He has a pout on his pink lips and just blinks his pretty eyes at me.

Fuck. How am I supposed to say no to him?

I slide into the water next to him, our bodies touching, and then he swings himself onto my back, wrapping his arms around my neck and his legs around my waist. I almost sink with him on me like this, but I reach out and grab onto the wall to keep us afloat.

"Show me what you got, big guy," he says.

I crane my neck to see him and he smiles widely at me.

"Scared?" he asks and I scowl.

I'm not scared. I haven't been scared in a long time. Well, not counting these confusing feelings I'm having about this guy.

I don't know what they mean. All I know is that I need to get rid of them, and fast.

Without answering, I dive under the water and Landon clings to my back, holding onto me tightly, and when I reemerge on the far end of the pool, Landon gasps for air.

"Oh my god. You're part dolphin," he sputters on a laugh. "I thought I was going to drown."

He still hasn't let go of me; his body is still plastered to my back.

"You could have let go."

"I'm not a quitter. Now, do it again," he breathes and I don't even question it. I just let us sink to the bottom of the pool, my legs catching the wall and pushing off it.

I'm breathing hard when we make it to the deep end. My hands reach out and pull us up, holding the two of us above water.

"You're going to make the team," Landon says suddenly.

He moves off of my back and hangs off the side of the pool next to me, his foot hitting mine.

"I know you will."

"We'll see," I say, not wanting to get my hopes up because I've done that before and have only been disappointed when it doesn't work out.

He nudges me with his shoulder and the contact has me shivering.

"Trust me. You will and I'll be there for your tryouts. I'm making you a sign."

I peek over at him. "Don't make me a sign."

He grins at me and then disappears under the water, leaving me to stare after him, and when he pops up at the other end of the pool, his eyes meet mine.

"I'm making you the fucking sign, Finn!" he shouts.

And he did. He showed up holding a big-ass sign with my name on it. His dad and mom showed up too, both looking so proud.

My heart leapt in my chest when I saw him in the stands.

I didn't even care that my dad didn't show up because *he* was there.

And when I found out that I made the team, he engulfed me in a hug, holding me tightly to him.

"I knew you could do it, Finn. I'll always believe in you."

Fuck. I hope my dad doesn't make us move again. I'm not sure my teenage heart would survive it.

I want to stay. I need to stay.

eight

LANDON

"WHICH ONE DO you think we should get?" I ask Finn who is hovering behind me with the basket. We woke up late and then made our way to the gym where I watched Finn swim while I lifted weights.

I mean, I sort of lifted weights…kind of moved them from one spot to another, and then spent the rest of my time just avoiding the treadmills. I've always loved running, but I just can't manage it yet. I'll start that up again when I'm fitted for my new prosthetic. But who knows when that will be.

Instead, I watched Finn's arms slice in and out of the water as his body glided from one end of the pool to the other. It never gets old, watching the way he moves.

"Your dad just said to get red wine."

"Yes, but there are a bazillion, and since when does he drink wine?" I ask, scrunching up my nose at the selection.

Actually, my dad said to get the "fancy" red wine, whatever that means. I think he's just trying to impress my brother's boyfriend, Theo. The two of them are visiting today and my dad is going a little crazy.

He stayed up late building another addition to the kitty hotel. Like it isn't big enough already. It takes up half the wall.

Now he's baking up a storm. Finn and I don't get this fanfare when we visit. Maybe we should both move away and only come home every once in a while. I want cake and cookies when I come over.

"He wants us to get it because Theo mentioned that he wanted some at Christmas. Don't know why he can't just have beer like the rest of us," Finn grumbles.

I glance back at Finn and see his scowl. "He's just trying to be accommodating. Don't be such a boob about it."

Finn's eyebrows lower even more and then he sighs, running a hand over his face. "You're right. God, I'm turning into my dad, aren't I? Shit, I said I'd never let that happen..."

I smile at him and run my finger over the deep crease in-between his eyes.

"You kind of are, but you're adorable. Such a grumpy old man."

He pulls me into him and rests his head on mine. "Shut up. I'm going to have an attitude change, okay? I will *not* be like him."

I snort as he moves away from me, grabbing onto a random bottle.

"Just get this one. I'm making an executive decision

because if I don't, we will be here all day. And it's not in a box, so it's fancy enough," he says.

"Yeah, you're right. Good plan. Let's grab a few more. That way Theo has options."

Finn sets four more bottles in the basket, and I stare down at them before grabbing two more for good measure, and then we make our way to the counter.

"What are the chances your dad starts growing grapes for wine after this week? He had that crazed look in his eyes when Theo mentioned it," Finn asks.

"Oh, I'd say pretty good. Although mom might kill him if he takes on another project."

Finn sets the basket on the counter and pulls out his credit card to pay for it. I'm not twenty-one yet, so he still has to do this shit for me. Soon enough though. I can't wait to see what Finn has planned for me.

"Oh. Romantic night or party animals?" the man behind the counter asks as he starts scanning the wine bottles.

I lean into Finn and bat my eyelashes. "Romantic night. This man is going to take me home, get me wasted, and make me beg for it."

"Jesus, Landon," Finn mutters under his breath, his hand tightening on my waist. "Ignore him," Finn tells the cashier.

The man just smirks and waggles his eyebrows. "Oh. I can't ignore that. I love dubcon. You two have all the fun."

"Oh, you know it," I say and then grab the box stuffed with wine bottles. Finn reaches out and pulls them from my arms.

"You do that shit just to fuck with me, I know it," he mutters. "And what the hell is dubcon?"

"Dubious consent. Like, if you get me drunk and fuck me then consent can be a little unclear."

"Oh my god."

"I know. I mean, I think it's kind of hot, to be honest. If we were together and you wanted to fuck me after a few drinks, I'd be down. Just bend me over, Finn, stick it right in." I bump his hip and waggle my eyebrows at him.

"Stop saying shit like that," he grits out and I cackle. I love seeing him all flustered like this.

The bottles clink lightly as we make our way to his car, and he stuffs them into his trunk.

I lean against the car, just watching him with a dopey smile on my face.

"What, what's the look for?" he asks, moving toward me. He stops right in front of me and his hand reaches out, tucking a piece of my wayward hair behind my ear.

"I just like watching you."

He exhales slowly and then steps a little closer to me.

And that's when I notice it, a low buzzing in my ear. My eyes dart around and I see a bee floating near us and I lean farther away, not wanting to get stung. I'm not allergic, but those little fuckers hurt.

"Damn thing," Finn mutters, swatting at it.

"Don't kill the bee!" I say, grabbing his flapping hand. "We need them. They pollinate shit. We're one squished bee away from a dystopian future!"

Finn's eyes meet mine and then roll. "Is that so?"

"Yes," I sniff. "And my cousin would be offended if you offed one of them."

"He'd never know."

"He *knows*," I say, the bee still happily buzzing around us.

"Fucker. I thought they were in hibernation this time of year," Finn mutters and I laugh. "Just let me kill it."

I grab onto his hands and pull them into my chest.

"It will lose interest and fly away."

"But what if it stings you?"

"I'll survive."

His eyes meet mine and we just stare at each other for a long-drawn-out moment.

"You must smell good or something," he says and I tilt my head, exposing my neck to him.

"Take a whiff and see, Finn. Do I smell sweet?"

Finn's eyes darken as he leans forward, his nose drifting across my skin, and my entire body tingles.

He comes to a stop with us nose to nose, his lips so fucking close.

"What's the verdict?"

"Smell the same to me."

"Maybe I taste sweet," I say. "Maybe you should check."

It's a joke, a teasing comment that usually gets Finn blushing, but instead of leaning back like he normally would, he moves closer.

"Maybe I should," he whispers.

My breath stutters out of me because, shit, when has Finn ever played along?

His lips brush over mine and I completely stop breathing. My lungs burn as his tongue snakes out and traces the seam of my lips.

The bee's buzzing has faded away and all I can hear is the

sound of the wind whipping around us and my heart pounding in my chest.

My tongue sneaks out, the tip touching his, and his eyes close as he slants his mouth over mine, gently, slowly, like he's savoring this.

His hands move into my hair, cradling my head, and my hands fall to his hips, holding him against me.

More. I want *more*.

But he abruptly pulls away, leaving me standing there, my mouth open, my tongue lolling out of my mouth.

"What's the verdict?" I ask, breathless.

"You taste..." he wets his lips. "Fine."

My brow furrows, my hands falling from his waist. "Fine? That's it?"

He shrugs and I place my hands on my hips, feeling overly warm and flustered. I was not expecting him to do that.

And I also didn't want him to stop.

"We should go," he says.

"Um, Finn, our tongues were just touching and you said I tasted *fine*. Like I'm some kind of lousy buffet meal!"

His eyebrows shoot to his hairline and his lips twitch.

"All you can eat?" he asks and I shove him. Not that he moves. He doesn't even sway. He just stands there. Like a statue.

"I am at least a nice dinner at Olive Garden."

He rolls his lips between his teeth. "I do love their all-you-can-eat breadsticks."

"Gah!" I say, throwing my hands up and pulling the car

door open. "I am insulted. You have insulted me. I need to go find someone to kiss me and tell me how good I am."

Finn's hand slides around my arm, stopping me. I glance over my shoulder and see his lips twitch.

He's deriving pleasure from this. He's getting me back for how I teased him in front of the cashier.

My eyes narrow as I turn to fully face him.

"You're asking for it. Don't play games you can't win," I mutter and his dark eyes twinkle.

Fine, if he's going to do this shit, he can be prepared to lose. My hands shoot out, grabbing his face and yanking him toward me, and I crash my lips onto his.

He grunts as I hold him against my mouth and then my tongue presses against his lips, seeking entry.

Gonna go in there and snoop around. I'm going to burgle his mouth. But he's a locked door.

Open up, Finn. Stop being a stubborn asshole.

I bite down softly on his lower lip, sucking on it. He huffs at the sensation, his mouth parting, and I take my shot.

My tongue slides into his mouth and he freezes, his entire body locked against mine.

I win, I think as I lick my way through his mouth, exploring every corner. My hands are fisted in his hair as I kiss him with abandon, his arms bracketing me and clutching the car behind me.

He's still not moving, though. He's just letting me taste, explore. His breath mingles with mine as I plunder and my heart pounds wildly. This is exhilarating.

When I pull away a minute later, I lean my head back, watching as Finn's eyes flutter open.

"Are you done now?" he asks, his voice rough, and I roll my eyes weakly. Because I actually really enjoyed that and he's making it sound like a chore.

"Yes. I did an excellent job. If anyone is a buffet, it's you. You just stood there."

He pushes away from me, running a hand over his lips.

"Are you rubbing my kiss away?" I ask, feeling offended.

"And what if I was?"

I let out a choked laugh and then poke at his chest. "You *will* kiss me back one day."

"Not happening," he says brusquely.

"I mean we already did it. My tongue was in your mouth."

And his tongue stayed in his, but still. It counts.

He takes a step back and runs a shaky hand through his hair.

"We need to go. I bet your dad is blowing up our phones. We can talk about kissing later."

I purse my lips and then peck him on the lips once more, just for good measure, before sliding into the passenger seat of his car. Finn stands outside for a moment staring at his feet before finally getting into the driver's seat and starting the car.

He's quiet, but he's never been overly chatty, so I let it go, and when we park on the street outside my parents' house and Finn shuts off the engine, I reach over and thread my fingers through his hair.

His eyes snap to mine and I smile softly at him.

"You're so handsome. I just love looking at you."

He sighs and brings my fingers to his lips, pressing a soft kiss to them.

"Alright, enough of that, Landon. We need to go. We're already late."

I tug on his ear a little and then let my hand slide down his neck.

"Okay. But you gotta carry me inside, Finn. Like a bride. I have one leg."

He snorts, shaking his head, and then gets out. He rounds the car, throws my door open, picks me up, and slings me over his shoulder like a sack of potatoes.

"Finn!" I cry out, his arm bracing against the back of my thighs as he moves to the trunk and pops it open.

"Put me down. This is not how you carry a bride. Unless you're a caveman. Are you a caveman, Finn?"

He chuckles and I hear the bottles of wine clinking together again as he hefts the box into his free arm, and strides across the street toward the front door.

I pinch his butt, but just end up hurting my fingers because his ass is solid. I mean, like a rock.

"Damn you and your hard butt," I mutter as Finn rings the doorbell with his elbow.

"I work hard for that ass," he replies.

I slap at it as the door swings open and I hear my dad exclaim, "They're here, everybody!"

Finn steps inside, me still hanging over his shoulder, the blood pooling in my head and making me a little dizzy.

But he doesn't set me down.

No, he just stands in the living room, chatting with my dad about the cat tree he's been adding to. And my dad ignores me, like his youngest son isn't slung over Finn's shoulder, losing consciousness.

I wiggle my body, trying to squirm down him, but Finn just holds onto me tighter.

Fine, this is war. I slide my hand down the back of his pants, my cold fingers on his bare ass making him twitch slightly.

But still, he doesn't let me go.

Oh, this is a total power play now. Watch out, Finn. I play in the big leagues.

I cup a cheek in my hands, feeling how firm it is beneath my palm and I squeeze it roughly. His body jerks, but he still holds onto me, so I let my fingers slide over to his crack, tracing it with my finger.

But just before I can slide inside the crease, I'm on the ground, wobbling slightly as my blood flows away from my head.

Finn steadies me with his hands, his cheeks flushed and lips parted.

I peek over and see my dad at the cat tree, blathering on and on to no one in particular about the additions he's made, all while petting Curie's back.

"You play dirty," Finn whispers.

"I play to win. I would have stuck my finger right up your asshole too. Try me, Finn. Do it."

His cheeks darken, his fingers flexing on me, and I let out a muffled laugh.

"Guys, want to see the kitty bed I made her? Mom sewed her a little comforter too. It's so cute," my dad calls out excitedly, pulling off the roof to one of the rooms and peering inside. "It has little mice on the fabric," he adds and then beams at us.

Across the room, Vincent bleats loudly and then prances over to us as we peer at the little handcrafted cat bed. I *ooh* and *ahh* over it and my dad puffs up with pride.

Vincent bumps my leg with his head, and I lean down and pet him just as Logan and Theo step into the house from the backyard.

God, it's so funny seeing the two of them together. They couldn't be more different if they tried. The nerd and the jock, but somehow, they totally work. And I can see how far-gone Logan is for Theo. Theo is a little hard to read, but there have been times when I've caught him just staring at Logan, hearts in his eyes.

"Hey, you two! You took your time coming over," Logan says, pulling me into a bone-crushing hug. I wheeze a laugh as I smack a wet kiss against his cheek, so happy things are back to normal for us. It was weird for far too long. He swipes at the wet spot on his cheek and then moves to grapple with Finn, wrestling with him while Finn tries to hold onto the box of wine still clutched in his hand.

"Let me go, asshole," Finn mutters, the bottles rattling.

"Have to take advantage of you while your hands are full," Logan says.

A mortified laugh escapes Theo as he stares at his boyfriend.

"What? What did I say?" Logan asks, and Theo just shakes his head, moving toward Finn and taking the box from his hands.

"Here, let me take this for you," he says as Finn

straightens up, righting his shirt and hair. Theo glances down and his eyes widen, just now noticing what's inside the box.

"Those are all for you, dude," Finn says. "You're going to spend your week here drunk as hell."

"I didn't...I just mentioned that thing about the wine once. I didn't mean for you to buy the whole store."

Logan moves toward him and presses his lips to Theo's temple. "Relax, Theo. It's not a big deal."

"We all like a good red in this house," my mom chirps from the kitchen. "I like all the wines."

Theo nods, swallowing roughly, and then moves to where my mom is, setting the box down on the island.

My mom peers into the box, waggles her eyebrows, and then reaches into a cabinet, pulling down some mugs.

"I hope no one expected wine glasses," she says as my dad indiscreetly feeds Vincent a carrot. Curie has disappeared inside the cat tree entirely and I have a feeling we won't be seeing her for hours. She's probably plotting world domination.

"We all know we aren't fancy folk," I say as Finn moves away from my side to help her pour the wine.

"Yeah, that we aren't," my dad says, and then his eyebrows shoot up. "Hey, did I tell you guys? I'm thinking about growing some vines—"

"Over my dead body, Basil," my mom interjects. "It's more than just vines. It's all the equipment we'd need too. We've discussed this already."

My dad ignores her. "Look, I have some space near the shed. I could grow a few different kinds and see how I like them. Then we could have our own homemade wine for the holidays.”

My mom sighs heavily from the kitchen and gives herself a heavy pour as my dad pulls me into a hug.

“She wants to kill all my happiness and dreams. We’ll just ignore her. How’s it going, bud?” he asks, ruffling my hair a bit.

I glance over at Finn and see him watching me and my eyes inadvertently drift down to his mouth. I bite down on my lower lip and his cheeks flush red.

“It’s going really good, Dad.”

“Good. Good,” he says and then reaches to grab a mug from my mom. “God, I’m so glad you’re all here. Nothing makes me happier,” he says and then sniffles a little. Which only gets my brother going as well.

The two of them really like putting on the waterworks. It’s like the Bellagio Fountain in here. All we need are some lights and a classic Cher song to complete it.

“Stop that, Dad. Gonna make me cry,” Logan says, swiping at his eyes.

“Can’t stop,” my dad mutters.

Theo gulps down some wine as he watches us all. He still seems a little unsure about us, but I think we’re managing to pull him over to the dark side. I think the kitty palace helped. Curie adores my dad, and it doesn’t seem like she gives that out freely.

Logan pulls Theo into his side, nuzzling his face into his neck and sliding one of his hands into the back pocket of his jeans.

"So, you two are staying here for the week?" I ask my brother as I move toward Finn and lean into his side.

"Yep, we are," Logan says, grabbing onto a mug full of wine. He takes a sip of it, grimaces, and hands it to Theo who now has one mug in each hand.

"I don't know if I can drink all of this," Theo hisses.

"You can. Mmm," Logan growls. "Yeah, Theo. Drink all of it. Get all fucking loose for me."

Theo's cheeks flame.

"What is it with you guys and the sexual innuendos?" Finn mutters, and I roll my lips between my teeth, resisting a laugh.

Logan chuckles a little and then nods to the sliding glass door.

"You guys want to sit outside? We have the fire going," Logan says.

I glance over at my mom and dad and see they're still working on dinner and, at the moment, seem to be having a very serious conversation about growing vines in the backyard.

I have a feeling my mom is going to put her foot down, but then again, my dad has a way of convincing her to do what he wants. I get that ability from him. I have my ways of persuading Finn to do what I want. I can persuade him all day long.

Watch out, Finn.

"We're going to be outside, guys," I tell them.

My mom nods, waving us away and we all step outside into the cold night air, Vincent trotting along after us. We all gravitate toward the warmth of the fire pit on the deck and take our seats. Vincent prances off into the backyard, probably going to find something else to consume.

Situated around the fire are plenty of chairs for us each to have our own, but Logan just pulls Theo down onto his lap. I follow Finn to an empty chair, waiting for him to sit down, and then I wait some more for him to pull me down on top of him like he usually does, but when he doesn't, my eyes narrow.

"Are you for real?" I hiss and Finn leans back, his legs spread, his hands clutching the arms of the chair.

He smirks slightly at me.

"Oh, I see, you're mad. Punishing me," I say, plopping down on top of him. An *oof* escapes him as he adjusts me on his lap, and I nip at his chin.

"Stop punishing me for winning. I had to play dirty because you're bigger than me."

"I can't believe you did that."

"Believe it, Finn. I would have gone all the way too. I have nothing against anal."

Finn's entire body stiffens beneath me and I smother a laugh.

"So..." Logan says, his chin resting on Theo's shoulder. "Before you got here, Dad was talking about going camping with us."

"I don't know why he always suggests camping. He hates that shit," I say and Finn laughs because we all know how much Dad hates bugs. You'd think he'd be used to them by now, working in the garden all the time. But you should hear him scream every time a grasshopper flies out of the bushes. And don't even get him started on snakes. He vacillates between wanting to kill them and save them. He spends a lot of time crying over that shit. We've had many philosophical discussions over it. Usually when he's high, of course.

"He was going on and on about it. You should have heard Mom," Logan chuckles. "She was all *we have a fucking goat, Basil.*"

"We could bring him," I suggest, and then watch as Theo sets one of his mugs down and starts working on the other. Apparently, he's decided to get a little loose for my brother. Good for him. At least someone is getting some around here.

"He'd eat the tent. He already ate part of Mom's comforter," Logan says.

"He does look a little fat," I say, leaning back against Finn, who isn't touching me like he usually does. Normally, his hand slides up my shirt and lands on the bare skin of my stomach. I love it when he does it, and it feels weird and wrong now that he isn't.

Is he still trying to get me back for earlier? Because if so, I'm over it.

Stop being a sore loser, Finn.

Grabbing his hand, I pull it against my abdomen and his fingers flex against my sweatshirt. I wiggle in his lap and he sighs, resigned to his fate. Good, Finn, take a nice long look. I'm done playing these games. I take what I want.

"Probably needs to go on a diet. Cut down on the inanimate objects," Logan snorts and then asks, "Hey, so you remember Paulina?"

"Yeah, your friend from high school, right?" I reply.

"Yeah, so she's having a party tomorrow night. You guys wanna go?"

I glance back at Finn and shrug. "Sure. Sounds like fun."

"Cool," Logan says and then shifts Theo on his lap. "I can't wait to show off my man." His hand slips under Theo's shirt and Logan presses his face into the side of his neck. "You're so fucking hot. Everyone is going to be so jealous."

Theo mutters under his breath and then tugs his hood over his head, disappearing inside of it.

"Stop it, Logan," he mutters but my brother just tugs the hood off and shakes his head.

"No more disappearing or I'll cut that hood clean off. Don't make me shred your clothes, Theo. Although, that won't be a hardship. Actually, you know what, keep trying to hide. I'll enjoy stripping you down."

Theo flushes as he gapes at his boyfriend.

"Oh my god," he whispers and sinks back against Logan, trying to disappear into the shadows, but Logan just chuckles lowly and nibbles his way up his neck. Theo shudders against him, craning his neck a little, obviously loving the attention.

And meanwhile, here is fucking Finn, sitting still as a damn statue behind me. I wiggle on his lap.

"You're being weird."

"No, I'm not."

I snatch his hand, lift up my sweatshirt, and slap it right against my skin.

Finn shifts beneath me, and I lean back and whisper, "Touch me like you want to."

His hand slides up my chest and I instantly relax.

"Like this?"

I shift on his lap, pressing my face into his neck.

"Yeah. Just like that."

In the distance, I can hear Logan and Theo whispering, but right now all I can feel is Finn against me, his hand traveling across my chest, grazing my nipple, his face tucked into my hair. This is more like it. This, right here. I need this.

"I'm going to go show Theo the beets Dad is growing," Logan says abruptly as Theo vigorously shakes his head.

"They're radishes," Theo replies.

"Same thing," Logan says, pushing his boyfriend off his lap and then throwing him over his shoulder. God, these guys. Just because they're bigger than us, they think they can manhandle us.

Theo cries out in surprise as Logan jogs them toward the greenhouse, leaving Finn and me staring after them.

"They're totally going to have sex," I say, letting my lips slide up Finn's neck. He trembles beneath me as I nibble on his ear. I am taking after Vincent now. Maybe I'll start eating Finn's clothes next. Just chew them right off.

"I would totally have sex in the greenhouse too," I whisper in his ear. "Where's the craziest place you've done it, Finn?"

His hand tightens against me, but he doesn't respond.

"Tell me all your dirty secrets."

"I'm not telling you anything," he says.

I bite down roughly on his ear and he grunts.

"Tell me, Finn."

When he still doesn't respond, I slide my tongue into his ear and he shivers against me.

"Are you vanilla, Finn? Because that doesn't seem like you."

He's silent, and I can hear a lone cricket chirping somewhere under the deck.

"Come on. Tell me," I coax.

His free hand slides up into my hair, roughly moving my head to the side, and then his mouth is at my ear, his breath harsh and choppy.

"No. Not a chance. You're a nosy little fucker and I'm not going to feed you with my secrets. You'll only want more."

I turn to look at him, our lips grazing.

"Of course I will. Now tell me, what are you hiding?"

"You don't need to know everything about me."

"Um, *yes*, I do. We're best friends. That's like the definition of best friends. I thought we didn't have secrets between us."

His hand tightens in my hair when I grind my ass against him, feeling his half-hard cock against my thigh. Ugh, why do I want to kiss him again so bad?

He tilts my face away again, his words whispering against my cheek.

"Fine, you want to know something?"

"Yes," I breathe, feeling desire prickle across my skin. "Yes, I want to know everything."

His nose runs along my neck, leaving goosebumps in its wake, and then his lips are right there, about to tell me what I've been dying to hear.

"There you are!" my dad shouts, moving outside and interrupting the moment. Damn him and his terrible timing. He always does this shit. You should have seen him when I was in high school, barging through doors without knocking.

There were some very close calls there.

"Jesus, Dad," I mutter, turning to stare at him. I give him the evil eye, but he just ignores me.

"Where are Logan and Theo?" he asks, his hands on his hips, his eyes scouring the darkening backyard.

"They went into the greenhouse."

"Oh, are they looking at the radishes? Because I told Theo all about them..." he starts to move away from us and I jump up, stumbling slightly.

Because whatever Theo and Logan are up to in that greenhouse is not something that my dad needs to see. Although, payback is a bitch and all of us have stumbled in on Mom and Dad going at it one too many times. So maybe I should just let him get a taste of his own medicine.

But then I think of Theo and how mortified he'd be if that actually happened.

I hold out my hand. "Do *not* go in there, Dad."

He looks confused for a minute and then his cheeks darken. "Oh. *Ooh*. I hope they're careful with the squash. It's very delicate. I got those seeds from Aspen."

Finn stands up behind me, his hand grazing my side.

"I'm sure they're being very careful, Basil."

My dad eyes the greenhouse and sighs. "I suppose this is payback for the playlist."

He smirks up at me and I roll my eyes. "You bet it is. That shit is disgusting, Dad. Like traumatizing."

My dad chuckles and then says, "Hey, wanna see what I'm making in the garage?"

He pulls the sliding glass door open with a flourish and

Finn and I follow him through the house, passing by my mom who is opening another bottle of wine.

"Do not go in the greenhouse, love!" my dad says and my mom freezes.

"Why not?"

"Just don't do it," I say as she glances out into the backyard.

"Oh...oh shit," she mutters, uncorking the wine completely and pouring herself another glass. "Thanks for telling me. My brain couldn't handle seeing that."

"Me either. Steer clear," my dad replies as we step into the garage. The door slams behind us with a crash as my dad flicks the overhead light on.

Off to the side, next to the SUV, is a little wooden swing.

"It's for Vincent," my dad says proudly. "I built it this weekend."

"Goats like swings?" Finn asks.

"Um, yes, and get this." My dad's voice lowers. "I'm going to add a seesaw."

I eye the contraption as I try to envision it. What the hell is Vincent going to do with a seesaw?

"But to use it, Vincent will need a goat friend."

Ah, there it is.

Finn runs a hand across his jaw. "You're going to buy another goat, Basil?"

My dad glances back at the door leading into the house and nods. "Hell yeah. I fucking love goats."

A strangled laugh escapes me. "Mom is going to kill you."

"She won't know until it's too late. She's going on that girls' trip next weekend and I'm going to the 4-H fair."

"You will be dead come Monday," I say and Finn nods.

"Risky business, man."

My dad seems unconcerned but swears us to secrecy before leading us back inside the house. My mom is slurping on her wine, her eyes tracking her husband.

"I know, Basil," she says ominously, and my dad skids to a stop.

"Know what?" he asks much too innocently. But he's not fooling anyone. I'm sure he left a browser open with the 4-H website up and my mom has just been waiting to pounce.

"I *know.*"

My dad shifts nervously on his feet and I just tug Finn towards the stairs.

"Bye Dad, good luck!" I call out as Finn and I walk up the stairs toward my room. It hasn't changed since high school —posters of bands I liked in high school are still stuck to the walls, pictures of me and Finn line the mirror on the back of my door, and my twin bed with the navy-blue comforter sits below the window.

I close the door and lean against it, breathing a little too heavily for how little exercise I just did. Yeah, I need to get back into running.

"Should we rescue him?" Finn asks, flopping down on my bed.

"He's a grown man. He can manage," I say as I move toward Finn, who has his hands behind his head, his thighs spread open. His shirt has ridden up his abdomen a little, showing off his smooth, muscled torso and I run a finger across it.

Finn's breath hitches as our eyes meet and I fiddle with the button on his jeans.

"Finn, do you really have secrets?"

His eyes close and he nods. "Of course I do. Everyone does."

"I don't. I thought we didn't do secrets."

"We're not kids anymore."

"But, like, what kind of secrets do you have that you feel like you can't tell me?"

He swallows and shrugs. "Just stuff you don't need to know."

I slowly crawl over him, my elbows bracketing his shoulders, my face directly over his.

"I tell you everything. You know everything about me."

"I'm sure that's not true."

The tip of my nose touches his.

"It is. You've seen me at my worst. You've seen everything, and it hurts to know that maybe I haven't seen the entirety of you. Like maybe I don't know you as well as I thought."

His eyes pop open and we just stare at each other, gazing into each other's depths.

"I can't," he breathes. "I can't tell you everything."

My thumbs smooth over his cheeks.

"Why not?"

"It would change...it would change everything."

My entire body freezes as I watch him.

"What would change, Finn?"

He doesn't answer, just watches me intently. Aggravating man.

I press my lips to his, and his hands move to my back, whispering across my skin.

"Nothing would ever change how I feel about you," I say softly, my lips moving across his as I speak. "I will always love you, Finn," I add when he stays silent.

I nibble on his lower lip, pulling it between my teeth, our eyes connected, unwavering, unmoving.

"Do you love me?" I ask, letting him go and kissing the corner of his lips.

"You know I do."

"Say it."

His hands tighten against my back, grinding me down against him. "I love you, Landon," he whispers.

My lips quirk up and I press my lips to his once more, tasting him, letting my tongue trace the outline of his mouth.

His body trembles beneath me, one of his hands sliding down to my lower back, his fingers dipping beneath the waistband of my jeans.

And we just lie there, me licking at his lips, nibbling on them, kissing them until my dad bellows that dinner is ready.

nine

EIGHT YEARS AGO

FINN

"HEY, FINN," Basil says, his smile a little sad. "Logan isn't home yet, and Landon is upstairs sick."

I run a hand across the back of my neck and nod. "Yeah, he told me. I thought I'd hang with him a little. He said he was bored..."

Basil's smile widens and the gloomy look on his face disappears. "Oh, he'd love that. I'll tell Logan where you are when he gets home."

I nod and make my way up the stairs to Landon's room. I know where it is. I spend more time here than I do at my house. It's so warm and comforting here.

And *he's* here.

I knock on the door and peek in, seeing Landon lying on the bed, his cheeks a little flushed, a blanket pulled up over his shoulders.

"Hey, Finn," he says, his voice a little weak. God, my heart aches, seeing him like this. I hate it. I've only known him a few months and I'm already so far gone.

"I thought I'd come keep you company, if you want."

He sits up and a cough racks his body. "Yeah, if you're okay with maybe catching my germs."

"I'm immune. You can't get me sick."

To be honest, not much could keep me away from him. Not even throw up.

I move toward his bed, toeing my shoes off and slipping in next to him, sitting up against the headboard.

He leans into me, his body so fucking warm against mine. God, he's burning up.

I press my cold hand to his cheek, and he sighs against it.

"I hate being sick," he says, resting his head on my shoulder and then scooting all the way down until his head is in my lap. There's no shame here, just total and utter acceptance that this is what it is between us.

I kind of love it.

I stare down at him, his eyes closed, his cheeks red, and I feel butterflies erupt inside of me.

Without thinking, I thread my hand through his hair, pulling on the wavy strands lightly. Landon huffs a contented sigh and curls up closer to me. It should be weird, but it's not. No, this seems perfectly right.

He has to feel it too, right? He has to. This can't just be me.

Slowly Landon drifts off to sleep. I can tell by how his chest rises and falls beneath the blanket.

Holding my breath, I allow my finger to skirt over the bridge of his nose, mapping out the freckles there, and then it moves down to his lips.

I don't touch them, though. No, I just hover above them, staring, letting myself imagine what they'd feel like.

I'm not sure what I'd do if I ever kissed him.

Combust and fall apart probably.

Not that he'd ever want me like that. That's not something I should even think about. It will *never* happen.

I lean back against the headboard and let my head *thunk* against the wall. My eyes close, my fingers still in his hair as I try to divert my thoughts.

But they're stuck on him.

They're always on him.

I can't escape him. He's ensnared me.

The door opens a while later and Logan pokes his head in.

"Hey man," he whispers, his eyes swiveling down to his brother still curled up in my lap asleep.

I lift my chin in acknowledgment as Logan moves into the bed next to me.

"He was hoping you'd come by," Logan says, handing me a candy bar and a bottle of water.

I take it from him and set it aside, running my hands down Landon's back. He lets out a sigh and my heart just melts.

Logan nudges me with his shoulder. "Want me to grab

my laptop and we can watch a movie while he sleeps? Doesn't seem like you're going anywhere," he whispers.

I glance at Landon and nod.

"Yeah, that sounds good, man," I say and Logan disappears, leaving me to trace Landon's face with my eyes.

Taking him in. Drinking him up.

This feeling isn't going away. I'm going to have to live with this forever.

I'm doomed.

ten

LANDON

WE MAKE it home from my parents' a little after midnight, Finn carrying me up the stairs to my apartment, stripping me down and tucking me into bed.

I am pooped. After dinner, we went on a walk to "see the stars". There were no motherfucking stars. Just clouds and the whiff of pollution. But we did it because my dad had shown up with Curie in her Petpod and Vincent on his leash looking way too excited.

Like we could say no to him.

So, we bundled up and took a walk around the block before coming back and stuffing ourselves with cake. We sat out by the fire and chatted until I fell asleep against Finn.

Now he's crawling up behind me and pulling me against his warm body. His leg is thrown over mine, my ass nestled against his groin, and his face is pressed into my neck.

I feel his lips against my skin, the huff of his warm breath, and my entire body relaxes into him.

His hand slips down my stomach, leaving a trail of desire in its wake, and a low moan escapes me as the tips of his fingers dip just below the waistband of my boxers.

My dick perks up just being near a hand. It knows what those are for. Now I'm remembering how good it felt to have him knead my ass while I came.

It wants to do that again.

"Stop thinking and go to sleep," Finn mumbles and I reach back and thread my hand through his hair, holding his mouth to my neck.

"I can't. I'm horny," I say

"Again?" he asks, his breath coming out a little stilted.

"You started it by giving me that happy ending yesterday."

"Jesus. I did no such thing."

"You massaged my ass and I came. It counts."

A choked laugh bursts from him and his fingers tighten against me.

"I need to get off if I want to sleep."

"That's not a thing."

"Maybe not for you, but if I don't do it, I'll be up for hours…" I grumble as his hand slides up my chest and cups my throat, squeezing it lightly.

Gah. I like that. Really like it. My dick likes it too. It's so fucking desperate, leaking, and needy.

"Fine. Go on," he says softly, and I let out a shaky breath, shoving my boxers down with my free hand, my cock springing free.

"You sure?"

"What's the alternative? You getting up and doing it in the bathroom?"

My hand engulfs my dick and I give it a long, slow stroke.

"We both know that you have no shame."

He's not wrong, I think as I start to jack myself. Shame? What's that? I don't have it. Not anymore.

"You've seen it all before. I have no secrets from you, Finn...unlike you," I pant.

His fingers tighten against my throat, but he remains silent. I inhale deeply, trying to pull in air.

Fuck, I like that. It's not a hard pressure against the side of my neck, but it's enough to have me gasping.

My hand works faster as Finn continues to clench and unclench his hand around my throat, playing with my breathing as his own breath puffs into my ear.

My eyelids flutter closed and all I can sense is him—the feel of him against my back, the smell of his skin, the sound of his panting.

I grind my ass into his hard cock, feeling it press against my crease, and I turn my head, pressing my lips to his.

As our mouths collide, his hand tightens around my neck and I see stars, bright blinding flashes as my climax draws closer.

"More," I gasp against his lips and he lets out a pained groan, as he slants his head and sweeps his tongue into my mouth, diving in and then retracting. It's brief but it's enough. It's just enough. "Shit!" I rasp as I feel my balls draw up and my cock jerk. My cum splashes across the sheets and my hand as I continue to pump myself through the orgasm.

Finally, when the last drop has been squeezed from me, Finn's hand relaxes from around my neck and I draw in a long, deep breath.

"Finn, my god," I pant. "What was that? What the fuck was that?"

He leans back a little, his forearm resting on his forehead, his expression indiscernible in the shadows.

"It was nothing."

"You did some breath play stuff...and damn, I *liked* it. I'm having all sorts of revelations right now. I think you unlocked a new kink."

The click of his swallow permeates the room.

"And you stuck your tongue in my mouth."

He runs a hand over his face and sighs.

"I wanna do that again."

He shakes his head but continues to stay silent.

"It's either that, or I find someone else to do it with me," I threaten. "Don't make me scrounge, Finn. Who knows what kind of person I'll find. There are a lot of weirdos out there."

He groans and then rolls away and stands up.

"Fine."

He strolls out of the room without another word.

"Fine," I mutter as I roll onto my back and press my hand against my throat. "What does that mean?"

* * *

We don't talk again that night. Mainly because I doze off before he comes back and when I wake up at the first hint of sunlight, my naked body splayed across his, he's still asleep.

But his cock isn't. It's hard and pressed against me. It knows what's up.

I shift against him, feeling it drag against my stomach and Finn lets out a low groan, hoarse from sleep.

"Fuck off," he mutters and I drag my lips across his collarbone.

"No, Finn. I want to do it again."

"Ugh. Go back to sleep," he grumbles.

"I can't."

He pries an eye open and peers up at me. I bite down on his shoulder and he grunts.

"You're just not trying hard enough."

"Oh, I'm hard enough," I say and then arch my hips into him.

He rolls his eyes but he feels it, the length of my dick against him because his cheeks turn bright red.

"I'm needy, Finn, and in pain. It hurts. Make it stop."

"So fucking dramatic," he mumbles, and I half-expect him to ignore me, but then suddenly, I'm on my back and my hands are pinned above my head as Finn looms over me, his body stretched out at my side.

I'm completely naked, nothing hiding my straining, hard cock from his dark, searching eyes. Good. Nothing in our way.

My breath catches in my throat as I take him in—stubbled jaw, disheveled hair, flushed cheeks.

"What are you going to do to me?" I whisper, wetting my lips. God, I ache. This is so new, so different. But it doesn't feel wrong.

Nothing ever feels wrong with him.

His hand flexes against my wrists as he watches me, something warring in those dark depths.

And then he does something I don't expect. He reaches down and wraps his free hand around my thick, needy dick and strokes it.

My back arches off the bed at the sensation. God, that feels so fucking *good*.

His thumb brushes over the head, sliding against the slit, and I let out a small whimper.

"More," I breathe and his hand slides to the base of my dick again, flexing his strong fingers around me tightly.

"Finn," I moan, feeling overly warm and vibrating with *something*. God, first that kiss and now this. "More," I gasp.

He slowly starts to pump me, drawing it out, torturing me.

I want to reach up and pull him down on top of me, feel him against me, but I can't. He has me trapped against the bed, my body stretched out and at his mercy.

God, I knew he wasn't vanilla. I knew it. He's fucking rocky road.

I tilt my head up as far as I can, watching the way his hand works me over. His tanned skin against the deep purple of my dick. Shit, that's a sight I didn't know I needed.

"Faster," I grunt, my head dropping back onto the pillow because he's taking his sweet time and it's driving me crazy.

His gaze snaps from my dick to my eyes and he ensnares me. I can't look away.

"Please," I groan. "Please Finn. Fuck me faster." He lets out a shuttered breath, doing what I ask. I arch my hips up with each downward thrust, pressing myself into his fist harder.

God. More. More, Finn. Don't take your hand off my dick. Keep it there forever.

"Yes, yes, yes," I chant, and then his name is ripped out of me as I explode across my chest, cum hitting my face, as I writhe and pant.

When I finally come down from the high of it, Finn is staring down at me, his eyes hooded, his chest heaving.

"That was..." I begin, trying to find the ability to breathe. "...that was fucking amazing."

It's like I've been living in the dark for the past twenty years and now my eyes have been opened. Everything's in fucking technicolor now.

He lets go of my hands trapped above my head, but I don't even move them, just keep them right where they are, remembering how good it felt to have him restrain me like that.

"Want me to reciprocate?" I ask and his eyes snap to mine.

He shakes his head. "No."

My eyes swivel to his crotch and see a sizeable bulge there.

"It doesn't have to mean anything," I say and he narrows his gaze.

"Yeah, I know. And that's the problem." He sits up and hands me some Kleenex before standing up.

"I'll be back. Just give me.... Fuck, Landon. Just give me a few."

I watch him walk away as I absently mop my mess up,

and then I obsessively replay what just happened over and over in my mind.

God, that felt fantastic. I liked it. I want him to do it again.

And again. On repeat.

I hear the shower start and I lean up on my elbows and stare at the bathroom door.

What's he doing in there?

For a moment, I wonder if it disgusted him, his hand on my dick. But then discard it.

No, no, that's not it. He's seen me come before when we were in high school. We'd sat side by side and jacked off multiple times. And since then, he's been in contact with all my bodily fluids and never once seemed grossed out.

No, this is something different.

The water shuts off and Finn emerges, a cloud of steam behind him, a towel wrapped around his waist.

"I'm hurt I wasn't invited," I tell him, a smile on my lips. "I could have joined you. We could have washed each other's backs."

He meets my gaze and rolls his eyes.

"And each other's dicks," I tack on because he's being an asshole.

He stumbles slightly but rights himself quickly. When he gets to the dresser, he drops his towel and I admire his ass for a minute as he bends down and pulls on a pair of sweats and a long-sleeved white shirt.

"I'm making breakfast."

I pout and scoot to the end of the bed.

He peeks over at me and sighs, moving to where I am and holding out his arms.

"That's what I thought, Finn. Trying to be so cold. But you're just a big marshmallow. A hot, toasty one. You're a motherfucking s'more."

He snorts as I wrap myself around him and he picks me up, carrying me to the bathroom so I can shower. I nibble on his neck the entire time, just tasting him.

"Stop it," he mutters, his hands gripping my ass and I kiss his ear.

"I am taking after Vincent. Just get me a collar and tote me around."

He sets me on the counter and turns on the water.

"Maybe I'll get you a muzzle."

"Even better. And get me a cock cage too. Make me your bitch, Finn."

He stiffens, his brows raised. "Honestly, where do you come up with this shit?"

I huff a laugh and lean back on my hands, my happy dick settled right against my thigh.

"I have a weird brain. I think it's genetic. You've met my dad, right?"

"Right, why did I even ask." He picks me up and sets me down on the shower chair, the hot water raining down on me.

"I'll grab your prosthetic," he says and closes the curtain, leaving me to sit and wash.

When I'm done, I dry off, put on my prosthetic, and walk into the bedroom to dress before meeting Finn in the kitchen.

"Ah, cooking me breakfast," I coo and then peer over at the coffee maker.

"You're out of coffee beans," Finn says, and my eyebrows meet.

"For fuck's sake," I mutter. "I need my coffee, Finn. You know how I get."

"Yeah, well you also need to eat, or else you turn into a real bitch. Let's do that first and then we can grab something on the way to your parents'."

I groan and flop down onto a seat, stretching my prosthetic out in front of me and rubbing my thighs.

"I won't survive."

"You'll be fine," Finn says, bringing me a plate of toast and eggs.

He joins me and we eat in silence, my ankle wrapped around his, and when we're done, we stride out the door, my eyes on Finn in those sweatpants.

Hmm, they look good on him. I eye my own torn jeans and sweatshirt and realize Finn looks like fucking sin in pajamas while I look kind of like.... Well, not like that.

I reach out and grab onto his ass and Finn turns to look at me.

"Hands to yourself," he says and I lean up and smack a kiss to his lips.

"You just look sexy in those," I say and pull my hand away, tucking it around his arm.

"You're delusional," he mutters as he leads me down to the car.

"You've opened my eyes, Finn. I can see clearly now."

"Stop fucking joking," he scolds as he slides into his car.

I buckle myself into the passenger seat and turn to look at him.

"I'm not joking. That was amazing. Why haven't we done that before?"

His hands flex on the steering wheel and he peeks over at me. "Because that's not what we do."

"Well, it's what we should do," I say, my lips turning down in a frown. "Unless you don't want to."

He backs out from the spot and then moves onto the street, not answering me. Oh shit. Is he trying not to hurt my feelings?

I fiddle with the zipper on my sweatshirt and watch him. His jaw is clenched, the muscle there moving back and forth as he grinds his teeth.

My hand reaches out and I stroke my hand across it and his eyes flash to mine.

"I won't pressure you about it," I say and let my finger trail down to his shoulder, massaging the stiff muscles there.

Finn nods and then fiddles with the radio, turning up the volume and drowning the silence with new beats.

I let my hand settle between us and I turn to look out the window as we drive toward downtown.

The entire time my mind conjures up images of Finn over me, his hands on me, stroking me, choking me.

God.

I shift in my seat and adjust my hardening dick.

Of course Finn sees it. His eyes snap to my crotch because he sees everything when it comes to me.

"Just having a situation," I reply, waving my hand around awkwardly. "Don't mind me."

His eyes move back to the road and then minutes later he's parallel parking on the street. Always so capable. I have never been able to do this. But for Finn, it seems effortless.

He shuts off the car and steps outside and I follow, tucking my hard dick beneath the waistband of my jeans.

It has all sorts of ideas despite the fact that Finn doesn't seem all that thrilled to go along for the ride. Maybe that was a one-off. Maybe he didn't like it. Maybe it was an experiment and he found me lacking.

Shit.

Finn is oblivious to the turn my thoughts have taken, slipping a hand around my waist as we walk across the street and enter the coffee shop.

The warmth slowly starts to defrost my nose as I tuck myself into his side, breathing him in.

"Want to drink it here or head over right away?" he asks as we move forward in line.

"Here, that way I can get a second one to go."

"Go grab our seat," he says and I leave his side reluctantly to nab our oversized chair before someone else does.

When I'm settled in it, I move my gaze back to Finn who is chatting with the cashier, a very cute guy who is smiling a little too wide. He has very straight, white teeth, and amazing hair.

I sit up a little taller in my seat, feeling my heart pang in my chest.

Finn leans his head back and laughs loudly and my eyebrows meet in confusion. Finn never laughs like that with me. Usually he's grumbling, and occasionally chuckles. He never full-on belly laughs.

The guy behind the counter waves his hand dramatically and Finn runs a hand across his jaw, grinning.

What the fuck?

His hand was on *my* dick this morning. He had his tongue in my mouth last night.

And now there's this barista dude, looking so pretty. I glance down at my missing leg and something pinches my chest and I rub at it. My eyes snap back to Finn and I watch as he grabs a pen and scrawls something on the side of a cup, handing it to the man.

Is he…is he giving this guy his number? Does Finn like dudes? Since when is that a thing?

What the hell is happening?

My mind is reeling when Finn finally grabs our drinks and settles down next to me, his body wedging against mine, all thick and warm and strong.

"What was that?" I blurt, taking my drink from him and gulping a big sip. I need the comfort of the drink because my worldview is shifting, tilting, and I'm feeling things. Uncomfortable things.

"Huh?" Finn asks, eyeing me innocently over his drink.

"Don't play games with me, Finn," I say, meeting his dark eyes. "Did you give that guy your number?"

He glances away from me and takes another sip of his drink.

"I did."

"Why?"

"We were friends in high school…."

My eyebrows fly up. I don't remember this guy. I would have remembered this guy.

"And because he asked for it."

My mouth just opens and stays that way. I cannot even think.

"Are you...Finn, are you gay?" I ask softly, feeling my eyes sting. Because since when does he not tell me this shit? Is this the secret he was talking about earlier? Has he been secretly into men this whole time?

"Does it matter?" he asks, and my eyes widen.

"Of course it fucking matters, Finn. Especially if it's a part of you. Part of your identity," I hiss.

He mulls that over and then tilts his chin down, staring into his cup. "I'm pan."

"You're pan?"

"Yeah."

"How long have you known?" I whisper.

"I don't know. Since middle school, I guess."

"Why...why didn't you tell me?" I ask, and he shrugs. He motherfucking shrugs. Like *no big deal I kept this part of me from you for years.*

My eyes water and I feel my chin start to wobble. Because he never told me. Why didn't he tell me?

"Does Logan know?" I ask, my voice raspy.

Finn frowns. "It never came up."

I bite my trembling bottom lip and Finn's eyes snag on it.

"Landon," he begins, but I just shake my head, turning my gaze, unable to look at him. How had I missed this? My mind scrambles for an explanation, but I don't have one. I'm a terrible friend—terrible to have missed this and terrible that he didn't trust me enough to tell me.

Finn's hand snakes out as if to touch me, but then it falls to his lap, tapping an uneven rhythm onto his leg.

We sit in silence, me drinking my coffee, feeling a little nauseous and hurt, and all the things.

I feel *all* of the things.

When I'm done with my drink, Finn sighs and moves to stand up.

"I'll get you another," he says and I reach out, grabbing onto him.

"I don't want one."

His brow furrows, but he nods and leans back, his hand flexing on his thigh. His jaw is clenched again, his teeth working back and forth.

"This is why I didn't tell you. I didn't want you to feel weird around me," he says quietly, and my eyes narrow and I feel the flush of anger rise inside of me, hot and blistering.

"Oh, *fuck you*," I hiss, and then stand up as quickly as I can, moving with a purpose out of the coffee shop. Gah, this man. I need space.

I need all the space right now or I'm going to bite his head off.

Finn and I have never fought. I have never felt like this before, this ugly pinched feeling in my chest. When I'd lost my leg, I went to a dark place, but that was me lashing out at him. At everyone. I wasn't angry with him, not really. But now I am.

I am a furnace. I'm going to burn the world down.

"Where are you going?" Finn asks, trailing after me and I come to a stop on the far end of the sidewalk, a slight mist hanging in the air. But I don't feel it. No, I feel nothing but fury.

"I am going to walk to my parents'. You can meet me there," I say and then move to stomp off, but Finn reaches out and grabs onto me, pulling me against him.

"You're not walking. It's too far."

"I am walking, Finn. I'm too upset to be in an enclosed space with you."

Then a tear slips from my eye and rolls down my cheek. Finn's eyes trail after it and he groans, his hands tightening on my biceps almost painfully.

"Don't cry. Don't fucking cry," he whispers, broken.

"It would have changed *nothing*," I reply, my words coming out fractured. More tears slip out of my eyes and wet my cheeks. "I am offended..." I hiccup. "I am offended that you thought you had to keep that part of you hidden. From me." I poke at my chest roughly. "From motherfucking *me*, Finn. Like I wouldn't accept you...like I wouldn't still fucking love you!"

He pulls me closer, his forehead resting against mine.

"I'm sorry...."

I inhale shakily, unable to stem the flood and just grasp onto his shirt and cry.

"Please, don't be upset with me. I can't bear it," he grunts, and I turn my face up and our lips brush.

"I'm hurt. You hurt me, Finn."

He groans and presses his lips against mine, not opening his mouth, just resting it on mine.

We stand like that, our clothes growing damp from the

mist until we finally pull apart, my cheeks wet, his eyes bloodshot.

"Forgive me," he whispers, his thumbs brushing the tears away and I sniffle.

"I'll consider it," I say and he rolls his eyes slightly.

"You already have."

I nod. "Of course, Finn. Always. Just...fuck, don't...please don't hide things from me. I want to support you, you're my best fucking friend, but I can't do that if I don't know these things. Don't hide who you are. Not from me."

He glances at me and then tilts his chin down and mutters, "Okay."

My heart stutters in my chest and I feel the fractures slowly start to mend. I peek up at him.

"Do you like that guy you gave your number to?" I ask, suddenly so very invested.

He stiffens and slowly lets me go.

"He seems fun."

I nod, my chest constricting. Because I'm fun, right? I'm the funnest.

"He's cute too," I say, trying to get him to admit...admit something. Because I have to know. Maybe that guy is his type. Do pan people have a type?

God, I don't know. I need to research this stuff.

"He is."

I roll my lips between my teeth and swipe at my cheeks.

"Are you two going to go out?"

Finn's gaze shutters and he shrugs. "Maybe. We'll see."

I don't want him to see. I don't want him to have to split his time between me and someone else. I thought we had

January to ourselves, but it seems that maybe that won't be the case. Maybe I will only see him a few hours each week, his time so consumed by another.

Maybe I should find someone to distract myself with too.

The thought turns my stomach. Can't think about this right now. Under the rug it goes. I need a bigger rug.

I wobble a little on my feet and Finn reaches out to steady me.

"You okay?"

I manage a small nod, even though it's a lie. I am a liar now. Because I don't know what this feeling is inside of me. It's new and fresh and confusing.

"We should go," I say, moving back toward Finn's car. "They're all waiting for us."

Finn eyes me warily but we still drive to my parents' place in heavy silence—Finn's eyes on the road and mine on him, seeing him through a different lens for the first time in years.

eleven

FINN

THE MUSIC PUMPS through the speakers in the school gym and my eyes strain from trying to see through the darkness and pulsing lights.

But I can't see him.

My date is with her friends, probably tired of me ignoring her, but I can't focus when he's here.

With someone else.

It's my junior year in high school and the feelings that consumed me when I first laid eyes on Landon haven't disappeared. No, they've only grown, twisting up within me. I'm sixteen and totally and utterly wrecked for my best friend.

My eyes snag on a familiar figure in the corner, pressed up against the bleachers and I move toward him. Drawn in.

Always fucking pulled toward him. He's the sun, warm and impossibly bright, and I just orbit around him, enraptured.

As I edge closer, my steps falter because there he is, his lips on someone else's. His head slanted, his tongue pressing into her mouth, his hands on her hips.

My chest aches, my heart thundering in my ears.

Of course. Of fucking course this is happening. I shouldn't have expected anything different. That he'd be my first? That I'd be his.

Insanity.

My breath falters and I turn my head away, unable to look a moment more and then I stride away. Pushing out of the gym doors and out into the cool night.

I'll let this go. I can let this go.

But I can't let *him* go.

No, I'll hold on just a little longer.

twelve

LANDON

"THIS IS A CIRCUS!" I shout into Finn's ear as we stand in the living room of the crowded house party. God, if I would have known Paulina's party would be this nuts, I probably wouldn't have come. I mean, I like a good party, but this is like next-level shit. "I'm waiting for the clowns! And those dudes on stilts!"

"I'm waiting for the bears," Finn says and I snort.

Him and bears. Ridiculous. It's a little bit of an obsession.

"We don't have to stay long," he says, his lips brushing against my ear.

"Let's hang for a bit, for Theo," I say, eyeing my brother's boyfriend who is looking completely overwhelmed. "He looks scared."

"To be fair, this is scary," Finn grumbles, his hand tightening on my waist, his fingers slipping against my bare skin.

I rest my head against his shoulder. But there is still something frustratingly lodged between us, something microscopic, but it's there. I can feel it.

I think he has more secrets, things about him that he's tucked away and kept from me. My cracked heart isn't mending as fast as I'd like it to. I still ache from earlier.

His finger tucks itself under the waistband of my jeans and I sigh.

At least he's still touching me. I couldn't stand it if he stopped.

Does he touch his other friends the way he touches me?

We move forward through the throng of people, Logan and Theo moving out from beside us and toward the drink table.

"You guys want anything?" Logan shouts and I shake my head.

Although maybe I should have something to drink. I'm a terrible dancer.

Glancing over at Finn, I see him looking down at his phone and my lips turn down in a frown.

Maybe if I slide up against him, he will forget all about that cute guy who got his number and who texted him almost immediately.

I saw the way Finn's eyes lit up over it. How quickly he texted him back. How his hands had dropped from me and went straight to his phone, flying across the screen.

Fuck.

I've never had competition before. I don't like it.

I am a terrible loser. I pout and whine.

I turn into a three-year-old.

"Actually, you know what? Get me drunk, Finn," I say with a wide, frantic smile. "And then dance with me. Let me stand on your feet and move me like a marionette." I bat my eyelashes at him.

Finn glances down at me, our eyes locking. He's a good dancer. I've seen him at our high school dances, moving seamlessly with the beat.

I never could do that. I was bad enough with two legs and now I'm one leg down.

Send help.

But I know that if he were to place his hands on me and guide me, I'd be able to look somewhat decent.

I may even enjoy myself.

Maybe he will too.

"Dance with me, Finn. Teach me," I say, and he ponders it a moment because we've never done this before. My high school dances were spent with girls from my class. But then Finn tugs me onto the dance floor and that's all forgotten. My body falls into him, my chest against his, my hands snaking around his neck, and he moves his thigh between my legs, pressing up against me. Right there. Right *fucking* there.

A gasp escapes my mouth as my hands slide into his hair at the nape of his neck, tugging lightly.

"I'll fucking teach you," he growls into my ear and I bite back a moan.

Because *yes, please*. Teach me all the things, Finn.

His hips arch into mine, his fingers digging into my waist as we move in time with the beat.

Shit. He's all I can feel and see.

It's just me and him.

Us.

One of his hands trails up my back and he cups my neck.

I lean back to stare into his eyes, those fucking penetrating eyes, as we rock into each other. We move like we're fucking.

Is this what it would be like to have him inside of me? I mean, now that I know he likes guys, I wonder if he's ever considered me. Has he ever wanted me like that?

Gah, now I want to know.

I mean, he did have his hand around my dick this morning, making me come. The memory of it wakens me. My body alight with...something needy and insistent.

Finn leans forward and his lips brush against mine, breathing into me and I part my mouth to inhale him.

The lights are pulsing around us, in time with my heart, the beat thick and heady as it pumps beneath our feet.

My dick is thick and long, pressed against him, rubbing, aching.

"Finn," I groan against his lips, feeling overly flushed and warm.

But then the haze is pierced and slowly starts to fade when I feel someone moving against us. My head turns along with Finn's and I see *him* standing right there.

The guy from the coffee shop.

Goddammit. Of course it is. I couldn't make this shit up.

His eyes are on Finn, his lips turned up in a sensual smile, his body moving smoothly and sexually.

"Hey," he says, the word carried away by the noise around us. Finn moves away from me, his hands slipping from my waist, and he smiles back at him.

"Hey," he replies, leaning down toward him. My hands tighten around his neck, still not letting go. Just holding on.

He's mine.

Mine.

The guy's eyes move to where Finn and I are connected, and he cocks his head.

"This your friend?" he asks.

Finn nods and reaches back, unclasping my hands from his neck. They fall to my side, tingling and cold.

Why did he do that? He's never done that before.

"Landon, this is Archer," Finn says.

Well, shit, he even has a badass name. And two legs. Motherfuck.

I wave at him with my empty hand and then stuff it into the pocket of my sweatshirt.

"Nice to meet you," I say, forcing a smile onto my face.

Archer flicks a wave at me and then leans toward Finn, saying something into his ear, something not for me.

I suddenly feel incredibly alone in this crowded space. Because Finn's going to leave me to go off with barista guy.

Finn, who is pansexual. Finn, who likes men.

Who likes *whole* men.

I shift and then awkwardly fling my hand out to the side.

"I'm going to...go. I'll go over there," I say, feeling my throat tighten and my eyes sting. I turn on my heels, half-expecting Finn to follow me, hoping he will. But when I make it to the drinks table, I notice that he's still with Archer, faces tucked close to each other, talking animatedly. Archer, with the nice hair, and the white teeth, and the cute clothes.

My heart sinks, just crumbles to the floor.

I'm being replaced.

I should just leave. I should go.

That way he can flirt without me awkwardly looming, watching.

I pull out my phone and open a ride app, not wanting to bother anyone with driving me home. I'm not far, just ten minutes away.

I don't even have the energy to find my brother to tell him I'm leaving.

I don't want to have to explain. I just need to get out of here.

I slip through the crowd and out the front door, and get in the waiting sedan.

When I arrive home, I move up the stairs, shooting a text to Logan, letting him know I'm home safe. I don't text Finn, though. I don't want him to feel obligated to come home to me.

I want him to have fun. I want him to be happy. I do.

Fuck, I want him to come home.

Come home to me, Finn.

The door shuts behind me and I shuck my sweatshirt, tossing it onto the couch and feeling my nose prickle, my eyes blinking rapidly.

Is this how it will be when he's with someone else? When he finds his person and I've been replaced? I hate it already. Dread it.

Moving into the bathroom, I peel off my shirt and

stumble slightly, my hands grasping onto the counter to steady myself. My eyes meet my watery gaze in the mirror and I shake my head.

I am not going to keep crying. Jesus. I'm a full-grown man. Get a grip.

A tear slips down my cheeks and I swat it away.

I'm going to take a shower. I'm going to wash the day away and try not to think of Finn with someone else.

Someone who isn't me.

I fumble to unzip my jeans, my throat working dramatically, my hands shaking.

I sit down on the toilet, pulling them down my thighs and working my prosthetic off, then reach over and turn on the warm water.

Then I just stare at the shower chair.

Fuck, I wasn't paying attention and I did this all out of order. Now what the hell am I supposed to do? I don't feel like starting over. What a fucking chore. Fuck it, I'm not putting my prosthetic back on. I can do this. I push myself up, grabbing onto the edge of the tub but my hand slips from the condensation and I tumble to the side knocking my ribs roughly against the tub and then falling to the floor, my forehead hitting the tile with a smack.

Fuck.

Fuck!

I push myself up and sit on the mat, leaning against the tub and feeling disoriented, dumb, and sad. What the hell is wrong with me? I've never done that before.

I gotta get my shit together.

I press my fingers to my throbbing forehead and pull my hand away. No blood, so that's good, but hell, there's a bump there.

A big goose egg. Stupid fucking leg.

I grab onto my toppled prosthetic and tug it on, my entire body shaking with pent-up frustration. I will not cry again. I'm just feeling sorry for myself and it's stupid. I can take care of myself; I just need to focus. Just because Finn is off doing who-knows-what with sexy barista dude doesn't mean I need to fall to pieces.

I work myself up, standing on wobbly legs, and look at myself in the mirror. A large bump sits right in the middle of my forehead. I look like a rhinoceros.

Just put me in the zoo. Everyone can gawk at it.

I touch it tenderly, and then drop my hand down to my side and take a deep breath.

Nothing to be done about it now, so I just climb into the shower, trying to follow my normal routine but end up just sitting, eyes closed, beneath the warm spray, my mind everywhere.

And always settling on him.

Suddenly, the shower curtain is ripped open and Finn is standing on the other side, his chest heaving, his eyes wild.

When they land on the lump on my head and the purple bruise blooming across my side, his countenance darkens.

"What happened?"

"Nothing. It's fine," I reply, turning to face forward. I haven't even washed yet. I just sat here like a sad, pathetic sack.

I reach for the soap and quickly run it over my body and hair, not even bothering with shampoo. When the suds have finally run down the drain, Finn hands me my towel, watching me like a hawk as I dry off.

Without asking, he hefts me into his arms and carries me into the kitchen.

I'm completely naked as he sets me on the counter and digs out a bag of lima beans from the freezer. That's all that vegetable is good for. Disgusting pieces of shit.

He hands the bag to me and when he notices me shivering, he strides to the couch and grabs a throw blanket, placing it over my shoulders.

"What happened?" he asks again, this time more sternly, as I press the frozen beans to my head.

A sigh escapes me. "I fell."

"When?" he asks.

"Getting into the shower."

He pulls the blanket away, eyeing my side and then his eyes fly to mine.

"Why did you leave the party?"

"I wanted to give you space..."

"I don't want space," he says, his hands flexing into fists at my side.

"You looked like you wanted space. You were happy with him."

Finn's eyes flutter closed, his chest heaving.

"Archer is handsome," I add. "And whole."

Finn's eyes snap up to mine, locking me in place.

"What did you just say?" he growls.

"He's handsome and...*whole*. Not disabled."

Finn takes a step forward, pushing between my thighs.

My breath stutters from my throat, my hand drops from my forehead, and the blanket from my shoulders flutters onto the counter.

"Do you think I care about that?" he asks lowly, tilting my chin up.

I swallow and manage a small shrug.

"Maybe."

His hand grabs onto the thigh of my residual limb and he slides it down, over the knee, until he's right there, pressing against the end, cradling it.

"It changes nothing," he whispers, his forehead dropping to mine. "It changes *nothing*."

My hands fly up to grasp his face and I crash my lips to his, slanting my mouth over his, pushing my tongue into his mouth.

God.

He groans loudly, his hand still on my leg, his other cupping my cheek, angling me just how he wants me.

His tongue presses against mine and I combust. Just go up in flames.

I gasp and pant as we devour each other's mouths, my leg wrapped around his waist, his hard cock pressed against mine.

Straining, reaching, wanting.

"Finn," I groan as he kisses his way down my neck, his hand tilting my head back so he can lick across my Adam's apple.

He shoves the blanket away from me, revealing my naked

body, as he bends over and engulfs my weeping cock with his mouth.

My eyes roll back as I cup the back of his head.

"Finn," I pant as his head bobs up and down, his warm mouth sucking me down his throat. I can hear it, the wet, slurping sounds and depraved moans emanating from him.

God, I never expected this. *Never.*

And he's so good at it, all tongue and spit, his throat contracting around me.

My mouth hangs open, gasping as he works me toward the edge. I lean back slightly and watch him, my chin on my chest, my hands fisted in his hair. I watch how his hands grip my thighs so tightly, possessively. How his back flexes and bunches with each movement.

I try to tug him off because I'm going to come, this feels too good, but he grunts and latches on, pulling me even deeper as I unload into his throat. My entire body quakes and rocks until I am utterly spent.

When it's done, the tremors of my orgasm subsiding, I lean back on my hands, pulling in air and just staring in awe as Finn slowly pulls his mouth off my dick.

He gives the tip a little kiss before he stands up slowly, his lips swollen, wet, and dripping.

"Finn," I whisper. "*Oh my god, Finn.*"

He wipes his mouth with the back of his hand and then takes a step back.

"Fuck," he says, moving even farther away from me. "Shit, I don't...."

"Come here," I say, reaching out to him.

He eyes my leg, remembering that I'm not wearing my

prosthetic, and moves toward me. He grabs onto me and pulls me into his chest, carrying me back to the bedroom with trembling hands and shaking legs.

He sets me on the edge of the bed, and then stands before me looking unsure and maybe even a little afraid.

I'm not sure what to say, so I go with my normal teasing tone, "Stop looming. Come hold me. I'm injured, Finn. Look at my head. Come make it better."

He runs a hand down his face and glances away, his throat bobbing.

"I want you to hold me," I plead.

He bites his lip, eyeing the floor, and then strips off his shirt and shucks off his pants before crawling up against me, pulling me into his chest. A hiss escapes me as he makes contact with my bruise and then he's over me, pressing his hand gently to my ribs.

"Damn you, Landon. What did you do to yourself?" he mutters, and I huff out a laugh.

"No, damn you, Finn. For having an incredible mouth and not using it on me before. You've been holding back on me."

He huffs out a laugh.

"Suck my dick all the time, Finn. Just cockwarm me."

"Stop saying that shit," he mutters as he pulls me gently on top of him, and I tuck my face into his neck, inhaling him.

"I'm being serious. I'm not even joking. You've opened a can of worms, Finn. First that incredible hand job and now this. You're stuck with me and my one leg."

"Jesus."

"Even he can't save you now."

Finn chuckles gruffly, his hand threading through my hair.

"Go to sleep," he mutters, and my eyes close.

The last thing I think before I fall into the abyss is how happy I am he came home.

To me.

thirteen

LANDON

I CAN'T STOP THINKING about the blow job and the hand job. All the jobs. Work me over, Finn.

But he hasn't touched my dick again since the night on the kitchen counter.

No, his fingers are too busy texting Archer.

I had hoped he would forget all about the annoyingly sexy barista now that he's had me, but no such luck. Apparently, I wasn't that memorable.

My inability to get Finn to stick his hands down my pants isn't for lack of trying. He pulls away each time, leaving me disappointed.

I have spent the last two days practically naked, wandering around the apartment, sticking my dick out, pointing to it, just to make sure he remembers it's there.

But every time, he just lifts an eyebrow at me and wraps

me up in a blanket instead of wrapping his hand or mouth around my dick. It's really starting to frustrate me.

Maybe it's this bump on my head turning him off. I mean, it's gone down a lot, but mostly it's a nice shade of ugly purple.

Who wouldn't want me like this? Huh? I'm a total catch.

"Are you done?" I ask, eyeing Finn whose thumbs are zooming over the screen of his phone.

We're currently parked in a dirt lot about to take a short hike to Felton Bridge, a large wood-covered bridge that spans the San Lorenzo River. We should have been out of the car minutes ago, but I've just been sitting here watching Finn ignore me.

I can tell he really likes the guy. Maybe they're rekindling something. I don't remember Finn dating anyone specific in high school, but apparently, there's quite a bit I don't know about this best friend of mine.

When I pried, he told me they're just friends. But I've never liked a friend like that before. I mean, not since Finn.

But Finn is different. He's always been different.

He peeks over at me. "Yeah, one second," he says and slips the phone into his pocket. "Ready."

I'd rather he left the stupid thing in the car so Archer doesn't interrupt my time with him, but I don't mention it because I don't want to seem jealous. I'm not jealous.

Lies. I'm so fucking jealous.

Finn links his hand with mine as we move down the path leading to the bridge.

"So, what were you guys talking about?" I ask, trying to sound nonchalant. Just open that door for me, Finn. I wanna know why you're so into this guy. What does he have that I don't, besides two legs, awesome hair, a cool job, and a nice wardrobe?

Finn glances at me and smirks. "Not telling you shit, Landon. So might as well stop trying."

"I know your password."

"You would never."

I meet his stare. "Oh, wouldn't I?"

He rolls his eyes, and we continue walking. He stays silent. Motherfucker.

"Just give me a hint. Like a few words. I can do all sorts of things with those."

His hand tightens in mine and he shakes his head. "I know you can."

A pout forms on my mouth and I slow down a little, feeling suddenly sluggish. Light rain has started to fall from the sky and Finn tugs me forward, trying to get me to move faster. But I have lost all motivation.

"Come on, Landon. Stop pouting."

"I like pouting. I do it so well."

"Yeah, you fucking do," he says, and then drops my hand and squats down in front of me. "Hop on. We're going to get soaked if you keep walking like a turtle."

"Are you insulting my missing leg?"

"What? No, I'm insulting you being a brat," he replies as I climb onto his back. My arms link around his shoulders, my thighs held in his hands.

I bounce against his back as he jogs us forward, and he's not even breathless after a few minutes.

God, he's so strong. I am not a tiny guy.

One of my hands slips down the collar of his shirt, pressing against his flexing pec, and then I pinch his nipple.

He grunts. "Keep your hands to yourself."

I don't listen. I just keep roaming, letting my hands wander. Finn's breath starts to puff out of him, almost winded, finally showing some semblance of weakness. I was beginning to think he was a robot.

"I like your nipples, Finn," I say. "I want to bite them."

"I'm going to toss you off of me. Just chuck you right down the hill."

"You would never," I say as I move my hand over to the other nipple and pluck at it.

He huffs, adjusting me on his back. His threats are empty words. I don't believe them. He would never hurt me.

Never.

In the distance, I see the covered bridge so I make sure to let my hands roam freely until he steps inside and gently sets me down, just as the rain starts to pour from the sky.

"God," he huffs, his cheeks flushed and his chest heaving.

"I know. I'm that good with my hands...almost as good as you," I say, smiling. I arch my hips a little and his bottom lip disappears between his teeth.

"Jesus, you and your dick," he says, and I huff out a laugh.

"You've been ignoring it." I glance around, noticing that there is no one around. No, it's just me and him. Alone.

We could do so many things out here, where no one can see.

He runs a hand through his hair and eyes me. "I have."

"Why?" I ask softly, feeling small in this moment, so utterly consumed by him.

"For my own sanity," he mutters and then lets out a shuttered breath. "We should watch the rain."

"That's boring," I say, but he spins me around, tucking my back against his chest. His hands slip around my waist, his head resting on top of mine.

"Watch the fucking rain, Landon."

My eyes move to the wet earth outside our little shelter. Rain splatters onto the ground, creating muddy puddles. I can hear the rush of the river beneath our feet.

Slowly, I feel his finger sneak under my sweater.

It's soft and tentative, but it's there. I can feel it all the way to my bones.

It slides across my stomach, dipping into my belly button before tracing the line of my happy trail.

My head leans back, my heart thundering in my chest. It's just Finn and me on this old bridge in the middle of nowhere. Just us.

His finger slips down to the button of my jeans, and it pops open.

Magic fingers. So fucking skilled.

My breath grows labored as I stand perfectly still, waiting in anticipation for what he's going to do.

His fingers creep down below the waistband of my pants, and my dick immediately thickens. It grows, inching toward him, like a plant arching into the sun.

I need it so bad. He's kept me waiting *days*.

His finger brushes against the tip of me and I let out a loud moan.

He stills behind me and I bite my lip, telling myself to be quiet, to shush. I don't want him to stop.

Thankfully he's not still for long. No, his long fingers brush over me again and I tremble, one of my hands reaching back to clasp onto his head, pulling his lips down to my neck. They brush against my overheated skin as he thumbs the slit of my cock.

It's leaking now and I know he can feel it. The tips of his fingers are slick with my precum, and then his hand surrounds me, squeezing my cock. I lift onto my toes, grasping onto his forearm tighter.

I don't even see anything outside anymore. It's just white noise and the feel of him behind me, pressing, cupping, stroking.

"Finn," I gasp as he rolls my balls in his hands before moving back up to pump my straining dick.

God, don't stop. Just don't. I'm fucking myself into his hand, needing *more*. Needing something to take me off the ledge I'm teetering on.

His teeth graze the side of my neck and I hear a low rumble begin in his throat.

"Is this what you want?" he asks, and I just nod. Just once. A tilt of my head because I'm unable to do more.

I've lost the ability to speak.

"You've been asking for it. Begging for it," he growls, his teeth pulling on my earlobe, and I nearly melt—just liquefy into the wooden planks below my feet.

"Yes," I moan, my throat dry.

And then suddenly his hand is gone, my pants buttoned,

his hand resting on my stomach. I let out a whimper as Finn exhales shakily.

Why did he stop? Why the fuck did he stop?

Then I hear it—voices steadily approaching.

God, do these people have the worst timing, or what? First my dad and now these assholes. Honestly, do I have the worst luck or what?

I swallow roughly, trying to calm myself, because anyone with eyes can see what we've been doing. I'm sure I look flushed and utterly wrecked. I take a step away from him, subtly adjusting myself in my pants, tucking my hard dick beneath the waistband of my pants.

"We should go," I say, feeling fluttery and unsteady on my feet.

His eyes meet mine and I see him adjust himself, his cock pressing out from the thigh of his jeans. And my cheeks heat.

So he did like it.

He liked *me*.

"Stop looking at it," he says quietly and my eyes fly up to meet his.

"I can't not see it, Finn," I hiss. "It's huge. You look like you're smuggling a squash in your pants. Tuck it away like I did."

He does not, in fact, tuck it away. Instead, he just runs a hand down his face and sighs.

I take a step closer, not wanting anyone to see his dick but me.

Pressing into him, I feel our hard dicks brush against each other and need punches through me once more.

"Not helping," he says, and I snort a laugh.

"Yes, well, I don't want people to run screaming in the other direction when they see it pointed at them."

He turns to the side, reaching into his pants and tucking it away. Thank god.

And then he looks at me.

"We should go. We have to meet Logan and Theo soon."

"Yeah." I glance out at the rain still coming down hard outside. "But we should go home first and change because we're going to get soaked on our way back to the car."

"I thought you said it was going to be sunny today."

"I didn't actually look at the weather."

He sends me a look that only makes my dick harder. Those dark, cynical, grumpy glares are not doing what he thinks they are.

"You're only making me hornier."

When he doesn't reply, I lean into him and press my lips to his.

"You touched my dick. Three times, Finn. You can't take it back now."

"I'm not...shit, I'm not taking it back. Let's just.... We should go."

"Yes, take me home Finn so you can finish what you started."

The people are approaching the bridge now, wet and smiling and chatting happily. I turn to Finn, taking him in.

His hair is slightly wet and his cheeks are flushed. Damn, he's so beautiful. I can't help it; I slip my hand into his and we make our way out into the rain.

* * *

We make the drive home in silence, one of Finn's hands on the steering wheel, the other on my cock.

I put it there. Just grabbed it and stuck it right over my hard dick.

He hasn't moved an inch, except for his chest expanding with each shaky inhale.

When we step inside the apartment and the door clicks shut behind us, our eyes meet, tension snapping in the space between us.

I pull my sweater over my head, tossing it onto the couch, leaving me bare-chested. I feel goosebumps break out across my skin from the cool air.

Finn's eyes consume me, fire lighting in those dark depths, sparking something inside of me.

"We have an hour," he says, his voice rough and deep.

"I can do so many things in an hour," I whisper and then move toward him.

I press myself against his chest, my hands sinking into his hair, and his breath stutters out of him. My lips connect with his and he sags into me, tilting his head and licking his way into my mouth.

And I explode. Just a mess of colors and sensations as his hands lift me up and he walks me to the bedroom. He sets me on the edge of the mattress, leans down, and pulls my pants and boxers down, letting my cock spring free.

It hasn't gone down. No, it's only grown harder, bigger, needier.

He eyes it and then gently removes my prosthetic, setting it to the side. His fingers trail over my scar and up the inside of my thigh until I'm trembling.

"Don't stop," I whisper, and Finn's eyes snap to mine.

He steps back, pulling his hoodie off over his head, and along with it, his shirt.

I watch it all, my breath trapped within me as he slowly peels himself out of his clothes until he's completely naked in front of me.

My eyes take him in hungrily—the dusting of hair on his chest, his cut abdomen, his thick thighs.

His dick is thick and long, pushing straight out from his body, right toward me.

I lean back on my hands and eye him, challenging him to take me. To wreck me.

"What are you going to do to me, Finn?" I ask with a raised brow.

He runs a hand down his stomach and grasps his dick.

"What can I do?" he asks, and I scoot back until my head is on the pillow and spread my thighs a little for him.

"Whatever you want. You can have anything you want."

And it's true. Finn can do anything he wants to me. I trust him implicitly.

He crawls up the bed, blanketing my body as he just stares down into my eyes.

"This changes things," he says.

I shake my head gently. "It changes *nothing*. It's just you and me, Finn. Always."

He watches me intently and then his lips fall onto my chest, biting and licking his way across my nipples, pulling them into his mouth and nipping at them until I'm writhing and pulling on his hair.

When he's finished thoroughly torturing me there, his

lips move down my abdomen until he's right against my aching dick. He buries his nose in my groin and inhales deeply, his fingers clutching onto my thighs, digging his fingers into the muscle there.

"Fuuuuuck," he groans and then he licks his way up my cock and swallows it whole.

My back arches off the bed and I let out a moan. "Finn!"

He doesn't let up, ignoring my pleas. He just drags me out of his mouth and then right back in until I'm so fucking close. I'm not going to last.

But then his lips are suddenly gone and he's pulling my balls into his mouth, rolling them around with his tongue and my eyes cross, my hands clutching the sheets, tugging them right off the corners of the mattress.

His finger presses against my hole and I clench around the tip of it, imagining his dick sliding inside me. Imagining him over me, grunting, working his way in. *All the way in.*

But my thoughts are cut short when suddenly I'm being flipped over, my stomach hitting the bed, my face turned to the side. His strong hands lift me until I'm on my knees, my ass thrust out, my arms splayed out above me.

"Finn," I whisper, not sure what he's going to do, but ready for it nonetheless. "Please."

And then I feel his hands on my ass, spreading my cheeks apart. And there it is. The brush of his stubble against my sensitive skin.

His tongue snakes out and licks up my crack, the feeling so unusual, so *hot*, that I wiggle up the bed to escape it, but he pulls me back, doing it again. It's wet and warm his tongue circling me and I squirm and writhe underneath him until he finally impales me on his tongue. It slides into me, opening me, wetting me, loosening me.

A sob escapes my mouth, desperation and need laced in the sound.

Finn is eating my ass and I never want him to stop. I need him to stop. I need more. I need to come.

Suddenly I feel pressure, and my body arches up as Finn slides a finger into my wet hole.

And then his mouth is back. His tongue and finger simultaneously fucking into me as I thrash at the bed and moan, completely at his mercy.

His finger crooks and he pegs something inside of me that sets my entire body aflame and I chant his name, begging, pleading.

Please, Finn. More. Don't stop. Fuck me. Fuck me.

His one finger becomes two and I'm thrusting back against it, sluttily.

Such a whore for it.

For him.

He spreads me wide, licking, thrusting until my balls draw up and I shoot my release across the sheets. Wave after wave tumbles through me until I'm just a shivering, whimpering mess.

My cheeks are wet from tears, my body covered in a light sheen of sweat.

I roll to my side, missing the mess I made, and stare up at Finn who is watching me. His jaw is damp, his hair tousled, and he's panting wildly.

He reaches down and swipes up the cum from the sheets, spreads it on his dick, and pumps himself.

I watch in awe, ragged breaths escaping me, loving the way he grunts and how the vein in his neck protrudes as he jerks himself roughly and blows his load all over me. Unrepentant, wild, gone.

"Holy shit," I mutter when I'm fully covered in him and he's slumped on the bed, his entire body trembling.

He peeks up at me and I manage a small, weak smile. God, I'm tired. He wore me out. Who knew ass-eating could be so much work?

"That was incredible," I say, and he huffs out a laugh.

"Good."

"I've never had anyone eat my asshole before."

He runs his tongue over his lips. "It was fucking delicious."

A smirk lines his lips and I roll my eyes. "Do not even—"

"Like an all-you-can-eat buffet."

I reach over and pinch his thigh. "Do not compare my ass to a buffet. Olive Garden, Finn. It's motherfucking Olive Garden."

He reaches down and smears some of his cum across my abdomen. He stares at it for a long time, as if he's committing this to memory before he draws his hand back.

"Let's get you cleaned up before we leave."

"Same goes for you..." I say and then bite back a laugh. "And brush your teeth. And your tongue. Use all the mouthwash, Finn."

He rolls his lips between his teeth and stares down at me. "Maybe."

"Disgusting," I mutter, but feel something move through me. Lust. Need.

Yeah, this is hot. He's so hot.

He pushes himself up and that's when I hear it, the buzzing of his phone from his pants pocket. I glance down at it and wonder if it's Archer texting him.

Wondering if Finn is going to answer it.

But he doesn't. No, the phone stays tucked away in his pants, ignored.

Archer is ignored.

Because Finn has me now.

Motherfucking me.

fourteen

FINN

FUCK, I hate coming home. I'd much rather be at the Lewis' house where I feel like I have a family. Where I feel welcomed and alive.

"Is he home?" Landon asks, his eyes wandering around the space. It's not a large place, but since my mom died when I was four, it's just been Dad and me, and we don't need much.

The size of the place isn't the issue, though; it's how barren it is. It's just four walls and a roof. There is nothing personal hanging up or decorating the surfaces, despite us living here for the past two years. It's plain and empty.

But to be honest, I don't really care. I'm just glad we

haven't had to move again, and that my dad seems content with us staying here for the time being. I never expected to spend my sixteenth birthday in this town, but fuck, I'm glad I did.

I'm waiting for the other shoe to drop though. Anxiously. It lingers in the back of my mind like a ghost. It's all going *too* well. Something has to give.

I glance over at Landon who is pressed up against me, his lips pulled between his teeth.

God, I don't want to leave him. It would kill me.

Please don't make me leave.

"I just have to grab some clothes," I say, planning on spending the weekend with Landon and Logan. It's what I do most days anyway. My dad doesn't really seem to care where I am, as long as I check in with him.

And he's met the Lewis'. He likes them.

Thank god.

I move to my bedroom. It's as basic as the rest of the space. I still have unpacked boxes sitting in a corner.

Landon flops down on my bed, the bottom of his shirt riding up his stomach, exposing some of his skin. I wrench my gaze away and grab my duffle bag and begin stuffing it with clothes.

"So, I'm thinking we go to the movies Saturday and then the Boardwalk Sunday..." he says and stretches up a little farther, exposing more of his stomach and that small happy trail.

I've dreamt of tracing it with my finger, of dipping below the waistband of his jeans...

I shake those thoughts away as I zip up my duffle bag.

There is no way that will happen. He's not into guys. And he's definitely not into me.

This is an unrequited love.

I will forever be wanting him, it seems.

"Ready?" he asks, smiling softly at me.

"Yeah." We move through the dim hallway toward the front door.

And that's when I hear it, my dad getting home from work.

"Hey," he says with tired eyes as he steps into the kitchen, his skin a little drawn. Fuck, he looks old and he's only forty. "Hey, Landon."

Landon lifts an arm in a friendly wave and smiles at my dad.

"Hey, Mr. Ledger. How are you?"

"Fine. Fine," he replies and then eyes me.

"I'm going to spend the night over at Landon's," I say awkwardly. Our conversation is always stilted. It's nothing like the warmth of Finn's parents. "I, uh, texted you."

"Yeah, shit. I got it. I just..." his eyes meet mine and my heart sinks. It full-on crashes onto the floor. I know that look.

I know it.

My head shakes and I start to tremble. No. No. *No.*

"Can I speak with you?" he says, nodding to the other side of the room.

But I can't breathe. I just shake my head, my fingers tingling, my heart racing. Shit.

"Hey," Landon says, rubbing circles on my back. "Hey, come here," he says and leads me to the sofa. He presses down on my shoulders and I sink down onto the cushions, my head between my legs, trying to suck in air.

Because I *know* that look. It means we're leaving. He's found something else. I knew it was too good. It was too fucking good for too long.

"What's wrong?" Landon asks, his voice concerned.

I glance up at my dad and see the sadness in his eyes. He was always too wild to have a kid. He can never put down roots. I was never made for his life and he's too selfish to make any kind of sacrifice for me.

"We're moving," I say.

Landon's hand stills and he meets my watery gaze.

"What?" he whispers, his face falling.

God, I never want to see that look on his face again. I only ever want to see him happy.

"We...we have to leave."

"When?"

I glance up at my dad and he runs a hand through his hair. It sticks out to the side and he nods. "Next month."

Landon swallows loudly, his leg bouncing frantically.

"Where?"

"North Dakota," my dad says.

"That's...*far*," Landon breathes and I press the palms of my hands into my eyes until I see stars.

I hear my dad's footsteps retreat into the bedroom, the door close, and the shower turn on.

"That's not true, right? It can't be true," Landon asks and I turn my head to meet his sweet, innocent gaze.

"It's true."

"But you can't leave!" he cries, growing upset. "We have plans!"

I reach out and clasp onto his hand, threading my fingers through his, feeling the weight of the ages settle on my soul.

"I'm surprised we stayed this long, to be honest."

Landon blinks and blinks, processing what I've just said. He knows that I've been waiting for this to happen. I've whispered it to him in the middle of the night when everyone else was asleep.

"We'll talk to my parents. You can move in with us," Landon says, sounding determined. "You're like a brother to us."

I rub at my chest because hope is blooming. But I can't get attached to the idea, just like I shouldn't have gotten attached to him.

Everything I love is only ever ripped away.

"Sure," I say, clearing my throat because I don't want to tear this away from him.

He can hold onto hope, even though I can't.

Not anymore.

fifteen

LANDON

I CAN'T STOP STARING at Finn and his mouth. His tongue was up my ass and I liked it. My eyes drop to his hands. Those fingers were up my ass too. And I really fucking liked it.

But my best friend doesn't seem to be as enamored with me because that phone he ignored earlier is now in his hands and he's texting frantically.

I glower at him.

"Who's he texting?" Logan asks me.

I meet my brother's stare and shrug. "I think he's texting some guy he likes."

Finn's eyes snap up to meet mine. "That's not what's happening."

"Oh, so now he wants to be a part of this conversation," I try and tease, but it comes out biting.

Logan's eyes fly between us and he taps his hand on the counter.

And then realization dawns on me.

"Logan...did you know that Finn...did you *know*?" I ask, not sure how to ask that question.

"Huh?" he asks, his brows drawn in confusion. "Know what? Know that Finn likes the occasional dude? Yeah, I guess...saw him watching some gay porn once..."

Finn mutters something under his breath and runs a hand down his face, pushing himself up from the sofa. "God, Logan. Not now."

Theo's cat takes that opportunity to hop down from her kitty chateau and meows loudly by Logan's feet, brushing up against his ankles.

"Shit, I need to feed Curie or she'll bite me," Logan says. "Hold that thought."

He moves away from us and I turn to face my best friend...*my* Finn.

"Great, so do Mom and Dad know, too? Am I the only one out of the loop here?" I ask, my arms folded across my chest. I'm feeling that bloom of hurt inch its way inside of me again.

I hate it, feeling like this. Like I'm the last man standing, the only one who hasn't figured it out.

Am I dumb? How did I not know this?

"Look it's not a big deal and I don't think he really thought much of it."

I narrow my eyes at him as his phone buzzes in his hand once more.

My eyes are slits now.

"Answer that and die," I hiss and Finn's lips twitch. "Put it down and come here," I demand. I need some privacy. My mom is out at the grocery store and my dad, Theo, and Vincent are in the greenhouse. But Logan is just as nosy as me and I don't want his ears homing in on this. And they will home. Like a drone.

Finn wraps his arm around my waist and I lean into him despite being annoyed.

When we make it to the garage, I open it and step inside, seeing Vincent's goat swing still inside, now with a seesaw attached to it. Apparently, my dad hasn't given up on this. Vincent is getting a friend.

The door shuts behind us with a click and Finn turns me in his arms.

"Yes?" he asks.

I glare up at him.

"You know what you did," I say.

His hand cups the back of my neck.

"It wasn't done to hurt you. It just never came up. There was never a good time..."

He's massaging my shoulder now and I arch into it, loving his hands on me.

I try to keep my eyelids from drooping but am doing a terrible job. They want to close. I want to nuzzle into him and fall asleep.

"God, your hands," I groan. "I am still mad, but you're making conversation impossible."

He chuckles, his thumbs working up the side of my neck now and I'm pressed into him, purring.

"Will you forgive me?" he asks lowly and I peer up at him

through drooping eyelids.

His lips brush mine and I just melt.

"Maybe," I manage to mutter against him because I will not be giving in so easily.

His tongue sweeps into my mouth and I clutch onto him, my irritation dissipating as he eats at my mouth.

"Forgive me, Landon. Say you do. I can't stand you being upset with me."

I groan as he sucks on my tongue, grinding slowly against me, driving me mad in the best way.

"Ugh. Logically, I know there really isn't anything to forgive. I know you weren't obligated to tell me. I just feel... sad everyone knew but me."

"I wanted to tell you," he murmurs, kissing his way across my cheeks and down my neck. "I just...I couldn't."

I hold him against me as he sucks a mark onto my skin, but suddenly his lips are wrenched away when the garage door starts to roll open. And we peel apart, my dick hard, my breathing labored.

"Shit," he says and then adjusts himself as my mom pulls the SUV into the garage. She waves at us as she hops out, her hair a mess of curls, her eyes bright.

"Waiting with bated breath to help me carry in the groceries?" she teases, probably noticing my swollen mouth and what I'm sure is a red mark on my neck. I adjust my sweater, making sure to cover the bulge in my pants and the mark on my skin.

Kind of useless because nothing gets past this woman. My dad never stood a chance with the goat.

"Uh, yeah," Finn mutters, moving away from me and

reaching into the trunk, grabbing all the bags in one hand. It's impressive, actually.

I watch his muscles bunch beneath his shirt as he moves back inside the house.

"I forgot how nice it is to have him around. I forgot he carries all the bags in at once."

"It's a skill."

She closes the trunk and pulls me into her side and squeezes.

"You going to help me make dinner?" she asks.

I shrug. "Depends on what it is."

"Well, your dad has all these vegetables that are going to go bad, so...soup. I need help chopping."

Finn is unloading everything in the kitchen when we go inside and I check out his firm, tight ass. Just ogle it for a long minute. Hmm, does he want my tongue up his ass? I've never done that before, but maybe he'd want me to. I'll have to ask. I'd be happy to repay the favor.

He catches me staring and he fumbles with a box of crackers, dropping them onto the counter.

"Shit," he says and it's my turn to smirk.

I sidle up to him, brushing against him as often as I can as I help him unpack the groceries. My mom is humming as she moves to the fridge to place the milk inside and grab the veggies, so I take my shot.

"Do you want my tongue up your ass, Finn?" I whisper, and he snaps his gaze to me.

"You did not just ask me that in your mother's kitchen."

"Oh, I sure did." I waggle my eyebrows at him. "You want it, don't you? Want me to return the favor?"

"What favor?" my mom asks, and Finn blushes the color of the tomatoes on the island next to him.

"Oh, hey guys," my dad says with a smile as he lumbers inside, Theo following closely behind. "Why's Finn's face so red?"

It only makes him blush deeper. Gah, so cute.

"No reason," he mutters, and I can't help myself from leaning up and pressing a big kiss to Finn's lips.

Everyone stills and just blinks at us for a moment. Suddenly Logan slaps his hands together loudly, startling Curie who is licking her paws on the ground. She leaps into the air, glowers at Logan, and then saunters over to her kitty castle and disappears inside.

"I knew it!" Logan says, pointing at us, and then looks over at Theo who has a streak of dirt across his cheek. "Told you! Motherfucking told you all. They're together!"

He looks around and everyone just continues staring at us.

"We're not together. We just kiss...among other things," I say and Finn looks like he's about to put the plastic grocery bag over his head.

"I'm going to kill you," he mutters.

"You won't. You love me. You'd miss me if I was gone."

"Right, um," my mom begins and then nudges Finn with her elbow, "help me wash these veggies, and Landon, leave the poor guy alone. Get the knife and chop."

She eyes my dad and then says, "Pour me a mug, babe. I need all the wine."

My dad smacks a kiss on her cheek as Vincent bleats forlornly at the sliding glass door.

"Can someone let Vincent in, please," my dad asks and Theo moves to the door, sliding it open. Vincent bounds in and my dad bends down, making kissy noises at him.

"He's so lonely, babe," he tells my mom who just rolls her eyes. "Did you just hear him? He was crying out for a friend."

"Friend, my ass," my mom says, and Finn snorts as he washes the vegetables.

I move toward him and set out the cutting board as he quickly peels the carrots.

"So, you never gave me an answer," I say softly, and Finn eyes me, setting some carrots on the cutting board in front of me.

"I'm not answering that here."

I jut out my bottom lip and blink up at him.

"Stop with the doe eyes."

I continue to blink at him, and he smacks me with a carrot.

A gasp escapes me, and I shove at him. Finn doesn't even move, though, he just bumps me with his hip.

"Behave."

"So boring and predictable," I grumble and then lean in closer and add, "I'd do it. I'd so give it a try if you wanted me to."

He shifts on his feet. "I'm good."

I nudge him with my hip, my eyes focused on cutting the carrots into little cubes.

"Why not?" I ask.

"Because," he says.

"We both know this is not an acceptable answer in this house. I need a reason, Finn."

He's quiet for a moment and then leans down, his mouth a breath away from my ear. "Because the only one getting anything up their ass...will be you."

The knife slips and I slice the pad of my finger.

Blood seeps from the wound and I glance at it. Then up at Finn.

"Look what you did."

"Shit," he mutters, reaching over and putting my finger under the water, then wrapping it tightly with a paper towel.

"Shit. I hope you don't need stitches," my dad says, peeking over my shoulder.

Finn gently pushes him out of the way, picks me up, and carries me toward the stairs.

"I'm fine," I say, my finger throbbing as I press the paper towel against it. "Finn, I can walk. I literally had my leg chopped off. This is just a tiny cut..."

"Shut up," he says, taking the stairs two at a time, not even winded from the exertion, and then sets me on the counter in the bathroom. He bends and pulls out the first-aid kit from under the sink and washes his hands.

"Finn," I begin, but he shuts me up with a long-drawn-out kiss.

"Let me fix it. I did this," he says when he finally pulls his lips away from mine.

I just stare at him, letting him peel the paper towel away, spread antibiotic ointment on, and seal it with a Band-Aid.

"There," he says. "We'll keep an eye on it."

"Okay," I murmur and thread my good hand through his hair, pulling him closer to me, right between my spread thighs. "Now show me how sorry you are with that mouth of yours."

He falters for just a second, but then his hands move to my hips, tugging me roughly to the edge of the counter. He leans down as I tilt my chin up and our lips brush.

"I'm sorry," he whispers, pulling my bottom lip between his teeth. "I never want to hurt you."

"You hurt me so bad," I whine. "You owe me the *biggest* apology."

He huffs a laugh and deepens his kiss. Yes. Just like that. More. *More.*

My fingers claw slowly down the front of his chest and then move to the front of his jeans, unbuttoning them with a flick of my wrist. Finn's stomach flexes and a gasp escapes him as I brush my hand across his happy trail.

"What are you doing?" he breathes against me before kissing me again.

I don't answer. I just show him by unzipping his pants and tugging them down. Finn groans into my mouth as I slide my hand across his hard cock, straining against his boxers.

I squeeze it gently, getting a feel for another man's dick in my hand. Has Finn done this with anyone else? Has he let another man touch him like I'm touching him now? Or am I his first?

God, I want to be his first.

My fingers slide under the waistband of his boxers, and I tug them down until they're bunched around his thighs. All of this is done without detaching myself from his mouth. I'm too busy ravishing it as my hand roams.

My palm runs down the front of his smooth, firm cock and then I enclose him in my fist.

He clings to me, his hands grasping my head, his fingers digging into my scalp. He's almost frantic now, panting, groaning, his tongue desperately pushing into my mouth, fucking my hand.

I stroke faster, needing to feel him come, needing to make him feel good. I want to watch him fall apart.

He wrenches his lips from mine and tucks his face into my neck.

"God, I can't believe this is happening," he groans as I pump him slowly. "I can't fucking believe it."

"Believe it, Finn. I'm your dream come true."

He grunts his agreement as he returns his lips to mine and arches his hips up into my hand. Again and again. Slow, small thrusts until he's pulling his head back and meeting my hooded gaze.

"Tell me you want me, Landon. Say it," he says gruffly.

I nip at his chin. "I want you, Finn."

He groans, my words pushing him over the edge and he erupts all over my hand, some splashing onto my jeans.

Finn collapses against me, his hands bracketing my thighs as he leans into me.

"Fuck, that wasn't...that wasn't supposed to happen."

I press gentle kisses to his jaw. "It was. Everything that happens between us is meant to be."

His eyes meet mine and then they travel down to the mess on my pants.

"Jesus."

"Mmm, yes. You erupted. Like a volcano."

"Goddamn you, Landon."

"You were on fire," I add and he pinches my side, making me giggle.

"We need to get you changed. Your parents can't see you like that...shit, neither can Logan."

"Calm down. I think I have some extra pants in the dresser in my room...."

"God, I hope so," he says, trying to wipe up the mess he made, but being mostly unsuccessful. He just smears it around. It's totally noticeable.

Oh well, I have nothing to hide.

But Finn looks a little frantic, biting on his lip and eyeing me warily.

"What?" I ask, tossing the tissue toward the trashcan and missing by a mile.

Meh.

But he doesn't respond, just keeps those sexy lips of his zipped up.

I run my finger across the crease in his forehead, trying to soothe his worry.

"Stop worrying."

"I can't help it."

I press a kiss to his nose and hop onto the ground, wobbling slightly before turning around and washing my hands, doing my best to keep my bandaged finger out of the water.

When I turn back around Finn's put back together, his pants fastened and his hair combed back into submission.

I kind of miss messy Finn. I'd rather he be wrecked and ruined for me.

He wears it so well.

"Come on," I say, pushing the door open and striding as quietly as I can to my bedroom. Inside, Finn moves to the dresser and rummages around inside.

"You only have sweats."

I flop down onto the bed. "Put them on me, Finn."

He shakes his head but does as I ask. But then we get distracted, his lips gliding against mine. "That was an acci-dent," he mutters before doing it again. And then his tongue is in my mouth and I suck on it happily.

It's ages before we actually return to the kitchen, me feeling overly flushed and giddy.

My mom arches an eyebrow at me.

"Do I want to know why you have different pants on? And why you're smiling like that?" she asks.

"Uh," I begin and then shrug. "I got...blood all over them. Just spurting and gushing everywhere..."

My mom's eyebrows rise and Finn just nudges me. "You're playing it up too much. Just act normal."

"Do we need to take you to the hospital?" she asks.

I shake my head. "Nope! I'm fine."

My mom eyes us as my dad covers the crock pot and clasps his hands in front of his apron-covered torso.

Hi, Hungry. I'm Dad, it reads.

"Who's ready for mini golf?" he beams, bouncing slightly on his feet.

Vincent bleats loudly when my dad holds out the leash.

"Not the fucking goat, Basil," my mom mutters.

Vincent bleats again sadly, and my dad gives my mom a look that has her fidgeting on her feet.

"Fine," she says, "but if he eats something he shouldn't and we get banned, I will be pissed. You know how I love my mini golf."

My dad perks up and Finn glances at me.

"That's who you get it from. The pouting," he says, eyeing my lips.

"It's a skill I've honed over the years," I reply with a smirk. "I learned from the master."

I jut out my bottom lip and blink up at Finn.

"Kiss me again, Finn."

He lets out a huff. "Later."

Mmm, yes, Finn. Later, I'll hold you to it.

sixteen

SIX YEARS AGO

FINN

HE'S CRYING, tears slipping down his cheeks as he clings to me, and I feel so helpless.

"Stop," I say softly, brushing the wetness away with my thumbs, but Landon is too worked up. They just cascade down his face, dripping off his chin.

I glance at my dad who is sticking the last box into the U-Haul before closing the back with a loud clatter.

"We'll talk every day," I choke out, feeling the sharp sting in my eyes. I blink it away rapidly. My stupid heart can't handle this.

It's breaking. It hurts to breathe, to move. I have ceased existing. Soon I'll just wither away into nothing but dust.

"Promise?" Landon chokes out, his lip wobbling. It's been Logan, Landon, and me since I moved here, but while Logan is my best friend, Landon is so much more. He holds a piece of my soul.

"Yeah," I say, swallowing the lump in my throat. "Every day. I promise. You're my closest friend. I won't forget you."

"I'll never forget you," he says, his words coming out muffled.

He throws his arms around me and presses his face into the side of my neck, clinging. My dad calls my name. Just once, but it's enough. It's time.

I'm leaving him.

My home.

Landon's arms slowly release me, and I press a gentle kiss to the top of his head, just breathing him in. And then, like he can't bear to step away, Landon throws his arms around me once more and squeezes.

We pull away slowly, Landon swiping his hand across his wet cheeks and I turn to look at Logan. Goofy fucking Logan who is pretending not to cry. And doing a terrible job of it.

"Text me, yeah?" Logan says with a sad smile.

I nod and then throw my arms around him too. Because while I'll mourn the loss of Landon, I'll miss the fuck out of Logan. God, I've never had such a good friend before, so unwavering and true.

"Finn!" my dad calls again, the unfeeling asshole. But I know it's time to go.

I make my way to the truck and hop inside, my eyes fixed on Landon as we drive away, his head on his brother's shoulder. Until I can't see him any longer.

I don't know how I'm going to manage this, this distance. I feel like I won't survive it.

Landon: I miss you already.
Landon: I love you.

The texts stare up at me and then smear across the screen as my first tear rolls down my cheek.

seventeen

LANDON

"LIKE THIS," Logan says, moving up behind Theo and running his hands across his boyfriend's arms, helping him putt the ball across the green. We made it to the mini golf place across town and are currently working our way through the holes.

I look over at Finn whose tongue is poking out from his mouth as he narrows his eyes on his target.

Yeah, Finn won't be moving up behind me to be all romantic like Logan is with Theo. No, we're competitive as shit at this game.

Vincent bleats loudly from behind me and I hear my dad chastising him. The little terror has been munching on the artificial grass and sampling people's clothes. He even tried to abscond with a lady's purse ten minutes ago.

"Your turn," Finn says, looking smug.

"Hole in one?" I ask, and Finn nods.

"Well, I still have a chance," I say. "I can still win this."

"Doubtful."

I nudge him, and he eyes my lips again. He's been doing that since I had my hand wrapped around his cock earlier. Good. At least he's thinking of them. Because while he was driving us over here, his phone kept buzzing and he was driving with his knee to answer them.

Halfway through the ride I finally snapped and took his phone away. I stuffed it right down my pants.

It vibrated on my dick. Good. Archer thinks he's flirting with Finn, but really, he's flirting with my penis.

"What do I get if I win?" he asks me as I move onto the green and eye the hole in the distance.

I turn to glance over my shoulder at him.

"Hmm," I say, running my tongue across my lips. "My mouth. On your cock."

Finn's jaw drops and his putter falls to the ground.

Now it's my turn to smirk. I step up to the line and whack the ball. It bounces off the side of the curb and misses the hole by a mile.

"Seems like you're still losing," he says and swipes his putter off the ground.

I glance over and see Theo and Landon cuddling, Logan pressing kisses to the side of Theo's neck.

"You should take a lesson from my brother, Finn. Look how romantic they are," I say, pointing to the two love birds.

"You want my hands on you?" he asks as we walk down the green to where our golf balls lie.

Finn gets his putter ready and just as he's about to tap it

into the hole, I lean in close and utter, "I want your fingers in me again."

The ball goes wide and I let out a small laugh.

"You're cheating," Finn grumbles.

"I'm using what God gave me to my advantage. We all know you're better at mini golf than me."

"I'm ignoring you now," he replies and I move into his space, pressing my hand to his chest, feeling the steady thump of his heart beneath my palm.

"Maybe I want to lose, Finn. Maybe I want that big dick stuffed down my throat."

He lets out a shaky breath and he meets my playful gaze. "I'm going to win fair and square."

"Sure, we'll see about that," I say, and then step up and hit my ball wide on purpose. Just to fuck with his mind. Let him think he won because I *let* him.

We play like this for two more holes until my parents catch up to us, Vincent trotting next to them happily. My mom is putting on the green just behind us, her eyes scarily focused. My dad, on the other hand, is hitting the ball around one-handed, not even trying to make it in the hole. For as much as he insists on coming to this place, he doesn't take it seriously at all.

"This is so fun, you guys. Next time, let's smoke a bowl before we come. Really amp it up."

"We are not doing that, Basil," my mom says. "This game requires concentration. And I cannot hit a hole in one when I'm high."

Basil snorts and then leans toward us. "Fun killer. Hey, I brought edibles. You want some?"

Finn eyes the gummies my dad has in his palm. "I'm good. I have a game to win."

"Gimme," I say and pop one into my mouth. My dad tosses one into his mouth right after me and then ends up fumbling with and dropping two to the ground, which Vincent promptly gobbles up.

My dad gasps as he stares down at the goat. "What did you do?" he asks Vincent and then turns his worried gaze on me. "He ate them. He ate the weed!"

"He's gonna be hella high," I say, chuckling.

My dad nods and then glances down at Vincent again. "Bad goat. Stop eating shit like that. I don't know if that's bad for you."

I snort a laugh as Finn taps me on the shoulder with his putter.

"Your turn."

I waggle my eyebrows at him and aim to the far left, skipping the ball into the koi pond. Finn's lips turn down in a frown.

"Stop losing."

"I want to lose."

He adjusts his pants a little and I smile widely.

"I want this to at least feel like a fair fight," he grumbles.

I take another gummy from my dad and pop it into my mouth.

"Do you like it better with me kneeling or laying down? I'll just open wide..."

Finn blinks at me and then shakes his head, moving his focus back to the game.

Thirty minutes later when we've finished up the course

and I'm feeling slightly buzzed, I lean into my best friend and say, "Take me home. Take me home and make me your slut."

He chokes a little, his arm snaking around my waist, and he runs a hand through his hair.

"God, you like fucking with me, don't you?"

"I love it. But I'd like it better if you were doing the fucking. Take me home, Finn. Claim your prize."

He walks us to his car, his fingers caressing my hip under my sweatshirt, but before he opens the door for me, he pushes me up against it.

"Fuck. This mouth. I want to shut it up." Then his lips crash down on mine.

He ravages my mouth for a moment, his hot, hard body pressed against mine. I can feel his cock hardening and lengthening. I want it.

"You can shut it up. With your dick," I groan, sinking into him, letting him tongue-fuck me as I arch up into him.

I want it.

I've never wanted something so badly in my entire life.

"Bye guys. See you at home for soup," my dad calls, and Finn rips his mouth from mine, muttering curses under his breath.

I turn my head and see my parents walking side by side, Vincent in my dad's arms looking dazed. Yeah, I feel ya, buddy. I'm feeling a little dazed myself.

Although, that could be from Finn's lips. I could be high on *him*.

Finn reaches around me and tugs the door open and

when I'm seated inside, he closes it softly before getting in the driver's seat.

I watch him, the way his hands move, the way he shifts in his seat. I reach out and run my finger across the vein in his neck.

"I can't wait to get back to my place tonight," I say.

"You're high."

"I'm buzzed."

He hums lowly and my finger dips beneath the collar of his sweater, running along his collarbone.

"My mouth is a little dry, Finn," I say, wetting my lips. "Let me drink your cum. Don't be stingy."

His eyes widen and he blows out a breath. "God, your mouth."

"Yes, my mouth. You love it. You love my dirty, filthy mouth."

"Yes, well, that mouth needs to wait because your parents are expecting us at their place for dinner."

"Fuck that. I want you instead. I'm hungry for you."

Finn chuckles and I lean toward him, my seatbelt straining against my shoulder. "Let's make a pitstop. Feed me your cum and then we can go eat the motherfucking soup."

His foot presses down harder on the accelerator and we speed back to my place, stumbling into the apartment, winded from racing up the stairs.

The moment the door clicks shut and Finn turns the lock, he's on me. His lips devouring mine, his tongue sweeping into my mouth.

He's hungry. For me.

I groan as he picks me up and carries me to the bedroom, tossing me onto the bed and ripping me out of my clothes. My cock bobs against my stomach as he peels my pants from my thighs, pulling off my prosthetic, and then I'm watching him undress, his clothes tossed across the room.

"Do you think I'm hot, Finn," I say, running my hand up and down my hard length, rolling my balls into my palm.

"You know you are," he breathes standing above me, his eyes roaming my naked form.

"Tell me."

"You're so fucking hot," he says and then lowers his head, sucking my cock into his wet, warm mouth.

My back arches off the bed, the haze of my buzz making everything so much more vivid. I want more. He drags his tongue up the underside of me, tracing the vein there and my eyes flutter closed.

More, I want more, but I owe him. I *owe* him for winning.

I yank on his hair and pull his face up. His lips are swollen, and my cock is pressed against his cheek.

"My turn. It's my turn."

He groans, turning his face and pressing a kiss to the side of my dick.

"I don't want you to do anything you don't want to."

"Finn, if you don't get that big dick in my mouth right now, I'm going to rampage."

He chuckles as he moves up my body, kissing wet trails across my skin until he's straddling my chest and his cock is right at my lips.

I look up at him, my gaze meeting his, as my tongue extends out and I press the tip right into his slit.

"I want you to gag me."

"Jesus," he pants.

"Don't go easy on me, Finn. Make me work for it."

I part my lips and he slides the head in slowly. I suck on it, relishing the feel of his smooth skin and the taste of his precum against my tongue. It's different, but it's not bad. Nothing is bad with Finn.

I take a little more, Finn's hand cupping the back of my head, his chin on his chest as he watches me swallow him inch by glorious inch.

His cock hits the back of my throat and I gurgle around him, pulling back a little to be able to breathe.

"Shit. *Shit*," he huffs as I suck on the tip once more before bringing his big dick back into my throat.

I gag and he groans, the sound lighting me up and making my own cock throb between my legs.

I love the sounds he makes when he's letting go, becoming unhinged. I've never heard him make them before, but I crave it. I want to hear him do it again.

I continue torturing him slowly, getting a feel for having him in my mouth. And just when I'm getting the hang of it, he pulls back, his slick cock bobbing inches from my mouth, his chest heaving.

"I can't.... I want us to come together."

"What did you have in mind?" I ask, swiping at my cheeks, wet from tears and saliva.

Finn doesn't answer with words. Instead, he flips his body around and shifts me to my side before sucking my cock into his mouth. I gasp, the sensation overwhelming and I hoover his dick between my lips to return the favor.

We're suddenly choking on each other's dicks, competing in a hot-as-fuck race to see who can make the other come first. Our moans travel through our bodies, our hips thrusting, our hands clutching on for dear life. And when his slick finger suddenly breaches my hole, I explode without warning into his mouth.

Damn, that's bad manners.

But Finn just groans around my cock and slides his finger into my ass a little further as his hot cum hits my tongue. It's new and unexpected. But in the best way.

I drink him down, some dribbling out of the corner of my mouth and falling onto my shoulder. I continue to just hold him in my mouth, feeling his spent, twitching dick on my tongue, laving at it like an animal. And he does the same to me, his finger still halfway inside of me.

I clench my hole around him and he moans.

See how tight I am, Finn.

"Fuck, Landon," he says softly, my dick slipping from his lips and falling against my thigh. His nose is in my groin, his words whispering against my skin.

"I'm just that good," I tease, pressing a kiss to the tip of him. His dick jerks and I do it again, loving how responsive he is.

"You are. That was...." He sits up, leans over, and presses his lips to mine, his words disappearing into the ether between us. We kiss for a long minute, tasting each other until he pulls away. "That was a dream."

"Mmm," I hum in agreement. But as I do my stomach grumbles. "Your cum was delicious and I am so not opposed to doing that again, but I'm hungry."

He pulls back, his finger tracing my nose.

"Soup?" he asks, and I nod.

"Feed me, Finn. Need to wash all that cum down."

"Oh my god."

* * *

"Do not even tell me where you were. I don't want to know," my mom says, pointing to the crockpot. "There is plenty left over for you. And there's the bread."

I rub at my growling stomach as Finn pulls two bowls down from the cabinet.

Logan meanders over, setting two bowls into the sink, and leans toward me, munching on a piece of bread.

"So..." he says and then lowers his voice. "It's so good, right?"

I peek over at him and shrug. Because I'm not telling him shit. The nosy bastard. What Finn and I are doing is sacred.

Finn's eyes catch the movement, and he fumbles with the ladle.

"Oh, come on.... I need someone to share the wonders of the prostate with."

I roll my eyes at him. He's trying to fish for answers. I hate fishing, Logan. You know this. Do better.

"Logan," Theo says, eyeing his boyfriend from the table.

Logan turns his head and lifts his hands as if to say *what?* before moving toward him.

Thank god for Theo. I love my brother and I love that things are better between us now, but shit. I don't know what I want to share yet. I don't even know what Finn and

I are, to be honest. And I'm not sure how to bring it up either.

I'll just shove it under the rug, stashing it for later. There are mounds of things under there, waiting to come spilling out. Maybe I'll go exploring later, really take a good look at what I find.

I glance over at Finn who is texting on his phone, the two bowls of soup forgotten on the counter, and my lips turn down at the corners.

Grabbing the bowl he dished up for me, I glower at him.

"Archer?" I ask and Finn's eyes meet mine.

"Yeah."

"Must be *so* important," I say childishly, and Finn turns slightly, so I can't see what he's typing.

I huff in annoyance, and then lean in a little closer, my words meant only for him. "I just want to remind you that your dick was in *my* mouth."

Finn freezes, turning his dark gaze to mine.

"How could I forget?"

"Yes, that's what I want to know."

He stuffs his phone into his pocket and then grabs his soup, walking over to the kitchen table. I watch as he sits down, his back to me, feeling suddenly forlorn. But then he tugs the chair out from the table and peeks back at me.

"Get your ass over here, Landon."

And all is right in the world once more. My mom and dad are discussing adding two apple trees to the backyard, and Logan and Theo are whispering to each other, Theo's cheeks pink. I turn to my best friend and he smiles softly at me.

"What?" I ask, and he bites down on his bottom lip.

"I like you jealous," he mutters with a slight smile, and I roll my eyes.

"I'm not jealous."

He snorts and rips into his bread, ignoring me. But he's right, of course. I am jealous.

Even more so when we get home after dinner and he tells me that tomorrow morning he will be getting up early to meet Archer for coffee.

At our coffee shop.

"We're just friends," he tells me as I curl into him, my face right over his heart. I can hear his heartbeat thudding against my ear, and I clutch onto him tighter.

Because I don't believe it.

Two beautiful people meeting for coffee isn't ever friendly.

I am one hundred percent sure there will be flirting involved. And touching.

And when Finn sneaks out of bed the next morning, his hands carefully tucking me back under the covers, I feel a sickening feeling coil inside of me.

I don't fall back asleep. No, I just lie there staring at the ceiling, wondering when Finn is going to leave me for good.

eighteen

SIX YEARS AGO

FINN

I MOVE through the next few months like a ghost. Barely eating, barely moving. I glance in the mirror each morning and see my thin frame, looking weak and tired, staring back at me. My eyes have sunken into my head. I'm slowly fading away.

I need Landon like I need air. I need him. This isn't just a teenage crush. It's more. It's always been more.

"Shit," I hear my dad mutter, when he sees me lying on my bed, the food he left me picked at and shifted around on the plate. But uneaten.

"You have to eat, Finn."

I eye him. He looks just as bad as me. Probably because

I've given him hell, in a quiet way. I don't talk to him anymore, not that we talked much to begin with. But I'm silent now, my lips sealed.

I slam doors silently, never meet his eyes, and haunt the small apartment in the middle of the night.

The plate rattles as he picks it up and sighs. "Look, I know this isn't going well and so I've been thinking," my dad begins, his voice gruff.

I don't even answer, just turn around and stare at the wall.

"I spoke with the Lewis' this morning." Just their name has me stiffening in expectation. What's he going to do? What's he got planned?

"And they said they'd be fine with you living with them..."

I hear nothing else, a loud ringing in my ears. Oh my god. Oh my *god*.

"What?" I ask, my entire body turning to face him. Because I need him to repeat it to me. One word at a time.

My dad rubs at his neck, looking sheepish. "You can live with them. If you want. Finish up high school in California."

As soon as the words leave his mouth, I'm up, my legs carrying me to the closet.

"When?" I ask, feeling lighter than I have in the past two months.

"Damn, won't even miss me, huh?" my dad mutters and I just stare at him, my heart thumping erratically in my chest.

"When, Dad? Tell me."

"I need to buy you plane tickets. So this week, if you want—"

"I want," I say, already packing my things. Because truth is, I won't miss my dad. Not like I've missed Landon. Never like I've missed him.

He holds the pieces of my heart together, and to be parted from him is a death sentence.

When I arrive at the airport three days later, my body a mess of nerves and excitement, Landon rushes toward me, his body flung against mine, a loud laugh erupting out of him.

His lips press against my cheek and I burst into colors.

"I missed you. You're home," he says, his voice cracking.

I bury my face in his hair and inhale deeply, holding him to me, feeling my heart stitching back together each second I'm with him.

Him.

Home.

Always my home.

"You've lost weight," Landon says when he pulls away from me. In the background, I make out Logan and his parents, but my gaze swivels back to Landon.

Sweet, perfect Landon.

"I haven't been doing well…"

Landon's eyes widen and he presses into me again, his head resting on my heart.

"I'll make it better…you'll be back to your old self now that you're here."

He doesn't understand how true that is. Because now that I'm with him, I can start living again.

* * *

That night, when I'm tucked away in bed, when the house is finally asleep, Landon sneaks into my room and slips beneath my covers. I can feel him, even though he's not touching me. I can sense his presence.

My breath catches in my throat with him this close to me and under the cover of darkness, too. The things we could do together, what no one would see. If only he'd let me. If only he'd want me.

"You okay?" I ask, clutching onto my pillow and staring at the shape of him.

He wiggles around, his foot knocking into me, and then he shuffles a little closer.

"I just can't believe you're here," he whispers. "It's a dream."

God, yes, it is. I still pinch myself to see if I'm asleep.

"Can I stay with you tonight?" he asks, moving even closer to me until I'm panting. His arm brushes against mine and I can smell him. God, to press my lips to his skin, to taste him.

"Of course," I reply as evenly as I can and Landon smiles at me.

"Good, because I couldn't sleep in my own room knowing that you're right down the hall."

And I couldn't sleep knowing he was just two doors down, but had been too paralyzed to actually get up and go to him.

"You can stay in here any time."

Landon wraps his arms around me, squeezing me tightly before letting me go and shuffling back to his side of the bed. I wish he'd stayed against me so I could hold him all night.

But this, right here, is as close as I'll ever get. Never more. Nothing more.

I vow to savor every moment I get with him.

So I keep my heavy eyelids open and watch the soft rise and fall of his breaths until he falls asleep.

$$nineteen$$

LANDON

I FEEL like a sad little ghost haunting my apartment ever since Finn left. He's been gone for ages.

I check my phone. It's been thirty-seven minutes, but really, what can Archer and Finn possibly be talking about for that long? Philosophy? How nice Archer's hair is? Sex positions?

I stuff my phone in my pocket, throw on a sweatshirt, and head outside. On the street is the ride I called for and I hop inside, letting the gruff, bearded man in the driver's seat take me across town to the little nursery where my dad works.

I need the distraction. I need to occupy my time until he comes back home.

I should probably text Finn and let him know where I am, but I don't want to bother him.

On his coffee date.

Gah!

I want to stop by and grab a drink because I'm dragging and need caffeine but I'm nervous. What if I see something I don't want to see? Like them holding hands or whispering to each other.

I'm caught between anxiety and morbid fascination, my knee bouncing up and down as I debate whether or not I should stop by. I shouldn't. I absolutely should *not*.

I end up stopping by the coffee shop.

My order has already been placed and all I need to do is walk inside and grab it. And maybe take a little peek as I stroll by. Casually. Like no big deal, Finn, keep having fun on your coffee date. That's not a date.

But then I see Finn—he's sitting on a couch right next to Archer, their heads lowered as they talk, Archer's hand holding Finn's. I feel my stomach churn and my heart rate skyrocket.

"Huge mistake," I mutter as I grab my coffee and try to sneak out lightning fast, but Finn's eyes catch on me. Something dark flashes in his expression and I shiver as his hand slips from Archer's.

He moves to stand but I scurry outside, not wanting to talk to him, and then I'm back inside my ride before he can catch me.

God, I'm an idiot. I just couldn't help myself. I just had to go *look*. I always do this shit. I can't peel my eyes away and then I have major regrets afterward.

I sip on my drink, feeling nauseous and confused. Because seriously, what did I walk in on? He says they're friends, but why were they holding hands? They were holding hands, right?

Shit.

By the time I make it to the nursery, I'm wrung out.

"Hey, bud!" my dad says with a smile, gardening gloves on his hands. His hair is disheveled and one of his cheeks is smeared with dirt. "What are you doing here?"

"Came to see if you needed any help." I glance around, taking in the buckets of plants lining the muddy floor. "Vincent didn't come?"

"Mr. Anderson banned him. He ate too many plants last time. He's with Logan and Theo."

I snort and then gesture to the pallet he's offloading.

"Can I help?"

"Sure!" he says with a wide smile. "You know Mr. Anderson doesn't mind."

I wave to the older man behind the register and he waves back, and then my dad and I get to work.

By the time Finn strides into the nursery, looking stormy and irritated, I'm covered in a sheen of sweat and soil.

"Oh! Hey, Finn," I say, managing a smile. It's fake. It's the fakest.

His eyes narrow on it. "Why are you smiling like that?"

I roll my eyes and run a gloved hand across my sweaty forehead, most likely smearing more dirt on myself. I ditched my sweatshirt ages ago, once the sun came out. It's hotter than I expected today.

"Smiling like what?" Dumb. I play dumb.

"Like that...it's weird."

My hand flops down to my side and then I gesture to my

dad. "You're hallucinating. I am smiling totally normal. And anyway, how did you find me?"

"I drove to your parents and when you weren't there, I texted Basil."

I glance over at my dad who is talking to a customer and then meet Finn's fiery eyes.

"Ah, well, doesn't matter. I'm almost done. You don't need to wait for me to finish. I can grab a ride home."

"Like hell you are. Why didn't you text me where you were when you ran away earlier," Finn says, moving to help my dad.

"I didn't run away. I walked briskly because I didn't want to bother you on your *date*."

That's a four-letter word now.

"It wasn't a date! We're just friends. Like I told you before."

"Yeah, well you were holding hands. Friends don't hold hands, Finn."

His eyebrows hit his hairline because we hold hands. Always have, always will. "Are you fucking serious?"

Yes, no. Maybe? I don't know. I just sigh and let it go because I don't feel like arguing. I move to help my dad, limping slightly because I may have overdone it a little. Just a tad. But the physical exertion helped me forget what Finn was doing all morning.

On a not-date with Archer. Whispering and touching each other. And probably talking about sex.

"You're limping," Finn grumbles, and I roll my eyes.

"I am."

"Let me take you home."

I eye him, watching him run a hand through his hair, his eyes a little wild.

"Ugh. Fine," I say, rolling over much too easy, but then again, I am a pushover. Plus, Finn looks like he's ready to burn the world down, and poor Mr. Anderson really loves this place.

I shout over to my dad. "We're going to go now."

"Oh yeah. Cool. See you later?" my dad asks.

I wave and nod. "Yeah."

Finn sighs, looking relieved and his hand slips around my waist, his pinkie finding its home on my skin. But it feels wrong this time, a little off.

Maybe because he was with someone else. Those hands were touching someone else.

I take a small step to the side and his hand falls against his thigh.

Finn looks at me confused.

"Uh, um, I'm going to go tell Mr. Anderson we're leaving," I say, shooting a thumb over my shoulder, feeling shifty and sick and just really sad.

Finn tucks his hands into his pants pockets as I move away from him. Mr. Anderson stuffs some bills into my hand and I tuck them away without argument. He insists every time. There's no use fighting it.

"Ready?" Finn asks, his hands still hidden from view.

I nod, swallowing a small lump in my throat.

We should talk about this. I should say something. But it gets shuffled around and makes a home under the hypothetical rug.

I need to clean house soon. It's getting very messy.

We make the ride back to the apartment in silence, Finn's hand clenching open and shut on his thigh.

When we're inside and I'm sitting on a kitchen chair, Finn eyes me warily.

"Can I check it," he asks softly when I lean back and sigh, my muscles tense and sore.

"I'd rather just take a shower," I reply, stretching out my tight muscles.

"Yeah," Finn says, running a hand over his face. "Yeah. Okay."

He moves toward me, but I stand up, not wanting to bother him. I've grown too dependent on him, too attached. It's not healthy, is it? But it's always been like this between us. From the minute I laid eyes on him when I was thirteen years old, this tall, gangly, dark-haired boy who held my hand was *mine*.

He had my heart from the moment we touched.

I'd always assumed this was how best friends felt about each other, this underlying, simmering need for one another. But I'm coming to realize that I was wrong. This is something else entirely.

But does Finn feel the same way about me?

Or maybe I'm too late?

I flinch a little at the thought and Finn lets out a loud huff. My eyes swivel to him and see his creased brow, that line growing deeper by the minute. I resist the urge to reach out and smooth it away.

Maybe I should try and put some distance between us. That way when Archer or another person comes along, I won't be left feeling like *this*.

Despondent and lost.

I close the bathroom door on him, locking it. The click resonates in the small space and I wince.

Fuck.

He looked so sad as I shut the door.

Maybe I should let him in and let him care for me.

But then again, that's dependence, isn't it? Codependency? Everyone talks about how unhealthy it is. But what Finn and I have doesn't feel unhealthy.

It never has. It just feels right. All the time. Always.

I let the door remain locked and go through the process of showering and drying off and when I emerge, the towel wrapped around my waist, Finn is there, leaning up against the wall, his phone in his hand.

"Sorry, were you waiting to use the bathroom?" I ask, all fake politeness when really my words just mask the awkward silence lingering between us.

His eyes move up to mine. He opens his mouth to say something and then snaps it shut.

"No."

"Hmm." I walk past him, grab some clothes from my dresser, drop my towel, and sit on the edge of the bed. Finn still looms by the door, his gaze alternating between me and the phone in his hand.

Texting not-date Archer, I'm sure.

But I don't bring it up. I don't even tease him about it. I just let it go. Because that's what I need to do.

I need to let it go.

Let him go.

When I'm finally dressed and heading toward the door, Finn reaches out and grabs my bicep.

"What are you doing?" he asks, his hand tightening around me.

"What do you mean?" I ask, wanting to sink into him, wanting to let him run his strong hands through my hair and press his soft lips to the skin of my neck.

"You haven't said a word to me—"

"I'm giving you space," I interrupt, and Finn's head rears back.

"Why the fuck would I want space?" he asks, and I shrug, picking at my cuticle and trying to look nonchalant about it. When in reality my eyes sting and I feel like I swallowed a brick.

"So you can have fun during your winter break. Without worrying about me."

His hand flexes, pulling me slightly closer to him.

"I'm having a fun winter break *with you*."

"And Archer. Can't forget about him."

He rolls his eyes. "For fuck's sake. Enough."

I shrug and fiddle with the bottom of his shirt. "Look, all I'm saying is we can have other friends—"

"I don't want—"

"And you can date whoever you want."

"I'm not fucking dating him!" he shouts and gently shakes me. As if to knock some common sense into me. Well, too late, Finn. That train is long gone. It never even made it to the station. It's not genetically possible for this family to have anything of the sort. It's a family curse. I mean, this family has the worst luck. Take my leg for example. I mean, it can't get any worse than that. And now, finally, when I'm starting to feel shit for Finn, he's into someone else!

Gah! It's just this never-ending cycle. One I can never escape.

"Why are you shaking me," I snark, as Finn jostles me roughly.

Finn's chest is heaving, his eyes shining and bright. "I want to rattle those fucking cobwebs loose in your mother-fucking brain."

I snort at the imagery. "Are you saying I'm dumb?"

"Sure feels like it right now," he mutters and I shove at his chest.

"You're so rude. Honestly, I don't know why I keep you around."

"Yeah, you do. You know why. So stop pushing me away. Don't give me space. I don't need it. I don't want it."

I stare at him, my eyes roving over his face, taking him in. God, he looks...tired. I don't want to upset him any more than I already have. This can wait. I can wait.

"But I may need to," I say softly, forcing my gaze away. "It's self-preservation."

Finn shakes his head, his hands falling away from me and he sighs, a long, weary exhale.

"Talk to me. Tell me what's in that head of yours."

"Can we do it later?" I ask. "We're going to be late to the movies."

"You're not shoving this under the rug like you do every-thing else. Not with me."

I gasp dramatically. "I would *never*."

A small snort escapes him and he reaches out for me, pulling me into his chest. And I lean into him. Just this once.

It hurts too much to be apart from him.

I'll deal with the inevitable pain later. I just don't know if I can handle it all right now.

* * *

Finn is in a mood. He huffed and puffed his way through the movie we saw at the theatre with Logan and Theo. Mainly because I didn't hold his hand.

I think.

But he was texting Archer anyways. His fingers were busy. I didn't want to bother him. And honestly, could either of them be any ruder? That light from Finn's phone was like a beacon in the middle of the theater, lighting up the space around him like a spotlight.

Now we're back at my parents' house and Finn is glowering at me because I sat in my own chair around the firepit. Despite the warmth from the fire, my body is cold from being parted from him. I peek over and see his hands clenched on the chair's arms and his jaw working back and forth.

I've never seen him so upset with me before. But now I'm feeling like I can't back down. I need to try and make it through this night.

I need to see if I can be strong enough to keep away. Even if it's just for a few more hours.

"Hey guys," my dad says lumbering outside with a tub of ice cream in his hand and a handful of spoons. "Want some?"

I smile softly at my dad, trying to ignore the murderous stare coming from Finn across the patio.

"Um…"

"No. No more. We're heading out," Finn interjects, standing up abruptly.

My dad looks flummoxed but just nods as Finn moves toward the sliding glass door.

And when I don't move fast enough, he turns his head and glowers at me.

"Get over here, Landon. Now."

I gulp and push myself up, giving my dad a quick hug and following Finn out to the car. He's quiet and cold and when he starts the car, I shiver slightly, my stomach rolling.

"Um…" I begin, when the silence between us becomes too oppressive. "Why are you so mad?"

His hand clasps the steering wheel so tightly I can see his knuckles turn white.

I swallow roughly, bobbing my head and whistling nervously. Jesus, Finn is really giving me the silent treatment.

I mean, it was just some itty-bitty space.

He turns on the blinker aggressively and veers onto the street leading to my apartment.

"Not going to talk? Just gonna keep it zipped…cool… cool," I say, my voice coming out a little higher with each word.

He pulls into my parking spot, slams the car into park, and then pushes the door open.

I scramble after him, trying like hell to play it cool, but unable to really manage it. I'm just worried now. I didn't realize that me trying to distance myself would make him so...angry.

I'm picking nervously at my poor cuticles when I finally make it to my apartment door, and Finn's just standing there, his arms folded across his chest, his eyes boring into mine. Like some kind of unmovable statue.

I shift nervously, dropping my keys onto the ground. And when I move to pick them up, those big hands of his don't go around my waist to steady me like they usually do.

Oh fuck.

I've really gone and done it now.

I manage to get the door open and hobble inside, my body shaking with nerves. I mean, Finn would never hurt me. Never. That's not why I'm scared.

I'm scared I ruined it. Whatever this was between us. That it's over before it started.

Finn flips the lights on and stalks to the bedroom, his long, muscular legs eating up the space with no effort at all and I scurry after him.

We really need to talk, but my words drift away when I see Finn moving to the closet and grabbing a duffle bag. And that's when my heart drops a hundred feet in seconds.

"What are you doing?" I squeak.

"I'm going to stay with your parents..."

My mouth opens and now anger, hot and furious bursts through me. Because now he's pulling shit out of the dresser and stuffing it into that stupid bag of his.

I stomp toward him, wrenching the canvas bag from his hands and tossing it at the wall. It hits with a *thunk* and plops to the ground.

And we both stare at it, his clothes scattered on the floor of my room, a pair of socks rolling under the bed.

My eyes swivel to his and I shove at his chest. He, of course, doesn't budge. But his nostrils flare, his cheeks red, his eyes wild.

Oh god.

"Don't run away from me," I hiss. "Don't be a fucking coward."

His hands become fists and then slowly flex open.

"You wanted space," he grinds out.

"We should at least talk about it!"

"You never want to fucking talk. All you want to do is shove shit under rugs and bury it."

Oh, that's not nice and entirely too true. But I'm mad now, so I shove at him again and his cheeks grow darker, his pupils blown out.

"Well, at least I'm not running away!" I practically yell. "I'm not abandoning you. This is fucking different, Finn."

My eyes well with tears and suddenly he's on me, pushing me against the wall, his hand around my throat, his thigh pressed up against my groin.

Oh god. *Oh my god.* My dick hardens immediately, my entire body breaking out in goosebumps, my heartbeat tripling

"You drive me so goddamn crazy," he says, his voice low and gruff, the vibrations moving through me, straight to my balls.

His nose runs up the side of my neck and my eyes roll back as I arch into him.

"Finn," I moan, clutching onto his arms.

His teeth sink into my ear and I gasp. Oh shit.

"I don't need space," he growls. "Not from you. Never from you."

I suck in air as he presses into me again.

"I am going to peel you out of these clothes," he breathes, his body trembling, his words choppy. "And then I'm going to stuff myself inside your hole until you can't move. How does that work for your *fucking space?*"

I groan as he gently squeezes his hand around my throat and then his lips are on mine, his tongue forcing itself into my mouth and I just open. Like a good little slut.

He groans, his hands clasping onto me just tight enough that my breath comes out a little stunted, but then he's gone, his mouth wrenched away, his hands falling from me and I reach out, wanting him to do that again.

Don't stop, Finn. Impale me. Choke me.

"More," I murmur, my brain in a fog.

Finn eyes me for a moment as if gauging how much I want this. So I help him along.

"Fuck me, Finn. Stick that big dick right up my ass."

His eyelids flutter and then he's tossing me onto the bed. My breath comes out in a whoosh as I bounce, and then his hands are yanking the clothes from me, my shirt ripping audibly as he pulls it from my body, my pants wrenched off my legs, my prosthetic tossed haphazardly onto the floor.

I watch as he strips himself down, his hair mussed, his cheeks flushed red, and his hands trembling.

All I can do is gape, my chest heaving in uneven breaths as he lowers himself onto me, our cocks pressing against each other, our lips meeting once more in a clash of teeth and spit.

Suddenly he's pushing away, his hands pressing my knees up to my chest.

"Hold them. Right there," he commands, and I do as he says, my cock leaking profusely against my stomach.

I hear the snap of the lube being opened and the press of his fingers against my hole and I pant as he pushes his way inside.

"Fuck," he says, knuckle-deep inside of me. "Look at how ready you are for me."

I crane my neck up, watching his stormy, wild eyes as he watches his finger impale me over and over again.

"Just for you," I moan and his eyes snap up to meet mine. His finger crooks, pressing against my prostate and I cry out at the sensation, my head flopping back onto the pillow, my hands clenching onto the back of my thighs so tightly I bruise. I want this so bad, so fucking bad even though I've never done it before. I was made for this. I just know it. I fucking *feel* it.

Finn adds a second finger, scissoring me open. The sounds of the lube squelching as he moves in and out of me only makes me harder.

"God, hurry up," I gasp. "Stick it in, Finn."

But Finn doesn't do what I ask. No, he just leans down and sucks my cock right into that greedy mouth of his.

And now I'm dying.

I can feel my soul leave my body as he bobs his head, his tongue running over my sensitive cock, his fingers hitting my prostate with every thrust.

Hell, I'm not going to last another minute if he keeps this up.

My legs fall onto the bed and I clutch onto his hair, yanking him off of me, and he glowers at me, his lips red and swollen.

"Get that big dick in me, Finn. Don't make me beg."

His eyes narrow and something evil gleams inside of them.

"I want you to beg. Beg me for it, Landon."

I inhale shakily, happy to beg for him, for what I want. I push my bottom lip out in a pout. "Please, Finn. *Please.* Fuck me."

He groans as he sits up, grabbing the lube and smearing it onto his dick. His large hands clutch onto my waist, pulling me until my hole is right there, lined up with the tip of him.

"You asked for this," he says and I nod, spreading and wiggling down as far as I can, so he can push inside of me.

"Goddammit," Finn mutters and then his hips arch forward and the tip pushes in.

It stings, fuck, it stings, but hell if I'm stopping now. Finn's mine. That dick is *mine.*

"More," I groan and Finn sinks deeper, his dick stretching me out, splitting me wide open. I arch back, my body breaking out in a fine sheen of sweat as I take every fucking glorious inch of him until he's balls deep inside of me.

He stills when he's buried to the hilt, his fingers flexing against my skin, his chest heaving. God, why is he stopping? Does he need me to beg again, to tell him how much I need this? How much I want it?

"You going to fuck me so hard I cry?" I taunt, my eyes meeting his, desire and determination in my gaze.

His nostrils flare and he arches up, and I gasp, pain and pleasure flaring up inside of me.

"You better fuck me into the mattress, Finn. Show me who owns me."

That snaps something inside of him. He wants to own me, to make me his. He shifts his hips back and slams into me, my body moving up the bed from the force of it.

"Shiiiiiit," I groan, taking it like the good boy I am.

"Look at you," he hisses. "Look at your ass swallowing my cock."

I whimper and moan, writhing underneath him, impaled on his dick, and god, we should have been doing this ages ago. He's been holding back on me. *I've* been holding back on me. If I only knew....

"Touch yourself," he says and I shake my head. I don't need it. *I don't need it.*

He brackets my head with his hands, his face right above mine. I can see his parted lips, the sweat dripping down his temple, and can feel his abs brush over my cock with each inward thrust.

My hands move up and grasp onto his face, pulling him down for a kiss, a long desperate kiss as he fucks into me harder and faster.

My cum spills out of me moments later, my hole tightening around his dick, and he releases everything inside of me with a groan so feral that I will remember it until the day I die.

"Finn," I whisper, my entire body trembling from the strength of my orgasm.

He collapses on top of me, his weight nearly cutting off my breath, but I just hold him to me, his cock twitching inside of me.

"Jesus, I can't believe that just happened," he says and I huff a low wheeze.

"Believe it. Oh god. Believe it. I'm your slut now."

Finn laughs and pushes up, allowing me to take a long, deep breath in.

"My slut?" he asks, and I smirk at him.

"You think that this was a one-and-done? Think again, asshole. I want to try all the positions with you. Who knew you had that in you? You were like an animal...."

He stares down at me and then arches his hips once more, cutting off my words with a gasp.

"No fair," I groan and then wiggle against him.

"Are you sore?" he asks, and I shrug.

"Maybe. But I won't be for round two."

"There won't be a round two," he begins as he pulls out of me and my heart sinks. "Not yet at least," he adds and a smile splits my face.

"Already planning it?" I tease. "How are you going to have me next, Finn? On my hands and knees?"

He peers down at me as he leans back, spreading my legs and examining my hole.

"We'll see."

Oh god yes, we will.

"I can't wait," I say as his finger slips between my cheeks and swipes up the mess he made.

"You going to wash me, Finn? Or just stare at my hole you stretched out."

"Jesus," he mutters and then moves away from me. "Fine, shower and then bed. I want you to rest."

He sweeps me into my arms, and I bite at his neck tasting the salt on his skin.

"Does this mean you're staying with me tonight?" I ask, and he glances down at me.

"If you want me to."

"Of course, I do. You're the one who wanted to leave me."

"You're the one who wanted to have some space."

He bites those words out, still angry so I nip at his chin. "You were just inside of me, Finn. I don't know how much closer you want us to get. Want to skin me and wear me as a jacket?"

"Jesus."

"Want me to jack off into a cup and you can drink my cum each morning?"

He shuts me up with a kiss, setting me onto the shower chair and turning on the ice-cold water without warning me.

I jerk, a loud yelp escaping me and that asshole just laughs.

Probably getting me back for earlier. For trying to separate myself from him.

But Finn makes it up to me by climbing inside the shower once the water is warm and washing me tenderly, his big hands sliding soap across my skin until I'm melting against him.

This, here.

This is what I want.

twenty

FINN

"GUESS WHAT?" Landon says flopping onto my bed, a wide grin on his face.

I've been living with the Lewis' for the past two years and I couldn't be happier. I don't even miss my dad and I'm not sure he misses me all that much either. He makes the occasional call and has been out to visit me once, but other than that, I'm content. I'm never moving away from Landon and his family again.

In fact, when this summer is over, I'm starting at UC Berkeley with Logan, which is about a two-hour drive away. I'm going to study computer science, whatever the fuck that means.

I'm hoping Landon picks the same school as me when he graduates next year, but it looks like UC Santa Cruz—the university nearest home—will offer him a spot on the track team and a really good scholarship. They've been eyeing him for months now and I don't blame him for considering it. And they have a great human biology program there.

God, to be parted from him.

I can't bear to think about it.

"What?" I ask, setting my book down and facing him. He looks so pretty today, his shaggy hair tousled, his t-shirt just tight enough that it shows off the muscles in his chest, and those long legs...those fucking legs that I have envisioned wrapped around me almost every night, are crossed in front of him.

Landon waggles his eyebrows and then lowers his voice. "I lost my virginity today..."

My entire body freezes as I watch his mouth move because I knew this has been coming. But fuck if it doesn't *hurt*. God, it stings.

"What's that look for?" he asks, poking me in the side.

I clear my throat, shaking myself out of the fog I'm currently slinking through. I rub at my chest and shrug.

"Nothing, just some heartburn or something. I'm...uh, happy for you."

Landon's brows scrunch and he watches me intently for a minute before scooting closer.

"You sure?'

"Yeah, totally."

He wets his mouth and then scoots a little closer until

he's nearly on top of me. Fuck, to have him crawl onto my lap. To have him press his lips against mine.

"Can I tell you a secret?"

I roll my lips between my teeth and nod. Shit, don't give me the details. Please. I don't want to know.

"It was…fuck I feel bad saying this, but it was kind of lame. I dunno, maybe because I didn't know what I was doing. But it was just…meh."

He shrugs like no big deal and I look away, feeling something ugly flare up inside of me.

Like hope.

Because I'd make it so good for him.

He would be begging. Crying for more.

But Landon isn't interested in men. He isn't interested in me. It would never happen in a million years.

I shake my head, dislodging those thoughts, and pull him into me.

He sighs, crawling between my legs and resting his head on my shoulder. He tilts his head back to look at me, our lips so impossibly close.

Fuck, I think about those lips, about that mouth. About every part of him.

I've done things in the privacy of our bathroom that would send me straight to hell. If he only knew the things I've imagined doing to him.

"I know you're busy studying, but wanna watch a movie or something?" he asks, nuzzling his forehead against my jaw.

Hell, why does he do this to me? Every moment, every

touch is torture. But like fuck I'm asking him to stop. I'd take this over nothing at all.

My arms tighten around him, and Landon lets out a small groan, the sound shooting straight to my dick. Doesn't help that he wiggles against me, trying to get comfortable.

I shift back a little, trying to make sure he doesn't feel the bulge in my shorts, but it's impossible to hide with him moving against me.

"What is that?" Landon asks, pressing up against my hard cock. "Why's your dick hard?"

My cheeks flame, but I keep my voice even. There is no way I'm ever telling him the truth. I'd rather die. I would never risk what we have. So, I'll continue to suffer in silence because at this point I'll take whatever I can get.

"Because you're pressing against it. It's a natural reaction," I wheeze, biting my bottom lip.

Landon freezes a moment and then wiggles against it some more.

"It's huge. You have a big dick, Finn," he says and I huff out a nervous laugh. "How come I've never seen it? I feel like this is something friends would know about each other…"

I cannot even believe this is a conversation we're having. But then again, I shouldn't be surprised—this is Landon, after all.

"Because."

"You know that is an unacceptable response. If mom heard you right now…" Landon snorts, sitting up and facing me. He has that look on his face, the one that usually means he's going to blurt out something ridiculous…

"Let's jack off."

My mind sputters and shuts down. I have ceased living. Because what in the ever-loving fuck is he talking about? Am I dead for real? Have I died?

Landon shoves at my chest. "Why are you just blinking like a robot?

I blink some more, my brain flipping on as I reply, "Robots don't blink."

"Ugh, what is your deal? Come on, let's do it. Together. Having sex was a bit of a letdown and I kind of wouldn't mind getting off again. My dick is horny."

He blinks at me, those sweet, sexy eyes, and I sigh. This is a terrible, awful, no-good idea and I'm going to do it anyways.

Because I can't say no to him.

"You're gonna say yes, I know it. I can see it in your eyes," he says climbing off the bed and locking the door. "Just in case. You know how dad gets."

And then he's back on the bed, staring at me eagerly, his hand on my knee. I peek down at his crotch and yep, there it is. His hard cock jutting against his jeans and my own just lengthens.

For fuck's sake.

"So how do we do it? Side by side? Facing each other," Landon asks.

"Just, fuck...just sit next to me. Don't want to make it weird."

Weird in that I'll watch him come if he sits where I can see it—will drool for it like the animal I am.

Landon bounces down against my side, his leg pressed against mine and he leans back, popping the button open on his jeans. I can't help but watch, my mouth growing dry.

"Come on. Hurry," he says. "No time to waste."

I don't know what the rush is. I want to savor this. But at the same time, I want to tell him to fuck off because this, right here, is going to destroy my heart.

"Take it out," he says and I watch as his hand pulls his cock from his pants. And it's perfect. The perfect size and shape. It's gorgeous, just like everything else about him.

He can do no wrong.

I desperately want to press into him, to wrap my lips around him and blow his mind.

I force my gaze away and quickly pull myself out, wrapping my hand around my hard dick.

"Oh, you are huge," he says and then holds his dick out a little, examining it. "I can't compare."

"You're fine," I mutter, clearing my throat.

"God, this is good," he says. I can hear the sound of him jacking off to my left, the sound of his palm against his cock, and I stroke myself faster.

"Is it weird we don't have porn on?" he gasps, a small moan slipping from his lips and I can't help but glance over at him. Seeing the way his cheeks are flushed, the bead of precum on the tip of his cock, the way his hips arch up with each thrust.

I don't answer, his question just fading away between us.

I'm not going to last. He's just sitting next to me, but the sound of his breathing, the smell of his musk, and the fact that soon I'm going to get to watch him explode is all too much.

"Fuck," I breathe, and Landon leans into me, our arms bumping as we stroke faster.

"Fuck, Finn, your dick looks like it's going to explode," Landon says and I groan loudly, feeling my balls draw up, and a second later, my cum shoots out of me. It hits my hand and my thigh, dirtying my pants. And the best-worst part is Landon sees it and it pushes him over the edge, his own dick twitching as he releases all over his stomach.

We sit, breathing, the smell of him making my mouth water. I want to lean over and pull his softening dick into my mouth. Lick him clean. But I don't. I grasp onto the comforter and hold myself in place instead.

"We should do that again. That was hot," Landon mutters, and I shake my head. Because I can't have a repeat of that. I can't. I will be using this one moment as jackoff fodder for years to come.

A stomping on the stairs has Landon scrambling off the bed and tossing me a box of tissues. The corner hits me in the side of the head and I wince.

"Oh my god," Landon giggles, pulling his pants up over his flaccid cock and trying to mop up his cum with the bottom of his shirt.

"It smells like sex in here," he says and then he gestures toward my still-hard dick. "Put it away! Why is it still hard?" he hisses.

I tuck myself away, wiping myself up as best as possible when the door handle jiggles.

"Finn!" Logan calls, and Landon slaps a hand over his mouth.

Fuck, he's cute.

I toss my used Kleenex into the trash bin and wrench the door open, just as Logan comes tumbling in.

"Hey, why was the door locked?" he asks, his eyebrows meeting.

Landon shrugs. "Dad needs to fix the door," he lies, pushing past his brother, the hem of his shirt scrunched up in his hands, hiding the evidence of his mess.

"Right, yeah, damn house," Logan chuckles and then punches me in the arm roughly. "I have to feed the chickens and then do you guys want to go grab something to eat?"

I shrug, moving around him toward the bathroom to wash my hands, to clean off the evidence of what we just did.

Logan bumbles after me, talking about something that happened at school, but my mind is replaying what just happened over and over in excruciating detail.

And a week later when Landon asks to do it again, I roll over and agree.

We do it three more times that summer, each committed to my memory, each making a home in my heart until Landon finds a girl to replace me.

And then, it never happens again.

twenty-one

LANDON

I WAKE up to the feel of Finn pressed against my back, his face tucked against my neck, his hand splayed across my stomach.

We're both naked, his cock sandwiched between my ass cheeks.

Hmm.

Yes.

More of that.

More cock near my hole.

I press back against him, his dick sliding against me, and he tightens his grip on me.

"You awake?" he asks, and I hum my response.

I'm awake and so is my dick. It's ready. I want more of Finn inside of me. I'm sore, but I take pain like a champ. I want to come again while stuffed full of him.

His lips press against my neck and I lift my chin slightly, letting him nibble his way across my skin.

"Is this a dream?" he mutters, and I snort a laugh.

"Yeah, because I'm your motherfucking dream, Finn," I say and he bites down on my neck hard, a yelp escaping me.

Not that it deters me. No, it only makes me harder. I'm throbbing now.

"I'm not fucking you," he says lowly, his hand engulfing my dick and pumping it slowly.

"Yes. Yes, you are. I want it."

"You're too sore."

"Don't tell me how I feel, Finn," I grumble. "My hole was made for sex."

Finn chuckles but doesn't lube me up, no, he just tortures me with his hand until I'm writhing.

"Please," I beg, my hands grasping onto him for dear life, and thank fuck Finn takes pity on me. Because he flips me onto my back and then that mouth is on me. The sounds he's making as he devours me set me on fire.

"You love it," I gasp. "You love sucking my cock."

His eyes meet mine, his mouth stuffed full of me, and I thrust my hips up, pushing myself deeper into him. He groans and my entire body zings with pleasure.

It's one thing to have your dick sucked, but to have that person desperate to do it only makes it better.

"Shit, that mouth," I say, threading my fingers through his hair as he bobs and groans. One of his fingers tentatively presses against my hole and that's all it takes. Just the thought of him inside of me again has me unloading down his throat. He swallows it all, not missing a single drop.

When I'm spent, my sensitive dick slipping from his mouth, he laps at it, slowly and carefully licking up every last trace of cum.

"The sounds you make," he says, breathing heavily, his lips pressed into my groin. "God, I could come to those a thousand times."

"You're just that good," I say, feeling lazy and spent. "Now jack off all over my ass. If I can't have you inside of me, I at least want it on me."

"Goddamn you," he says, but he still positions himself right near my ass and jerks himself, that vein in his neck popping out, his muscles straining.

And when he comes all over my crack, his release dripping down my skin, I sigh, starfishing across the mattress, satiated and limp.

"I am just going to lie here all afternoon. You can suck me off again and again and then come all over me...."

"Not happening."

"You can just bukkake me."

"Landon," he says with a laugh, and then shakes his head. "We can't do that even if we wanted to. We have to watch Vincent for your dad."

"Ugh, that goat. Why can't Logan and Theo watch him?"

"Logan is taking Theo out for a romantic day in Half Moon Bay."

"Oh, is he?" I say, pushing up onto my elbows. "When do I get my romantic getaway?" I ask.

Finn's cheeks flush and he shrugs. "We can do that if you want."

"Oh," I begin flopping onto my back. "I want. Let's get a

hotel and bring a bottle of lube. I bet we'd go through the whole thing."

"Horny bastard."

"You started it by being exceptionally good at sex."

I lean up again and meet his stare, noting his cheeks are red. "How did you get so good, Finn? I don't remember any boyfriends or girlfriends in high school. Did you just have clandestine hookups or some shit?"

The question makes me a little nervous, but it's out there now, hanging awkwardly between us.

His hand grasps the back of his neck and his blush deepens.

Oh. *Oh.*

"Wait...no way," I gasp, and then smile, because... "I'm your first, aren't I?"

Finn looks away sheepishly and I feel smug.

"How is that even possible? Look at you! You're like a... sex god! You have big muscles! You're handsome as shit."

Finn runs a hand down his face looking...embarrassed? God, he has nothing to be embarrassed about. Him fucking me was perfection. I haven't had sex like that, well, in ever. That was the best sex of my life.

"God, I am so smug and impressed right now. Me. Your first time. And the fact that it was so good. My first time was...not good. At all."

"Shut up," he says. "I don't want to hear about that."

"Mmm, yeah, you so don't," I reply with a shudder. "I'm not even sure I made it into an actual vagina..."

Finn grumbles and then tackles me, my arms pulled up over my head, his strong body pressing me down.

"Shut your mouth."

"What are you going to do if I don't?"

His jaw clenches, his pupils dilating, the brown of his irises almost disappearing in an instant.

"Make me, Finn. Shut me up," I whisper. "I'm such a brat, such a bad boy."

His eyes flash down to my lips and he tightens his grip on my wrists.

My spent cock twitches between us and I wiggle beneath him.

"You could fuck me into submission. I bet that greedy cock could get hard for me again."

Finn huffs and presses his lips to mine, shutting me up for minutes as he slowly eats my mouth.

And when he finally pulls away, we're both breathing hard, our cocks thick and leaking.

"I'm not fucking you again today."

"Fine. Tonight. And that's final."

He pushes up off me, straddling my thighs and I reach out and stroke my finger along his hard dick, his eyelids fluttering when I press my finger into his slit.

"Finn, if that was your first time, I can't imagine what your second time will be like. It will be epic. I am *so* ready."

I wrap my hand around him and tug, making him grunt.

"Come on. Change your mind, Finn. You're ready. I'm ready. Let's do it again."

I can see him thinking about it, those gears turning, but suddenly his eyes snap open and he rolls away from me.

"Not today, Satan," he mutters, swooping me up in his arms and carrying me to the bathroom.

"Ugh, you're so stubborn. I don't know what I have to say to convince you. I want to walk crooked for days, Finn. I mean, I kind of already do with one leg—"

He shuts me up with a kiss.

* * *

Finn teases me all day. Just by existing and touching me and breathing in my general direction. My dick is painfully hard and I'm growing grumpier and grumpier by the second.

I want it and I want it now.

Vincent is nibbling at my shoelaces as we lounge in the backyard of my parents' house. It's just the two of us. We could be doing so many dirty, filthy things, but instead, we're just sitting outside, staring at the gray, gloomy sky. I hope it rains so it gives us an excuse to go inside and mess around.

Although, doing it in public with Finn wouldn't be bad at all. Hmm, now that's an idea. I wouldn't mind a little library sex or car sex. Or any sex really.

I wiggle on Finn's lap and his cold fingers slip down my pants a little.

"Let's just go inside," I say. "We can go to my room and mess around."

"Your mom would kill us if Vincent ate something he's not supposed to and your dad would be crushed if the goat ends up evicted."

"My mom would never evict Vincent," I say, grinding down against him, trying to get him to slip that hand a little closer to my penis. It doesn't work, doesn't even move an inch toward its final destination.

I huff and turn my face so my cold nose is pressed to his skin.

"We could just bring Vincent with us."

"I'm not doing anything sexual with you while a goat watches."

I glance over and see Vincent eyeing us. Hmm, yes, that would be creepy.

"Gah! You are killing me with this."

"I'm not doing anything."

"You are teasing me. Logan has lube here. It's in his room. Go get it and bend me over, Finn. We can put Vincent in a closet and lock the door."

"We can't and you know it. Plus, your parents will be home soon, and you know your dad is excited about making the tie-dye stuff with us."

"Argh," I grunt. "Him and his projects. No one wears tie-dye anymore."

Vincent bleats and I look down at him. "Yes, except for you. You're getting a tie-dyed sweater, asshole, and my butt-hole will be seeing zero action because of it."

Vincent just continues munching on my shoelaces. I don't even stop him. Who needs shoelaces anyway?

Maybe Vincent could munch all my clothes off so I'm stark naked, then Finn couldn't ignore me and my horny dick.

"We have barely a few minutes. Even if I felt like it was a good idea, we couldn't."

"I only need two minutes, Finn. Maybe thirty seconds if you hit my prostate just right."

"Oh my god," he mutters, a laugh choking out of him.

I waggle my eyebrows, and he slides that big hand across my cheek, cupping it gently.

"Stop being ridiculous," he whispers, his thumb tracing my bottom lip.

"I'm being utterly serious," I say. "I want it. I want you."

He lets out a shaky exhale. "I don't want to hurt you."

I grind down against him again as I bite onto his thumb. "You'd never hurt me, Finn."

His lips are on mine a second later, his tongue in my mouth. I shift my body to be closer to him. I need to be closer. I want to be a part of him.

"Uh, hey guys. Shit," my dad's voice says interrupting the two of us.

"Jesus, Dad, you just know exactly when to interrupt, don't you," I hiss, turning to see my dad shuffling from foot to foot.

"Well, I heard Vincent calling my name and I had to come check on him...."

I press my forehead against Finn's and sigh.

"You have terrible timing," I say.

"Yeah, well, I know this." He starts to whistle nervously, and Finn huffs out a laugh behind me.

"Basil, no worries, man. Ready to tie-dye? Do you have the stuff?"

My dad lights up, the whistling cut short. "Yeah, I am so ready. I bought this dye that's supposed to be hella awesome..."

He starts to prattle on as Finn pushes me to stand, and we follow my dad inside. I feel my heart flutter like it always does with him because he's so good with my dad. My weird as fuck dad. Who makes goat swings and grows asparagus.

But here is Finn helping him fold shirts into patterns for dyeing right near the kitchen sink.

God, I love him. He is the best man I know. But I guess I've always felt this way about him. But now...now that I've had him like this, inside of me, I feel it tenfold.

"So, I was thinking. Windchimes..." my dad starts, bobbing his head, his tongue peeking out of the corner of his mouth as he scrunches the shirt into a heart-shaped design.

Finn stops folding the shirt he's working on, securing it with a rubber band, and eyes my dad. "What about them?" he asks as I settle in next to them to help.

"I was thinking I could make some. Chickens love them."

"Do they?" I ask as I grab a shirt and start to fold it. Hmm, this is harder than it looks. Why does my dad's look like a heart and Finn's looks like a flower and mine looks like a smooshed toaster waffle?

"Yeah, they like shiny things. And goats like them too," my dad responds.

I'm not sure what websites he got this from, but it doesn't seem legit. He probably saw it on Facebook.

Finn grabs the shirt from my hands and fixes it for me. So I let my bored hands wander down and feel his nice, round butt. Hmm, I like his ass. I really like it. I wonder if he'd ever change his mind about me licking it...

"And listen, I was thinking...shit, don't tell your mom, but I saw this on Pinterest...a goat bridge with instructions on how to build it. I can call it Golden Goat Bridge. Saw that online too."

He smirks at us and Finn just snorts a laugh.

"Where you gonna put that, Basil?"

"Uh," my dad looks around and shrugs. "Don't know quite yet, but Vincent and his buddy will love it. They could just lounge on it all day."

My hand slides into the pocket of Finn's jeans and I squeeze.

Finn peeks over at me and then smacks me on the arm with the folded shirt when I don't stop.

"Ah, you guys, young love," my dad says holding a shirt over the sink and squirting yellow dye onto it. "I remember when your mom and I were so handsy."

"You're still handsy," I say and then nuzzle up closer to Finn. "It's ridiculous. You act like you're sixteen."

"Can't help it. Still in love," he says smugly, and I rest my head on Finn's shoulder, wanting to crawl inside his clothes and just hold him against me. Skin to skin.

I don't think I'll ever get tired of this man. In thirty years, I can still see myself horny for him, wanting to be near him. I will be like this until the day I die.

I never want to be parted from him for the rest of my life.

Shit, I hope I die before Finn.

That thought depresses me for the rest of the night.

twenty-two

LANDON

I HAVE to pull Finn out the door. Asshole takes his time about it too, chatting endlessly to my parents. I've never heard him talk so much in his entire life. And don't even get me started on how he got my dad on some tangent about cucumbers. They spent thirty minutes discussing fun facts about them.

Note: the facts are not fun.

The only possible fun thing about a cucumber is if Finn took me home, bent me over, and put that cuke right up my hole.

"You took your sweet time," I whine, shoving him into the apartment. "What's your deal?" I ask, frantically stripping myself down.

Finn stands there by the door, watching me throw my clothes off.

"Why are you just standing there like that? Move, Finn."

I stumble slightly and fall back against the couch. Damn missing leg.

But I don't fall far because Finn is right there, his rough hands on my skin and I groan, my dick pressing up and eager for him. I want him to rub those hands all over me.

"Please," I say, threading my hands through his hair and licking my way up his neck. "I need it. I've been dying all day."

He presses his hips into mine, right against my cock, and I groan like the slut I am.

"Those sounds," Finn says darkly, his grip tightening on me. "What they do to me."

I'm panting now as his hands slide down to cup my bare ass, dragging my pants down with them. The cool air in the apartment hits my skin and I shiver as he kneads my ass cheeks.

"Turn over," he says roughly and I don't even hesitate. I flip onto my stomach, my torso bent over the couch, my ass up in the air.

"Like this?" I breathe and Finn grunts. Just once. And I can't help but peek back to see what he's doing.

He's just staring at me, his pants tented, his chest rising and falling with deep breaths.

"Look at you," he mutters, catching my gaze. "Such a good boy."

God, yes, yes I am. The best boy.

Finn wets his bottom lip and then pushes my pants down a little lower, spreading them over my thighs. Then his hands are on my ass cheeks, pulling them open. The sensation of his hands against my ass drive me wild.

"So fucking greedy and insatiable," he murmurs and spreads me wide, his finger running up my crack. My hips buck forward and then I press back against him.

"I told myself I wouldn't fuck you—" he begins, but I cut him off with a loud, angry moan.

"Don't you dare think about it."

I'm humping the couch now. Poor couch. It never did anything to deserve this. It probably wants a nice home with a family that doesn't sexually harass it.

"Don't make me wait another minute. I'm ready. I want it. I want you, Finn," I gasp when his finger presses lightly against my hole. "I can take it. I can take anything you give me."

Finn freezes and then he's gone, stepping back.

"Don't you fucking move," he commands as he disappears into the bedroom. I don't have to wait long for him to return, those strong legs eating up the floor as he moves back toward me, a bottle of lube in his hand.

I watch behind me as he wrenches his shirt off, tossing it onto the floor. Shit, that muscled torso. He's so fucking sexy.

How did I never really notice this before now? How have I existed in the same space as him and never wanted him like this?

Obviously, I'm an idiot who humps couches in his free time.

The sound of the lube snapping open echoes around us and my hole clenches, ready for what's about to come.

"Are you sure, Landon?" he asks, his finger swirling at my hole.

"Fuck yeah. I've never been more sure in my entire life."

My fingers tighten on the sofa cushions as Finn starts to work his fingers inside of me, the squelching sounds making my dick twitch and leak.

"I've dreamt of this," he says softly. So softly I almost miss it.

"Yes," I groan as he pushes a second finger inside of me. "Tell me. *Tell me.*"

Finn crooks his finger and I jolt up as he hits my prostate just right. Fuck, I'm sensitive there. I love it. I want him to play with it all day. Just make me come over and over. I don't even need my dick touched. I just need him to fuck me with his fingers, just like this.

"I imagined you bent over like this," he begins adding a third finger and I groan, my cock impossibly hard and rutting against the couch like an animal. "Taking it. Taking all of me."

"Do it. Do. It," I hiss and then suddenly Finn's fingers leave me, only to be replaced a moment later by the tip of his cock.

"And how you'd beg for it," he says as he presses inside of me, inch by inch. "How you'd moan and writhe and pant for me."

I'm doing all of those things, my sore hole stretched impossibly wide.

When I'm fully impaled on him—his cock so deep inside of me that I can feel it in my abdomen, he wrenches me up against him, my back to his front, forcing me onto my tiptoes to accommodate him.

God, I can't move. I'm stuck. My dick jumps in excitement as his hand wraps gently around my neck, his teeth sinking into the skin just below my ear.

"But what I never, ever imagined," he says softly, canting his hips, fucking up into me slowly. "I never imagined how perfect it would be. You, Landon, are *perfection*."

I cry out as his hand tightens slightly around my neck.

I claw at his arm as he ruts inside of me, my entire body on fire with sensations. I love it when he does this. When he owns me.

"I never want another. Never. You're mine," he growls.

He's grunting now, feral. A wild animal let loose as he fucks up into me. Suddenly his hand is gone, and he's pushing me forward onto the couch, his hands on my hips, bruising and rough as his hips slap against my ass with each forward thrust.

I'm a keening, crying mess as he fucks me so hard the couch slides forward a few inches. Just put it through the wall. Who needs it?

"You take me so good," he says. "Your hole was made for my cock."

Fuck, he has a filthy mouth. I love it. I want him to talk dirty to me all damn day.

"More," I cry out, slamming my ass back to meet his cock.

His thrusts grow erratic but never slowing in momentum until I'm weeping, tears lining my cheeks.

This is a full-on religious experience. Who the fuck knew this was a thing?

Sex has never been this good. Never.

Without warning, I combust, my orgasm cresting so hard and fast that I black out for a few seconds, the ringing in my ears so loud that it's all I can hear for a moment. But then Finn shudders and groans, his grip tightening on me as he releases inside of me.

I swear I can feel it, him marking me.

Finn was here.

"Oh. My. *Fuck*," I hiss, my voice rough from screaming. "The cops are going to come. They'll think there was a murder."

Finn chuckles breathlessly, his cheek on my spine, his hands sliding up my stomach. I can feel the tremble in his body. He's just as affected by this as I am.

"I'll just have to tell them you murdered my asshole," I add. "It's a crime scene now."

He bites down on my shoulder blade, and I yelp.

"Shut that ridiculous mouth."

I snort and wiggle against him, his half-hard cock still inside of me.

"You know how to keep me quiet, Finn."

He slips out of me and turns me around, his cum dripping out of me as his lips meet mine.

And we just kiss. And kiss. And *kiss* until I'm ready to go again.

But instead of putting me out of my misery, Finn totes me to bed, tucks me in, and kisses my forehead.

Well, I'll just have to sit on him when he's half asleep

then. Stick that big dick right up inside of me once more. That's how eager I am for it.

But just as that thought enters my mind, I close my eyes —just for a second to rest them—and I'm out like a light.

Hmm, it seems Finn fucked me to sleep.

* * *

I wake up needy and sore. But like the champ I am, I push through. I lost a limb after all. A sore ass is small potatoes.

"Finn," I whisper, scooting so I'm completely on top of him.

He harrumphs like an old man as I thrust against him, his hard cock sliding against mine. Hmm, nothing old about that.

It's as spry as a spring chicken.

"What are you doing?" he asks, his voice gravelly from sleep, his eyes still closed. Mmm, I love that sound.

"Um, I'm going to ride you. Duh."

He rolls his eyes behind his eyelids like I'm fucking joking. Like I would joke about something like this.

Pfft.

I poke at his eyelids gently and they pop open.

"Do not roll your eyes at me," I reprimand, leaning over and grabbing the lube from the bedside table.

But before I can squirt some on my fingers, he swipes it from my hand.

"No."

"Finn, I know you like to think you are, but you're not the boss of me," I say and lunge for it. But he has long arms, like ridiculously long swimmer arms and I have to shimmy up his torso to even make a grab for it.

"Finn," I grunt, grabbing onto it finally and wrestling it into my hands. "Stop telling me what to do. I want you inside of me again. Why are you always telling me no...?" My words trail off as realization dawns.

"Wait, do you not want to fuck me again? Are you tired of my ass already?"

His eyebrow cocks and he reaches up, his hand encircling the back of my neck.

"Fuck off with those theories, Landon."

"Then let me do it."

I uncap the lube as he mulls it over, like the overthinker he is, but his dick knows what's up. It's hard and ready right beneath me.

I squirt some gel onto it, running my hand up and down it, and a groan escapes his mouth.

Well, that was easy. Like I've said, convincing.

"That's what I thought. Pretending to not want me, but you do, don't you, Finn?"

"Hell yeah I do," he says as I let go of him and work some of that lube into my hole. One finger. Two. Just stuffing it right in. And when I'm nice and slick for him, I lift up on my knees, using my hands to balance myself and position his cock at my hole.

"Now, Finn, here's what I want you to do."

He arches an eyebrow at me, his hands flexing at his sides.

"Keep those hands behind your head. Yes, like that. And

don't move. I want this to be all about me. I'm in control this time. *Me.*"

His dark eyes just watch me and he gives me a small nod.

I preen. I'm the motherfucking king.

I feel even more powerful when I see Finn's biceps bulge in restraint as I lower myself down onto him. He wants to reach out and grab onto me because I'm a little off balance, but he doesn't. Instead, he just grunts and moans, but he keeps his hands where they belong.

He's letting me control this rodeo.

Because I always get what I want.

"I'm going to ride you like a bull."

"Fuck off," he mutters as I sink all the way onto him, the vein in his neck protruding from his skin as he huffs out a breath.

"Say it again, Finn. Tell me to fuck off again. Give me an incentive to torture you."

He clamps his lips shut and I smirk as I pull off of him all the way before lowering myself back down.

Hmm, I could go harder. When I was younger, I thought it would be cool to be a cowboy.

I slide up until his tip is just inside of me and then slam my ass down onto him. His entire chest is heaving with restrained breaths, his abs constricting as he leans his head up to watch me take him.

Oh, yes, he wants to participate. I can tell by that look on his face. And he will, just not yet. No, I want to feel in control, just for a minute. To reign in this man and make him desperate for me.

"Keep your hands where they belong," I gasp, rocking onto him.

"So fucking bossy," he retorts, arching his hips up in response, nailing my prostate in the process.

Fuck yes. Oh god, why did I want to be in control? No one fucks this good.

No one but Finn.

"More," I moan, grabbing onto my dick and pumping it in my hand. It's ready, ready to come all over him.

My man. *Mine.*

I throw my head back, my ass doing all the work. And hell, I'm tired. My thighs burn. I'm about to beg for relief, when Finn bends his knees and fucks his way into me over and over, jostling me up and down roughly. I cry out, my fingers digging into his sweaty chest and then I say it.

"Please."

It's just a whisper, but it's enough. Finn's hands move and land on my hips, lifting me up and bouncing me hard on his dick. Like it's no big deal, like he isn't just moving another grown man up and down, over and over.

Fuck, I love it, how strong he is.

He hits that spot inside of me again and again until I burst all over him. Finn follows me over seconds later, and when I'm curled up against him, lying in my mess, his dick still shoved up my ass, he sighs.

"What's that sound for?"

His hands roam up my back, massaging my sore, worn-out muscles.

"I'm just...happy."

A smile splits my face and I nip at his chest. "Yes. Happy. Me too. And my asshole is ecstatic too. So is my prostate."

"Jesus," he mutters.

"Logan is going to die when I tell him..."

"Do not say a word to him about it. He won't shut up if you mention that fucking word. I can't bear to hear about his sex life over and over," Finn mutters rolling me onto my back, his dick slipping out of me, leaving me feeling...empty.

So I distract myself by pressing my lips to his.

"I could be persuaded to keep my mouth shut..."

But before I can finish my sentence, he's tugging me to the end of the bed, throwing me over his shoulder, and carrying me to the bathroom where he washes me very, *very* thoroughly.

Thank fuck for the shower chair. Can really get in some good angles. And Finn is very creative with his tongue.

twenty-three

LANDON

NOW THAT FINN HAS ME, his texts to Archer are few and far between. But they still happen. And it bugs me more than it should.

Because really, why does he feel the need to keep that gorgeous anomaly around when I'm riding his cock every day? Twice a day, if I can convince Finn to let me sit on him.

Which, I usually can.

To be honest, Finn is a total pushover when it comes to me. I've realized this in the past three days. I just need to pull my pants down and he's on me.

"What are you doing?" I ask, peeking over Finn's shoulder, trying to see what the fuck he's doing. But his shoulders are so broad I can't really make out what's going on over there and every time I try to glance around the side, Finn shifts his body so I can't see.

His thumbs are still on his screen as he glances over his shoulder at me. Logan and Theo are in the greenhouse with my dad helping him weed and my mom is in the backyard with Vincent, leaving just Finn and me inside the house with the cat.

Curie is watching this entire exchange from her perch in the kitty lodge.

She's currently licking her paw and eyeing us with glee, probably relishing in my breaking heart.

What a soulless creature wrapped in a cute package.

"Nothing," he replies, and I bite down on his shoulder just hard enough to show him I mean business. But that doesn't stop him. Nope, he keeps on clacking away, ignoring me.

And dammit, my insecurities come rearing their ugly heads.

One leg. Not whole. Disabled. Burden. Not good enough.

"Why are you texting him when you have me?" I ask softly and Finn turns so quickly I stumble back into the kitchen counter, losing my balance.

His hands reach out and grasp onto me, pulling me against his chest.

"For fuck's sake, Landon," he mutters, his fingers threading through my hair, tilting my face up to meet his gaze. "Archer and I are friends and I was...shit, I was planning a trip for us. Which would have been a surprise if you weren't so fucking persistent and nosy."

I blink up at him trying to hold it back, but my grin breaks through and I wiggle against him.

"A trip?"

"God, yes. A trip. You mentioned it the other day and Archer recommended a place...."

My eyebrows meet my hairline, not expecting that. "He did?"

"Yes, because we're *friends*. And he's happy for us. I've told you about Archer and what he is to me a thousand times."

I snort. "You told me exactly *never*, Finn."

"I've told you at least once."

I roll my eyes and then press small kisses to his neck. "So, what trip are you planning?"

"I'm not telling you anything else."

"When do we leave?"

"Do you never listen?"

"I have selective hearing," I say and then drag his mouth down to mine, where I lick and bite until I'm ready to fuck again.

"Sweet baby Jesus, not again," my mom mutters, and I wrench my mouth away from Finn to see my mom grabbing a bottle of wine as Vincent trots along next to her wearing that tie-dye sweater my dad made for him, looking utterly ridiculous.

And fucking cute.

"I love you both but please refrain from making out in my kitchen. It makes me nervous."

A giggle escapes my lips, but I bite it back when she glowers at me, pointing her wine mug at me.

"I'm not fucking joking, Landon. Your brother is bad enough. I found nipple clamps in the laundry machine.

Nipple clamps...Jesus fucking Christ! I do not want to imagine him wearing those."

"Who said nipple clamps?" Logan asks loudly, coming in through the slider door, and my mom just sets the mug down and grabs the entire bottle.

"Nope. Not doing this," she mutters and moves back outside. "I'm too old for this shit."

"What?" Logan says and then calls out, "What's wrong with nipple clamps, Mom?"

She plugs her ears as best she can and my brother bellows after her, "This is payback for ruining slow jams for me! I can't even look at Beyoncé without having horrific flashbacks!"

He turns back to Finn and me and chuckles. "God, it's too good. Just wait till she finds the dildo."

Finn tries to move away from me, but I cling to him.

"Where you going, Finn?" I ask.

He chuckles and bends slightly, picking me up in his arms. My leg wraps around his waist as I hold onto him tightly, and Logan just beams at us, chomping on a piece of celery noisily.

"I am so fucking glad you both got your heads out of your asses."

"Me too. And I'm glad Finn got into my ass instead...." I say and press a kiss to Finn's neck as he sighs and carries me outside where Vincent is head-butting my mom's ankles. My mom sighs and pulls out a carrot from her sweater pocket, handing it to the goat.

Ha, I knew she liked him, carrying around snacks for him just in case.

"Oh, hey. Guess what! Finn is going to take me on a romantic getaway," I blurt, unable to contain my excitement.

"Oh shit, yeah?" Logan asks, following behind us, chomping away. Crunch, crunch. Like a horse. I mean, honestly, who eats celery plain like that? Is he a psychopath? Celery was made to be turned into compost. "Where you guys going?"

"He won't tell me."

"It's supposed to be a surprise," Finn retorts.

"We hate surprises," my mom says. "The family curse, remember? All surprises are bad ones."

Well, she's not wrong. Just look at my poor grandma. Surprised by a coconut to the head—ended up dead as a doornail. And that deer that bolted out in front of the car that night a year ago. Surprise! There went my fucking leg. Plus my scholarship and a year's worth of college while I recovered.

"Maybe you should just tell us so it's not a surprise, and then bad luck won't follow," I say, my bottom lip protruding out in a pout.

"For fuck's sake," he mutters. "I'm not telling you a thing."

But we all just stare at him until he caves, sitting down on a chair and sliding his hand up my shirt.

"Fine, Jesus, stop with the peer pressure. I'm taking him to Carmel."

Ooh. Yes. Carmel. It's this small beach city on the Monterey Peninsula. It's ritzy as fuck, but so, so pretty. I've never been there on vacation; I've only just passed through.

"Will we be staying there?" I ask.

Finn stares at me and I nuzzle against him.

"I want to keep that a secret at least," he tells me, his pinkie sliding down the front of my pants.

My dick lengthens in response, wanting to be touched.

My mom mutters under her breath and then yells, "Vincent, not the hose!"

Vincent bleats forlornly when my mom wrestles it from his little goat teeth. Then he headbutts her ankles again.

"You should break him of that habit," Logan says, and my mom sends him a death glare.

"Do not talk to me about parenting the goat."

My brother gives her this goofy smile, finishing off his celery with a crunch.

"Just trying to be helpful," he replies, and my mom sighs and gulps down some more wine.

"Yeah, right, okay," she mutters and then meets my stare. "Let's change the subject before I say something not nice.... Your birthday is coming up, Landon, what do you want to do?"

I shrug, not really having put much thought into it.

"Come on, man, you're turning twenty-one. You have to want to do something," Logan says.

My mom holds her mug out toward Finn. "I don't know why I even ask when we all know Finn probably has it all planned out already. Care to share with the class?"

I glance up at Finn. "Is that true?"

His eyes narrow and I wiggle in his lap a little. Oh, he so does. I mean, he always does. But I like to pretend I'm surprised.

"Yeah, I guess he does," I tell my mom and Finn sighs heavily behind me.

"I have some ideas because we all know Landon won't make a decision."

"Hey," I say with a laugh. "I just can't make up my mind. You know this."

"Well, share those ideas, Finn," my mom says. "We want to know."

"Well, I was doing some research and there's this escape room..." Finn begins as my dad walks upstairs to the patio with Theo.

"Oh, an escape room," my dad interrupts and thumps Logan on the shoulder. "You know how scared Logan gets with those."

Theo eyes his boyfriend in disbelief and Logan shrugs. "They're creepy. I mean, you have to figure out the clues to get out..." He swallows and shudders. "And you're trapped. Inside."

"Oh my god, Logan. You're ridiculous. They're fun," I say and then nudge Finn. "Go on, tell me what else."

I'm so excited. He always plans the best stuff. One year he booked us tickets to ride a hot air balloon—you should have heard the way my dad screamed. And when Finn came home from his first year of college, he took me, *just me*, to Big Sur. We stayed in a lodge and hiked and just chilled.

Fuck. I am obsessed with him. How did I never know what these feelings inside of me meant?

I should have known.

"Just no escape room," Logan blurts again and Theo nudges him.

"Logan, man, this is Landon's birthday. It's not all about you," Finn tells my brother.

Logan just sighs, as if the weight of the world is on his shoulders.

"Yeah, yeah. I know," he grumbles, pulling Theo into his arms and burying his face in his neck. "Theo can protect me."

Theo's cheeks darken in embarrassment, but he still leans into Logan and slides his hand across Logan's arm.

So fucking cute, the way they touch, how they're so comfortable with each other.

"Anyway, after the escape room I thought we could do some archery lessons," Finn adds.

I gasp because Finn knows how much I've always wanted to do this.

"Are you for real?" I ask, excitement lacing my voice.

"Yeah, well, you've mentioned it a few times."

"By a few, you mean every month," Logan replies and I send him a glower. Because doesn't he understand? Archery is sexy, and now that I've had Finn, I can imagine him standing there, bow pulled wide, his muscles bunching...his dick pressed against his pants.

Hmm, yes, his dick.

"You mock me, Logan," I reply, forcing my mind away from Finn's private parts. "But just think about Theo with a bow and arrow in his arms...."

Logan mulls that over for a second and then shoots me a finger gun.

"Genius. I bet you'll get all super smart and competitive,

Theo. Right?" he says to his boyfriend who just sinks further into Logan, trying to disappear entirely.

"You kind of look like an elf with those pretty eyes and your long legs," Logan adds and Theo mutters under his breath as my mom snorts loudly.

"Jesus, you guys," she begins but is interrupted when my dad holds up a finger and shouts, "Elves! Yes! Ooh! Hold that thought! I have a thing."

He disappears into the house in a flurry of bumbling steps, Vincent trotting along after him.

"What's he going to do?" I ask and my mom just shakes her head.

"Oh, I have an idea. Jesus, take the wheel. I need more wine."

A few minutes later my dad comes stumbling out wearing some kind of Renaissance costume, looking like mother-fucking Robin Hood. He even has the boots and the hood.

Logan gasps in delight and I just giggle at how ridiculous he looks. Because he does. He looks fucking silly.

"Guys, look! I can wear this when we shoot arrows!" he says as Vincent bleats loudly in agreement. "It would be so cool! I'm so cool!"

"Oh, you so should," I tell him as Finn's body shakes beneath me in laughter.

"Where did you get that, Basil?" Theo asks, genuinely curious. "Did you wear it for Halloween?"

"Pfft, Halloween. No, I worked at a Renaissance fair one year. It's so cool, right?" he bounces on his feet looking at us and my mom just arches an eyebrow in his direction. "Your mom is pretending like she's annoyed and embarrassed, but I know she really wants to take me inside and rip this off of me. Wore this once when we..."

"Basil Lewis, do not utter another word," my mom snaps and then blushes deeply. "Although I'm not sure they don't deserve it. Not with the shit that's been going down lately."

"She found the clamps," Logan tells Theo who just about dissolves into the patio. Poor guy. He's in it now. No escaping this family once we have our claws in you.

"Well, I'm going to wear it when we go. We can all dress up! We could be like the dudes from *Lord of the Rings*," my dad adds and looks to Finn for confirmation. "Fool of a Took! You shall not pass!"

Finn just stays silent, eyeing my dad with mirth. But my dad bounces on his feet some more, not deterred by the silence. No, he's steadfast. He's the ultimate nerd.

"I'll text you about it, Finn. I'll wear you down. I know you want to."

Finn snorts as my dad fiddles with his leather belt. "You know, I could probably craft some kind of holder for the arrows...could be really authentic."

He pretends to grab some arrows from his back and shoot them at random targets throughout the yard while everyone just blinks at him.

Finn sighs at my dad's antics and then presses his lips to the skin of my neck. And just like that, all of my focus is back on him. Always on him.

"I can shut him down, if you want," Finn says softly. "If you don't want us showing up looking like the Merry Men, let me know ASAP."

"But he's so happy," I say.

"Yes, well, it's *your* birthday. You just tell me what to do."

I arch my neck a little more and he drags his mouth across it, causing my skin to break out in goosebumps.

"Please tell me there will be drinking after all of these activities. I think we'll need it," my mom says and all eyes are back on us.

"Yeah, at one of the local vineyards," Finn replies, resting his chin on my shoulder. "Because you only turn twenty-one once..."

"I love it," I tell him, and he pulls me closer to him, his arms tightening around me.

"Good. I want it to be perfect."

"It is. It already is."

And when we make it home later that night, I make sure to show him how much I mean what I said.

And I do it all on my knees.

twenty-four

TWO YEARS AGO

FINN

AS EXPECTED, Landon decided on UC Santa Cruz. He was offered a scholarship to join the track team and he's majoring in human biology like he'd always planned to. I'm happy for him, I really am. He has everything he's ever wanted, but the separation between the two of us is palpable.

I feel the absence of him each and every day. It's been two years since I went off to UC Berkeley and seeing him on the weekends, holidays, and over the summer is never enough. I want to see him every day, to wake up knowing he's close. I cannot wait until I graduate so I can move closer to him.

Even if we don't live together, just knowing he's near makes breathing easier.

I should try and occupy my time while away at school, to take my mind off of him. For a moment, just the briefest of seconds, I thought I'd try and date, but I gave that up almost immediately.

Nothing felt right. Nobody felt like *him*.

No one could ever measure up to who he is.

And it just wouldn't be fair to compare someone else to him.

Even if I can never have Landon, I'd rather be alone and just enjoy the parts of him he gives me.

This weekend I'm driving to see Landon. I just can't stay away. Last weekend we had a water polo game and I about died knowing I'd be missing him. So this weekend, I told Logan I was going home and now I'm almost there. Ten more minutes. God, it's ten minutes too long.

My foot presses down on the pedal, my car rocketing forward. If I go faster, I can make it there in eight minutes. I just want to see him, to touch him.

It's all I'll ever get, but it's enough. It will always be enough.

It has to be.

As soon as I'm on the Santa Cruz campus, I'm jogging toward his class. I know exactly where he is. He told me and I remembered. I'll always remember.

The second he steps out of his class, his eyes land on me and he runs toward me, his smile wide, his eyes shining with excitement.

"Finn!" he says, that voice of his sending shivers through me.

He throws himself into my arms and clutches onto me as if we've been apart for years instead of just two weeks. I hold him against my chest, lifting him off the ground, tucking my face into his neck and inhaling.

God, he smells like home.

"Finn, you're early," he says, with a small laugh. "I thought I wouldn't see you until tonight."

"I ditched class," I tell him, still not removing my face from his neck, my lips brushing against the skin there.

"Don't do that. Don't do that for me. You have to pass your classes...."

But doesn't he see? I'd move heaven and earth for him. I'd die for him. What's a missed class or two?

"It'll be fine. I just missed you," I admit, pulling away and Landon grabs onto my cheeks, pressing a kiss to my forehead. I can see people staring, but I don't care. I'm just so fucking happy I'm here. With him.

"Come on. Let's go back to my dorm and hang out and you can tell me all about what happened this week..."

I open my mouth to respond that we talk every night. He already knows everything that's happened. In great, mundane detail.

"Okay, fine, we don't even need to talk. You can just hang with me. Hold me. Whisper sweet nothings in my ear."

I snort and set him onto the ground, wanting to carry him to my car in my arms, but resisting the temptation. He's not my boyfriend. He'll never be mine.

He's just my best friend. I have to remember that.

"Hey, Landon," a female voice says behind me, and my hands slip to my sides as I take her in. Curvy, soft, pretty. So different than me, all sharp angles and gruff.

Right, yes. He loves me. I know he does, but not like *that*. Never like that.

And when he tells me later that the girl who said hello is someone he's been with...well, my heart just shrivels a little more. But I'm used to it, the pinching in my chest. I shove it aside with all the other little pains.

Because this is enough. I'm lucky I have him in my life at all.

I'll take what I can get.

twenty-five

LANDON

I'M BOUNCING in my seat as we approach Carmel, the city by the sea. It was about a two-hour drive from Santa Cruz, and I'm itching to get out of the car and onto Finn.

And I mean that literally. I want to be on him. With him *in* me.

Not that he'd let me. Party pooper. He's already telling me to keep my hands to myself. I even offered a blow job while he was driving and he just shot me this look. He was not convinced by the waggling of my eyebrows either.

No fun, Finn.

"We already had sex this morning," he mutters, and I roll my eyes because why the fuck is he reading my mind?

"You are an old man. Guys in their twenties are supposed to want to fuck all the time. Like every hour."

"And I gave you a blow job behind the gas station. Wasn't that enough?"

"Pfft, like that counts. I mean, it was good, but my ass is empty, Finn. Empty. Squatters have moved in."

Finn just eyes me, his lip twitching. "Fine, I'll wreck that ass when we get to the hotel room."

"God, yes please," I say, feeling better already. "Wreck it and then feed me. I'm hungry."

Finn pulls into a parking spot behind the hotel, and I scramble out of the car, adjusting my hard dick as I grab my bag, which Finn promptly pulls from my hand.

I follow my man inside the fancy lobby. Probably should have dressed a little nicer. I look like a ragamuffin with one leg.

Finn looks nice. Really fucking hot. Everyone is staring at him.

My boyfriend.

Never had one of those before and don't mind if I do.

I should probably tell him that I'm labeling this now, but Finn's busy talking to the woman at the check-in counter of this cute little hotel overlooking the ocean. She is making some googly eyes at him and I want to poke them right out of her little head.

"We were able to upgrade..." she says and Finn smirks back at me. So fucking proud. God. I hope we have a balcony. I want him to bend me over it and do filthy things to my asshole with his tongue.

"Finn," I hiss when the woman clacks around on her computer. "Does our room have a balcony?"

He eyes me and I waggle my eyebrows at him.

"Jesus," he mutters, but he's smiling because he's just as filthy as me. I mean, have you heard the things he says to me when he's fucking me silly? That mouth. I had not been expecting that, but I am *here* for it.

"Don't pretend that you don't want it," I say, trying to whisper, but it's louder than intended. Seems to really echo through the marbly space.

The woman behind the counter eyes us and I waggle my eyebrows at her too.

I'm just going to waggle them all the way home.

Because in about five minutes, my boyfriend's thick dick is going to be all up in my business, and I can hardly wait.

When we finally make it into the elevator, I'm on him, my mouth crashing into his and he is helpless to do anything but take it.

His hands are holding our bags, one at each side, so I just climb him like a tree. Well, more like just hop up into his arms and cling to his neck because my prosthetic makes climbing a little awkward. I just hang from his neck, one ankle hooked around his back, my other thigh clenched against his hip

When the door pops open, he's then carrying the bags and me down the long hallway to our room as I nip and lick at his neck. And listen, my man isn't even breathing hard. Not even a puff, but he will be soon.

He always gets winded when we fuck. He just loves it that much. Gets all excited and pants like an animal.

As soon as our door clicks shut, he drops the bags and starts to strip me down, and when I pull out the gigantic tub of lube from my bag that arrived from Amazon yesterday, his eyes go wide.

"Are you serious?" he asks. "This is like a month's worth."

"It's more like two days. And Finn, do you even know me? I am always serious about sex," I reply, bending over and wiggling my ass. "Just do it already. I'm dying for it."

He wrecks it just like he told me he would.

Jesus, does he ever. Just pounds into me until I'm screaming. I'm surprised security hasn't come to investigate. They'd lock us both up.

"You're walking crooked," Finn says hours later, a smug smile on his face.

Well, good for him. He deserves an award for that performance. Ridiculously sexy man. I am kicking myself for not doing this with him sooner.

"Yes, well, we both know why. You didn't take it easy on me."

"No, I didn't. But you asked for it." He lowers his voice, "Begged me."

"I did," I reply, not at all embarrassed by the fact. Finn reduces me to a weeping, horny mess when he fucks me. Every single time. He has a magic dick.

"I have a reservation for two," Finn tells the hostess at the fancy Italian restaurant overlooking the ocean. He was able to keep this bit a secret and I'm so glad because this is so fucking romantic. I never thought I'd be one for romantic gestures, but I guess I am. I want flowers too.

Buy me flowers, Finn.

When Finn gives the man his name, I link my arm with

his, and then we're being led to a booth in the dimly lit space. God, the tablecloths, the candles, the cloth napkins—it's so intimate and classy. I wonder if I could get Finn to jack me off under the table. Jerking off is classy, right?

Hmm, yes I like this idea. I slide in right next to him and eye the menu.

"Holy shit, Finn," I say, my eyes widening in surprise. "This is so expensive."

"Yeah, well I have money saved up from when I worked in the gym last semester, and I want to spend it on you. So don't be weird about it..."

"Finn," I protest, but he just shuts me up with a kiss. A really filthy one with a lot of tongue. The waiter arrives, bringing bread and some kind of balsamic dip, and Finn shuts me up by feeding me pieces of it. Slowly.

By the time dinner is over, I am about ready to just roll my way back to the hotel room. I can't feel my leg and my stomach has expanded to the size of a balloon.

"Finn, if you stick your dick inside of me tonight, I might pop," I groan.

He chuckles, holding out a forkful of chocolate cake, and I lean forward and gobble it down.

Willy Wonka has nothing on me. Who was that kid who drank the chocolate river and got swept away?

Gluttonous little fucker. I would have done the same thing. Just drown me in chocolate sauce.

"God, this is good," I moan around my mouthful and Finn smirks. "Why is this so good?"

"Knew you'd like it."

"Yes, well, I do like it. I'm going to lick the plate and then I'm just going to keel over and die, Finn."

He chuckles again, feeding me another bite.

"You're going to have to carry me out of here," I warn him. I mean, I'm serious. I won't be able to walk out of here. Between my ass being wrecked earlier and consuming a small colony I won't be able to wiggle out of this booth.

"I can do that," he says, taking a bite of the chocolate cake himself. I watch the way his tongue slides along the piece of silverware, all sexual. That fork is a lucky bastard.

I want that tongue on me. Like all the time.

We finish off the cake slowly, my dick getting harder and harder each minute because he's assaulting that fork, trying to torture me.

And when I finally swallow the last bite of dessert, I sink down in the booth as far as I can and unbutton my pants.

God, that feels so much better. Who invented jeans anyway? They're constricting and awful. I want to wear sweatpants all the time, or maybe a dress. A long flowy one. I suck in a deep breath. Shit, the food is crushing my lungs. I can barely breathe. That's how full I am.

"I should have come here naked. I'm going to have to take my jeans off just to stand up. I'll walk out of here in my boxers. I have no shame, Finn."

Finn reaches over and wipes some chocolate frosting off my face with his thumb, that digit going into his mouth and that tongue that's been torturing me all night peeks out once more. Teasing me.

"You're doing that on purpose," I hiss.

When he just raises his eyebrows in question, I wave my hand lazily in front of me. "That thing you're doing with your tongue. You're teasing me with it. I want you to do things with that tongue, but I can't even move. I think sex would absolutely kill me right now. I doubt I can even bend over at this point."

Finn leans back against the booth and pulls his phone from his pocket.

"Yes, well that was my evil, villainous plan all along, you sex fiend. I need you incapacitated."

"Pfft. Asshole."

He smiles softly at me, and then says, "I want to take a picture. Of us."

"Oh god, but look at me," I groan, and Finn's eyes slide across me, eating me up. Like he hasn't just gorged himself on food. Like he wants to consume me too.

"You look so hot," he says and I stare down at my bloated stomach.

"Sheesh, you have low standards," I say and Finn rolls his eyes, but I'm too full to protest. "Fine, fine we can take a picture as long as you tell everyone your boyfriend looks better in real life."

Finn's hand freezes in midair, his eyes snagging on mine, his chest no longer moving. He's stopped breathing.

"What did you just say?" he asks, so softly that I almost miss it.

"I said that I want you to tell people that your *boyfriend...*" Oh. Oh shit. Yes, we didn't discuss this. I discussed it with myself in my head but never actually uttered the words. It's a problem I have.

"I mean, you know...um, well, we don't have to label it. If you don't want to."

"Shut up," Finn says and then reaches out gripping my chin. "Tell me again. Say it."

"I said...we're boyfriends."

That serious face transforms, his lips turning up at the corners, breaking into a glorious, bright smile.

"Hell yeah," he says. "Boyfriends."

He says that word almost reverently, rolling it across his tongue, feeling it. Tasting it.

"So, we're a thing? That's okay with you? Because we were a thing when you first sucked my cock, Finn. Just so you know."

"Yeah, you've been my thing for a while."

"Yeah?" I say, scooting as close as I can to him. "How long?"

He swallows and his eyes slide away from mine.

"Oh my god, Finn. How *long*?" I ask, desperate to know. My exploding stomach is forgotten and now all I can focus on is prying this information from Finn.

"Tell me."

He runs a hand across his jaw. "Since I first laid eyes on you."

The world stops, the Earth frozen in orbit, and I just stare at my best friend. My boyfriend.

"Are you for real?" I whisper, and Finn clears his throat, glancing at me and then turning his gaze away from me once more. But I don't let him escape. No, I grab his face with both my hands and force him to look at me.

"You've wanted me since middle school?"

"Maybe."

Oh my god. Oh my god. I can't believe it. Why didn't he tell me? Did he keep his feelings secret this whole time?

"Finn. Why didn't you tell me?"

His eyebrows meet and I want to throttle him. Is he for real? We could have been fucking this whole time. Could have been kissing and doing all sorts of romantic things, like going to prom together or I don't know...anything couples do through high school and college.

"Finn, we could have been together this whole time. We could have been *fucking* this whole time."

He freezes, his body stiff and unmoving and his voice comes out dark and cold.

"Is that all this is to you? Fucking?"

Oh, sweet Jesus, this ridiculous, overthinking man. Always doing this shit.

"Of course not. Fucking is a benefit. You're my boyfriend now. But we could have been boyfriends for years! We could be married by now!"

Finn just watches me, those gears in his head turning rapidly.

"Are you serious right now? Or are you just teasing me?"

I roll my eyes slowly, and then I do it again so he can really see it.

"Of course I'm serious. I'm slightly upset you've been keeping this a secret. First, the fact that you're pan, and now this."

"Well, I didn't know...how could I have known how you'd take it?" he asks sounding exasperated. But really, he has no right. Mr. Secret Keeper.

"You could have asked me."

"And risked it, our friendship? Risk everything? I couldn't do that."

My eyes fill with tears as I stare at him, my best friend, my man, mine.

"You'd never lose me, Finn. You're my heart. You're a part of me. I might have been confused back then, but I would have come around. I know it. I just *know* it."

His Adam's apple bobs, and he grabs onto the back of my neck, pulling me in for a long, bruising kiss. And when we finally pull apart, he rests his forehead against mine.

"Well, now you know. So there it is. I've wanted you for years."

"Okay, okay, yes, but do you have any more secrets in there, Finn? Anything you want to tell me?"

He shifts, and I lean toward him, poking him in the chest.

"Tell me. I want to know everything."

"When we get back. I'll tell you everything. Anything you want to know."

I flag down our waiter. I want to go back to the room now. I'm desperate for answers.

* * *

Finn carries me most of the way. I wasn't joking. I am stuffed.

"You weren't kidding."

"I never kid about food," I say as Finn sets me on the counter in the hotel room bathroom.

He turns on the fancy tub faucet, testing the temperature

and I throw my shirt off, ready to be naked. Ready to be wrapped up in him.

"Oh, use that bubble bath shit…. Yes, that one. It smells so good."

Finn squirts a liberal amount into the water, and I watch as bubbles bloom beneath the stream of water.

"Oh god, I can't wait," I groan, trying to work my pants off, but failing. I am too full to move, so I wait for Finn to strip me down, pulling my prosthetic off and setting me on the edge of the tub. I slide my foot inside the hot water and hiss.

"This is extra hot. Are you trying to boil me like a potato?" I tell Finn, but my words trail off when I see him strip down. Who cares if my skin melts off? I just want to straddle him and let our dicks slide together. Dick soup it is.

"Grab the lube, Finn."

He freezes, one of his legs still in his pants.

"No."

"Grab the fucking lube and set it right here. We may need it once I can breathe and move without wanting to die. I have one leg. Don't make me beg."

Finn complies because he secretly wants it too. He wants me bad.

When he finally sinks down in the hot water, his muscular arms on either side of the tub, I lower myself onto him, my thighs straddling his, my arms wrapped around his neck.

"Damn, this feels good," I say. "That lavender soap is really helping my sore muscles."

"That's all horseshit, you know this."

"I know nothing of the sort, Finn," I say wiggling against him, our cocks brushing against each other.

"Finn," I say gently. "I want you to tell me all your secrets now. Everything you've kept locked away from me."

His hands clench against the lip of the tub and he swallows. "Tell me what you want to know."

I wiggle against him.

"I want to know the first thing you thought when you saw me. It was at school, right? Your first day when you walked home with Logan and me?"

He nods, just once.

"Tell me, what did you think when you first saw me?"

"That you were so beautiful," he says. "I couldn't believe you were real."

I press soft kisses along his jaw. "I thought you were so handsome. And when you held my hand...god, that shocked me."

"Fuck. Your hands," he groans, bringing my fingers up his mouth and kissing each one. "I've been obsessed with them for years. Your fingers. Your palms. I want them on me always."

"Well, you can have them. Anytime you want," I say and then lean into him. "Tell me more. What do you love about me?"

"Everything." It's so simple. So definite. And I believe it.

"Everything?" I ask.

"Yes. Anything that is Landon, I love. I've loved you from the moment I met you."

"Even with a missing leg?"

"Yes. Of course. Nothing could make me feel any differently about you."

"Are you in love with me, Finn?" I ask.

He swallows and nods. "I am. Absolutely."

"Mmm, good. Because I'm in love with you too."

His eyes flash and I press a kiss to those lips I adore. "I think I always have been. I just didn't realize that's what it was."

He lets out a shaky exhale and I nuzzle his jaw.

"We're going to get married, Finn, you know that, right?"

His hands tighten against my back and he holds me to him.

"Fuck, I hope so."

I look up at him and I bite down on his chin.

"We'll plan the wedding later, but Finn, I have to know... have you jacked off to thoughts of me?" I ask and his cheeks flush. Which is silly really, there is nothing to be ashamed about. It's a compliment.

"Yes."

"For how long?"

"Years."

Oh god, I love that. Love that he's been so far gone for me all this time.

"And what did you imagine you were doing to me?"

"Everything. Anything I could think of. I was a horny teenager, so far gone for you, and you didn't even notice me."

"I did. I did notice you," I say, but it's not the total truth. I had noticed him, how hot he was, the strong planes of his body, how handsome his face was. But I didn't understand what those thoughts and feelings meant back then. I know them now.

I fucking *know* now.

I cup his face in my hands and press another kiss to his lips.

"I'm so sorry it took so long. That I was so slow to realize..."

Finn kisses me deeply and all thoughts just disappear into the haze of lust. It clouds my mind and I'm utterly consumed by him.

"I want details. I want to know *all* the filthy things you wanted to do to me," I say, my hard cock pressing against his.

I reach down and clasp us together and Finn groans.

"I wanted to suck your cock," he breathes. "That first time we jacked off together. I wanted to lean down and take you in my mouth."

"Oh shit, you should have. You so should have."

"I jacked off to thoughts of that for years."

I groan, stroking us lazily, the water in the tub sloshing up with each movement.

"Did you think of me sucking you?" I ask, and he nods, his pupils blown out.

"Yeah. All the time. What it would feel like, how you'd sound. God, but Landon, your actual mouth around me...it's so much better than I could have ever imagined."

"More," I say, working my fist faster.

"I had you in my dreams. In every position," he gasps. "Hands and knees, underneath me, on your side, riding my cock. But I never thought I'd have the chance to have you."

"Well, you have me. You have me and you can do all the

filthy things you want to me. I'm yours now, Finn." We both groan when I tighten my grip. "You've had my heart from the moment we met. Something about you was *different*. I didn't understand it then, but I know now.... I am obsessed with you. You're it for me, Finn. There will be no one else."

He lets out a shuddering breath and holds me to him, my hand trapped between us.

"Now make me come," I tell him, and Finn's eyes darken.

He yanks my hand away from our cocks and fists us together in his huge, rough hand, pumping hard and fast.

"I've imagined this," he groans. "My cock against yours, the way you'd moan for it. I want to have you every way I've ever imagined."

"God yes," I groan, arching my hips up with each of his downward thrusts. "Anytime. Always."

His grip tightens on us and he brings us over the edge with a groan, his teeth sinking into my shoulder as he shudders and shakes beneath me. Claiming me, marking me.

When the orgasms subside, and his hand finally releases us, he presses a kiss on the bruise he left on my skin.

"You marked me like an animal," I say, my voice shaking.

"Yes. Well, you're mine now."

"Hmm, I love it. An engagement ring should be next," I say, resting my forehead on his, trying to get my limp arms to move. But I needn't bother. Finn sweeps me up, dries me off, and carries me to the bed, tucking me in. And when he scoots in next to me, I just crawl on top of him.

Happy. Satiated. Content.

twenty-six

LANDON

I'VE NEVER HAD SO much sex in my life. It's like Finn's completely let loose. He made fun of that gallon-sized lube I got, but we went through most of it. When we weren't walking along the beach or eating, he had me inside the hotel room, fucking me in all the positions he's always wanted to try on me.

And I was a happy, willing participant.

My boyfriend is a sex maniac, and I am positively in love.

We made it home late last night and Finn fucked me against a wall, in too much of a hurry to even take my clothes off, and this morning, he entered me while I was half asleep.

Let me tell you...this is the best way to wake up.

But now the bubble has burst because Finn is leaving me alone for the next hour or so to meet up with Archer.

Fucking Archer. The guy Finn still texted on our weekend away. Not often, but enough to make me squirm.

"Do you really have to go meet him?" I ask, looking at Finn who is stroking my cheek so tenderly.

"Yeah, I want to.... I like talking with him. We're just friends," he says, reminding me. And I need reminding. I've come to realize I'm extremely possessive and jealous. I don't want to share him. Not for a single minute.

I guess I've always been like this with Finn, but now I've gone and taken it to a whole new level. Finn is allowed to have friends outside of me. I know this logically, but still, I feel this rage inside of me at the thought of him with someone so...

"Stop it," he says, cupping the back of my neck, reading my mind. "Don't even go there."

I feel bashful for even thinking what I was about to think.

"I know..." I groan. "I'm working on it. I just don't understand why these chats with him are so secretive. It makes me insecure that I don't know what you guys talk about."

I blink up at him, putting my bottom lip out and Finn rolls his eyes.

"It's just...fuck, it's too embarrassing," he says and I sit up in bed, my ass twinging from the movement.

"Why is it embarrassing?" I ask, now desperate to know.

"Because..." he runs a hand down his face. "Because I only ever talk about *you*."

He peeks up at me and then rolls his eyes once more when he sees me smiling.

"What? What about me?" I ask.

"When Archer and I first reconnected, I just needed someone to talk to about you and me..."

I scoot over until I'm draped across Finn's lap.

"I just needed advice because I was so confused after that first kiss. The one on New Year's. And I couldn't tell Logan."

I snort. "Yeah, good thinking."

Finn runs a hand through my hair and I arch into his touch. "I just...fuck, I just needed to process it all with someone. I've been...I've been *pining* over you for years, Landon, and suddenly you started kissing me all the time like you wanted me too. It kind of messed with my head. You have to understand that I just needed to talk."

I get it, I do, but I still ask, "Why didn't you just tell me?"

His hand tightens in my hair and I groan, loving how rough he can get with me. Just throw me around the room, Finn.

"I didn't want to lose you. I was scared."

"Oh, Finn. You'll never lose me. I will always be yours."

He presses his forehead against mine and inhales deeply.

"Forgive me, for keeping it from you, for going to Archer..."

"No, none of that. I'm just a jealous asshole. I'm glad you had him. I am, even if he is very pretty..."

Finn runs his nose along my cheek.

"I see no one but you. Why do you think I waited...?"

I puff up with that. "That's true. I was your first."

"And you're going to be my only."

"God, yes," I say, wanting to go again, but Finn is pulling away, already running late.

"Don't be mad," he says, shrugging on his jacket, looking way too hot for a casual coffee with a friend.

"Could you put on some rags instead? Maybe a dirty shirt? Or a ski mask?" I ask.

Finn chuckles, running a hand through his hair. "You're ridiculous." And then his eyebrows meet. "You're not upset?"

I sigh and shake my head. "No, go have fun. It's hard to stay mad when my ass is so happy."

"I like you jealous, you know," he says, glancing back at me from the doorway.

"Yes, well, I won't be jealous for long. I know it's an issue. I'm a work in progress. Pretty soon you can be out and about with all sorts of pretty men and I won't care."

Finn snorts a laugh and then walks back to me, pressing his lips to mine. I arch into him, wanting more, but he pulls away too quickly.

"I'll bring you a coffee to your parents' when I'm done."

"Fine. And a scone too if you really want to grovel."

He chuckles and then looks a little concerned. "Want me to drop you off...."

"Finn, just go! I'll be fine. I'll call a ride when I'm ready to head out."

He looks unsure, but still pulls himself away from me and leaves. Ugh, I miss him terribly and he's only been gone a few seconds. I can't even bring myself to think of those days in college when we were apart for weeks. That was just a torturous and bleak time, and now those feelings have multiplied tenfold.

I am a clinger and I'm not even ashamed about it.

I want to text him to come back to me, but I would *never*.

I'm an adult. Not really, but I can at least be an adult about this.

I flop back down on the pillows and stare at the ceiling. I need a hobby. Maybe some pottery classes or some shit. I can make my dad pots for his plants.

God, he'd like that. He would get all sniffly when I gave them to him. I just know it.

I shift on my side and grab for my phone to see if there are any community classes I could take, and a soft grunt escapes me when I move. My ass is mega sore, and my leg is kind of hurting me. If I'm honest, I probably overdid it this weekend. There was a lot of walking involved, not that I was about to complain. I wasn't about to ruin that trip for him.

I lift up my arm and sniff. Yep, I need to shower before I head over to my parents' place to watch Vincent for a bit.

I need to make sure that little dude doesn't headbutt his way into the greenhouse and eat my dad's beets.

Fucking goat.

I get ready and leave quickly because the absence of Finn is making my chest ache and I need a distraction. Luckily, I find it with Vincent while walking him around the block. He's dressed in a little yellow raincoat that my dad purchased for him online. It rained last night, and the ground is slick with puddles. Hopefully we make it home before another downpour starts.

I splash through a small puddle as Vincent bleats merrily, stopping occasionally to munch on pieces of grass growing from the road. To be honest, this outing is a bit shady. Without Finn next to me, the road seems a lot more uneven, this part of the city not having any sidewalks, and the rain we've had the past few weeks has made potholes in the asphalt.

Fucking California.

"Yes, well you have no trouble at all, do you, Vincent?" I tell the goat who is ignoring me in favor of eating soil. "You just prance around all day long. Not a care in the world. Must be nice."

He bleats loudly, some dirt on his chin. He looks ridiculous.

I stumble slightly when Vincent pulls to the right and let out a small gasp of horror at the thought of falling out here. I mean, I wouldn't be found for hours probably. We aren't in the suburbs and the houses are spaced quite far apart.

Cars come along this road, but not often. I could be face down in a puddle and no one would notice.

A morbid giggle escapes my mouth at the thought. Hell, Finn would lose his shit if I so much as scraped my knee walking Vincent around. I mean, he about died when Logan and I got in that car crash. I know it's not funny, it really isn't. But what do you do when something is so tragically ripped from you? Cry? You can't cry all the time.

So I laugh about it and joke. My dark humor keeps me sane.

And mostly, I've moved past it. I just hate that sometimes I'm wobbly on my feet, like right now. I should be able to walk around the damn block by myself.

Oh well, Vincent is almost done eating his way across the earth. We can head home now.

I tug on his leash and he cries out pitifully, a leaf hanging from his mouth.

"You little gluttonous goat," I say with a huff of laughter. "You just can't help yourself."

His jaw works back and forth, and I snort at how absurd he is, turning around to head back home.

And that's when I hear it.

The spin of tires, the thumping music, the rev of an engine.

When I look up and see the headlights rapidly approaching, I yank on the leash holding Vincent, because if this silly goat gets hit by this car my dad would sob for days. I don't even consider me. No, Vincent is at the forefront of my mind. I jolt us further toward the side of the road as the silver flash of metal advances so quickly I barely have time to think.

But as I step back, my foot catches on a root protruding from the pavement, and I feel myself start to fall. As I go down, I hear the screech of tires just as the back of my head thwacks against the pavement.

Pain, white spots behind my eyes, and the crunch of metal beside me.

Everything goes black.

twenty-seven

ONE YEAR AGO

FINN

I FUCKING hate that I had to stay back and work on a final project, missing my Friday evening with Landon. Logan got to go home early though, having finished up everything ahead of time. Since when does that guy ever finish things on time? Jesus. Lucky bastard.

I glance down at the text Landon just sent of him and his brother smiling goofily at the camera.

They're out having fun. Without me. God, I just want to be with them. Well, with Landon. I live with Logan, and I love him like a brother, but what I feel for him is nothing like what I feel for Landon.

It's been weeks since I've seen him and I miss him. I've been far too busy with classes and with water polo and his schedule has been just as hectic. I should have made him more of a priority, but I just wanted to finish the semester strong so I could spend all of January with him. I can't wait to wake up in the same place as him, and to spend our days doing fun things together.

I press down on the accelerator, speeding down the road, wanting to make it home as fast as possible. I'll break all the laws for him. Always have, always will.

My phone vibrates where it rests on my leg and I glance down, seeing Basil's name appear on the screen.

He probably forgot something at the store and needs me to swing by to grab it.

I press the green answer button, a smile on my face, just waiting to hear his bumbling, goofy voice. But all happiness evaporates when I hear the distraught breaths on the other end of the line.

"Finn?" he gasps, and my entire body sizzles with panic.

Oh my god.

Oh my god.

"There's been an accident. Landon…. He's alive but, shit, it's a mess. He…He needs you. He's asking for you…"

I can't breathe, I can't think. I don't even know how I make it the rest of the way to Santa Cruz, but by some miracle I do.

I stumble into the hospital and see Logan, his forehead a little bloody, his eye bruised from the impact of the airbag when his car hit the tree.

But when I swivel to look for Landon, my heart drops. "Where is he?"

"He's in surgery.... They're trying to save his leg..." and my entire vision grows hazy because if he loses...oh my god. He loves running. Shit, his life will never be the same after this.

I sit in the seat nearest Logan. He stares at the carpet looking utterly broken, like a piece of him has fallen out of his chest and he can't find it.

"I did this," he mutters, running a shaky hand across his jaw. "It's my fault. I did this."

His mom holds onto him, resting her head on his shoulder. "It was an accident, sweetie...it wasn't you."

But I know, I just know Logan will blame himself. He will carry this with him for years.

Basil swipes at his eyes, holding onto my hand and explaining what happened as best he can. Landon and Logan had gone for a drive to grab some food. A deer had run in front of the car and Logan swerved to avoid hitting it, and hit the tree instead.

Landon's leg was crushed by the dashboard and the doctors weren't sure if they'd need to amputate.

I listen to it all, numbly, just wanting to see him. To be near him and feel his heart beating.

I get my wish hours later when the doctors finally let us in to see him. My heart stutters in my chest at the sight of him, bruised, broken, and hurting.

I ache. I would trade places with him in a heartbeat. I would take it all if I could.

His eyelids peel back groggily and he blinks at his mom, dad, and brother who are huddled in the room before they finally settle on me.

"Could they save it?" he croaks, and his dad shakes his head sadly.

Tears leak from his eyes, his chest moving in heaving sobs, and Logan leaves the room, his cries echoing around us.

I can't stand to be separated from him a second longer. I move toward him, crawling in next to him, needing to just hold him.

"They took my leg," he says, looking at me, his eyes wet with tears.

"Yes," I say, cradling him. "It's gonna be okay. You're okay."

"What am I going to do, Finn?"

"Everything. The same things you've always done. Just a little differently now."

He sniffles and rubs at his face. "But who will want me like this? Who's going to want someone so broken?" Landon whispers, his entire body trembling.

"Me, Landon. I will. Always," I whisper, pressing my lips to his temple, inhaling him. God, even now he smells like home.

My home.

I just hold him, not leaving his side.

I spend the next few months by his side; every minute I can be away from school I'm with Landon. Because Logan can't be there. No, he's disappeared into his grief and guilt.

It's just me carrying Landon, soothing him, holding him when he cries out at night.

I whisper to him when he's fast asleep, hoping his brain absorbs my words even if he can't hear them.

"You are beautiful. Perfect. Everything I want. I love you. You. Only you."

twenty-eight

LANDON

I WAKE up in bits and pieces. My dad. My mom. A man with dark soulful eyes, they're leaking, crying. He's crying.

Who is he? He's someone. Someone to me. Someone important, I can feel it.

I can feel him.

But fuck, my head hurts. A sharp, incessant pain. It's too hard to remember right now. It's painful to think and so I just close my eyes and drift off back to sleep.

* * *

I wake up in a fog.

Are we moving? I feel a sway.

And *he's* there again. A name. His name.

Finn.

My Finn. My best friend. Yes, I know him. I feel him. He's mine.

His hand is clasped in mine, rough and strong. I've had those hands on me. I know it. He's a part of me.

Finn. My best friend. More than that. More. He's more. I can *feel* it.

"Finn," I say, my voice raspy and hoarse.

His face appears in my blinking, blurred vision. Those eyes, lost and sad. Why is he so sad?

"Hey," I say softly, my hand clasped in his.

"Landon," he replies, his voice cracking, raw. As if he's been yelling. Why was he yelling? Why? Did something happen?

God, my eyes feel heavy. So tired. Like when they put me under to amputate my leg.

My leg. Oh fuck. Not again.

I quickly wiggle my foot, and relief surges through me when I feel it. Okay, so I still have one. But something is missing.

Something I can't quite place.

"Finn," I say again, and there he is, my best friend, leaning over me, tears streaking down his cheeks.

"Hey," he says, that voice so familiar. "God, you're awake. Landon..."

He trembles, pulling me closer and I lean into him, my head splitting with a fierce headache.

"Say my name again," I whisper and he does.

God, yes. This. More. Something more.

"Again," I say, and he leans down, his lips brushing the lobe of my ear, and his voice trembles.

"Landon."

My entire body shakes with *something.* Fuck, what is wrong with my brain? Why can't I think? Everything is hazy.

"Do you remember?" he asks, his hand clasping mine so tightly, it hurts. But I don't pull away, I feel anchored by it. With him.

"Remember what?"

A broken sob is wrenched from his lips and he tucks his face into my shoulder. Breathing. Weeping. Why? *Why?*

"Why?" I ask, my head already throbbing. But he doesn't answer. No, he just pulls away.

"I just need a minute," he says, and his face is replaced by someone unfamiliar. Someone I don't know. But it's no matter. My eyelids shut and I drift into darkness once more.

When I wake up again, I'll figure it out. I just know I will.

Because there is a puzzle piece slightly askew, and I want nothing more than to put it back where it belongs.

And I will, but first...fuck. I'm tired. I just need to sleep.

* * *

"With the way he fell, there is a chance of some short-term memory loss. Not sure how severe, so only time will tell," a deep voice says. "We'll keep him here overnight to monitor him, but if everything looks good, he can go home tomorrow."

My eyelids blink open once more. I feel better, better than before. Things are clearer, more in focus. I'm no longer moving through a thick fog. Sleeping helped. Thank fuck because that niggling feeling is back, that feeling that I'm missing something, but maybe now that I've rested, I can decipher what it means.

"Um," I mumble, and all heads swivel toward me. But someone is missing. He's missing. I can feel it, the absence tangible.

"Where is he?" I ask, feeling frantic. Why isn't he here? I know he left earlier, but why isn't he back?

Did he leave for good?

"Where is he?" I ask again when no one responds.

"Who?" my mom asks.

"Finn."

Everyone is silent, my breath loud and piercing in the air. "Where is he?" I'm growing frantic. I need him. Need him.

"He's..." my mom's voice breaks off and then she's moving out of the room, her eyes red-rimmed, her face splotchy.

And there's my dad, moving up next to me. His hair is a mess, and his shirt is wrinkled. He looks sad, tired, and *weary*.

"He's coming. Calm down, son. Just hold on a minute," he says softly and then grasps my hand, holding it tightly.

"I just want to go home," I say and my dad's head bobs, his eyes watery. "I just want Finn."

"Yeah, bud. I know."

I stare at him, just really look at him, memories of my dad filtering through my mind. The time he showed me how to ride a bike, how to hold my hand open to feed the chickens, how he'd tuck me into bed at night, pressing a kiss to my cheek. But all of those memories are wrenched away when I feel Finn approach.

My eyes are peeled away from my dad and zero in on him.

Finn. My Finn.

I pull my hand from my dad's and shift up, wanting to just crawl to him.

Come here. Closer. *Closer.*

"Finn," I choke out, reaching for him, but he hesitates. Just stops right where he's standing and watches me, his eyes wet and red.

"Come here," I say and he eyes me, unsure, guarded, so fucking sad. "Come here. I need you."

He moves, those legs I love so much eating up the ground beneath him until he's crawling in next to me, jostling me on the bed, pulling me into his chest.

I inhale him. *Mine.*

"Why did you leave?" I ask, and his breath comes out broken and shattered, a window broken with force, the shards scattered across the ground.

"You'd forgotten me.... I needed...I just needed a minute."

"Forgotten you?" I ask, craning my head up, looking at him, the stubble lining his cheeks. I reach out, tracing it, feeling the roughness against my palm. "Never. You're a part of me. I can feel it."

"I know," he mutters, pressing a kiss to my forehead. "But I.... I'll be fine. This is about you. I just want you to get better. You hit your head...you hit it hard when you fell..."

"I know, but why are you so sad, Finn?" I ask, my finger tracing the tear falling down his cheek. For a moment, I imagine kissing his tears away, soothing him with my lips. The thought jolts me. Since when have I ever seen Finn this way? Not doing it feels painful, a pinch in my chest making me catch my breath.

Finn sniffles and swipes at his skin, rubbing it away.

"No reason. It's...just seeing you here again..." his words break and crack, a fracture.

He's lying. I know him. I feel him. Something is wrong.

"Tell me."

But he won't. Those lips I love so much slam shut, and he shakes his head. Just once, but it's enough to force me to let it go. He won't tell me. Not yet. So, I just nestle into him, and he holds me in silence until I fall asleep.

* * *

I'm released from the hospital a day later, my memories a jumbled mess. I have a severe concussion which has affected my short-term memory. The things that happened last week are fuzzy and gray around the edges. But I know that I just need time to sort through them and then that one missing piece will come filtering back. I know it. Because something isn't right. Something is still missing.

The brain is a funny thing, my doctor had said. Give it time.

And that's what I plan to do. Because Finn is acting strange, his eyes are so sad. Dark purple splotches sit under them, and he can't bear to look at me for too long.

I just want him to hold me and for him to smile at me. But he doesn't. Worry clouds his eyes. Worry and sorrow.

But why is he so sad? And why won't he tell me? We tell each other everything.

Don't we?

"I'm fine, Finn," I say when he carries me to my bed and settles me under the covers, tucking them under my chin. We made it back to my apartment, Finn driving so slowly that I about died from old age. He carried me up the stairs, not even breathing hard, and settled me right in my bed.

He's going to dote on me until I'm fully recovered, I just know it. He did that when I first lost my leg and I know he'll do it again. He just can't help himself.

"You need to rest," he tells me and stands there above me, not moving to crawl in next to me. Why isn't he? He always holds me when I'm sick.

I'll just have to remind him.

"When you're ready, can you hold me like you used to?"

He swallows loudly and nods. "Yeah. Okay, I can do this..."

He takes his shirt off and then slides under the covers, and I scoot toward him until I'm right against him. But it doesn't feel like enough, so I crawl onto his broad, strong body and spread myself out.

Yes, better. This is better.

And when his hands slide across my back, rubbing small circles with the pads of his fingers, I feel like everything will be okay.

"Don't be sad, Finn," I say. "I'm fine. It's just a knock on the head. I got lucky."

I don't remember the accident. I do know Vincent survived. Lucky goat. It was one of the first things I'd asked my dad when I woke up. He also told me the car that almost hit us hit a mailbox instead and sped off. Cops never found them.

"I know you'll be fine. You were so lucky," he chokes out.

I nuzzle against him, letting my hands slide up and into his hair. I'm completely stretched out on top of him, my cock twitching between my legs.

Fuck...that's new. Isn't it?

My dick doesn't seem to think so. It's getting harder and harder the more I writhe around on top of him. And then my ass twinges and I wiggle until Finn's hand stills me.

"Enough," he murmurs softly. "Please...."

I settle down, not wanting to upset him, and then my mind starts to wander.

"Finn. Why was I walking alone out there?" I ask, having a vague inkling, but not able to piece it together.

Finn's throat clicks loudly. "I should have been with you, but I was out..."

"Doing what?" I ask.

He pauses and then says, "Archer. Do you remember him?"

I don't, but I have a feeling about that name. It's a stupid name, makes me a little angry. But I don't know why.

"I hate that name. That's all I know," I say, and Finn lets out a choked laugh, his hands gentle against me, continuing to stroke my lower back.

"Can I ask you something?" he says.

"Of course."

"Do you remember us?" he asks softly, quietly as if he's scared to bring that question to life.

"Of course I do. You're my best friend."

"That's all?" he chokes out.

I tilt my chin up, my head throbbing from the movement, but still, I force my gaze to meet his. "Is there more? Because I have this feeling there's more…"

I peek up at him, his eyes are closed, his chin trembling.

"No, Landon, there's not more."

"Why do you look like you're crying?"

"It's…it's nothing. Don't worry," he manages to say, trying to reassure me, but his voice sounds off, cracked and rough. I'm not convinced that whatever happened was nothing. But my brain is aching, and my eyes are tired, so I just close them and let myself drift off to sleep.

Tomorrow. Tomorrow I will try and piece things back together.

* * *

My mom and dad visit, as do Logan and Theo. And there is Finn, standing in the kitchen, his head hanging between his shoulders, his face sunken, his eyes so very tired.

I woke up from my nap sprawled across him, feeling his warmth and just basking in it.

I don't think he slept. Instead, he just held me and when I was ready to get up, he carried me to the shower and turned it on. But he didn't stay, which…irked me. Why didn't he stay?

And everyone's not telling me something but no matter how much I try to get them to, they just blubber and deflect like we all usually do.

"Logan," I say, leaning over toward him. He's sitting on

the couch with Theo on his lap. Everyone's trying to pretend everything is normal, but it's not fucking normal. Something is bugging me. "You're not telling me something."

Logan flushes red and he shrugs, Theo on his lap squirming a little. So, Theo is in on it too.

"Tell me," I say and Logan swallows.

"He'd kill me. We promised," he mutters and then looks away, scooting over a little.

My eyes narrow as I grow more and more upset. My mind is all muddled and scrambled and I just want to know what they're not saying.

"Someone tell me!" I shout and the entire room grows silent. My mom and dad look over from their place in the kitchen and Finn looks at me through glossy eyes.

And when my mom looks at him, placing a hand on his arm, he shakes his head, just once but it's enough of a shutdown to have me pushing up off the couch. I wobble slightly and when Finn moves toward me, I slice my finger across my neck dramatically and he stumbles to a stop. I storm into my room and slam the door.

I stew in silence, my chest hurting, the secret everyone is keeping from me making me angrier and angrier until I'm panting.

God, I'm going to pass out from hyperventilating. I shut my eyes and I try to focus, but there are only vague feelings about something I can't put my finger on. Frustrated tears roll down my face and I curl up into myself, sobbing lightly.

Why does this always happen to me? Why can't I just catch a break?

The door creaks open and Finn moves in. I can smell him, feel him even when I don't see him.

"Landon," he groans softly, and my heart pitter-patters in my chest.

"I'm mad at you," I hiss and then swipe at my wet cheeks. "You're keeping secrets."

His hand falls on my side and I scoot away from him, despite my entire body revolting at the move.

"Tell me or sleep on the couch tonight."

His hand falls from me and he runs a hand down his face. "Shit, Landon, I..."

I peek up at him and he lets out a rattled breath.

"Do you mean it? I don't want.... Don't make me sleep somewhere else. Please."

I try to stay mad, but those dark eyes just swell with sadness, and I swipe at my cheeks, feeling myself cave.

"Fine, I'll make an exception, just this once, but you need to tell me, Finn. No more secrets."

"I'll tell you when you've had some time to recover. I just...I want you to focus on yourself."

"I can't focus on anything when this piece is missing. Something is missing and I can't stand it!"

He sits down next to me and brushes his fingers across my cheek, his thumb tracing my bottom lip and my entire body lights up.

God, I know this touch.

Know it.

"Finn," I breathe and he lets out a stuttered breath. "I feel like I need to kiss you."

He exhales as his thumb pulls my bottom lip down slightly.

"Not until you're better."

"I'm tired of waiting," I say, letting my tongue slide across the tip of his thumb.

Finn looks absolutely wrecked. "Rest, my love, and then we can discuss this tonight. When everyone is gone."

His hand falls away from me and then he stands, crouches down, and holds out his arms. Like before.

And when I'm in his arms, it feels right. It feels perfect, but something is still missing.

Something he's not telling me.

twenty-nine

FINN

GOD, my heart.

I can't.

I can't fucking *breathe*.

I had him and I lost him.

He's angry with me for saying nothing, but how can I force memories on him? Force an entire relationship on him?

No, he has to remember what we had himself.

If he remembers at all.

Or we'll have to build it again from scratch.

I can do that. I can start over. I can...

What if he never comes around again?

It took him eight long years the first time.

I clutch at my chest, feeling the organ beat unsteady beneath my hand.

It hurts.

It doesn't feel like I'll survive this.

But at least I *had* him.

Even if it was only for a short time.

It's enough.

He'll always be enough.

I press my lips to his hair and feel a sob well up within me.

But I suppress it. I'll be strong for him.

Always for him.

LANDON

I SPEND the rest of the day trying to remember that missing piece, and come up empty each time. It's right there on the tip of my proverbial tongue and I can't quite get it to materialize.

I say goodbye to my family as they leave, and with a frustrated sigh, I limp to the bathroom. Finn tries to follow me, but I wave him off, feeling the start of a headache coming on and just feeling defeated.

I'm going to make Finn tell me when I get out of the shower. He's going to tell me everything. I can't stand this anymore.

But in the meantime, I'm just going to sit on this fucking shower chair and mope.

I stare down at my residual limb and rub at my thigh, smearing soap into my skin.

And then it happens.

One second I'm watching the soap cascade down me toward the drain and the next second the flood of last week infiltrates my mind. It happens so quickly that I nearly slide off the chair and onto the floor of the tub, busting my head open again.

"Finn!" I shout and he comes barging in, his chest heaving, his eyes wild and I just stare at him.

Remembering.

His lips, his hands, his cock. Everything about him.

How he's mine and I'm his. How we are *us*.

Everything.

God, what it must have been like for him. To have me and then to have it ripped away.

My body is choked with sobs as I reach for him. He stood by me even knowing I couldn't remember what we had.

"I remember," I cry.

He staggers, his hands trembling as he clasps onto the counter.

"You remember?" he asks, his voice cracking.

"I remember everything," I breathe, tears streaming down my cheeks. "It just took me a bit but of course I'll always remember you, Finn," I say, and then hold out my arms and he rushes to me, pulling me into him and, wrapping me in his arms, sinking to the floor.

"Why didn't you tell me? Why didn't you say something? Why did you make me wait?" I gasp, touching him, pressing my lips to his skin.

"I didn't want you to be with me because you thought you had to…"

"Jesus Christ, Finn. Always the martyr.... Of course I want to be with you. Something was off this whole time, and no one said a word!"

I'm getting angry and at the same time, I'm just so fucking relieved. Now I know what was missing.

Now, I know.

"I'm sorry. Forgive me," he gasps. "Forgive me, Landon."

"Of course, I forgive you," I reply and Finn just shudders against me, my neck growing wet from his tears.

"Tell me what you remember," he says.

"Kissing you, touching you, fucking you.... everything."

He lets out a choked sob. "Do you remember Carmel?"

I blink, letting those memories come to me slowly.

"Yes. You told me you're in love with me."

"I am. Fuck. I am. *I love you.* Don't ever scare me like that again...." His voice cracks. "Don't ever forget me. Don't ever leave me. I couldn't bear it."

"Never," I whisper and press my lips to his. "And I love you too. I'm so in love with you. I'll always come back to you. Always. Sometimes I'm just a little slow at catching on."

He groans, pulling me even closer, wetting his clothes. His tongue plunges into my mouth, licking every corner of me. Tasting me. Memorizing me.

"Fuck, I want you. I want you so bad. I didn't think I'd ever get to...when you forgot.... I thought that was it."

I moan, clinging to him. This. This is what I was missing. Him around me, inside of me, filling in my empty spaces.

"That never would have been it. I'd always come back to you. Now fuck me. Please."

He stands with me still in his arms and walks me to the bedroom where he lays me out and crawls up against me.

"We should wait...your concussion."

"I'm fine," I say and Finn just presses his forehead to mine.

"We can't...shit, I can't. We need to wait."

"But my dick is hard. It was frustrated I'd forgotten. Now that I've gotten with the program, my ass wants in on the action too."

He lets out a choked laugh. "Jesus."

Then I feel the drop of tears against my cheek.

"Finn," I say, leaning up and kissing them away. "Don't cry."

He holds himself over me and sniffles.

"I'll give you a blow job, but that's it."

"Fine, but only because I think my brain needs a little help remembering how good it was...actually, we should do that with all the positions, just refresh my memory."

Finn just stares down at me and then presses his lips to mine.

"I adore you."

"Show me, *show me*, Finn," I say.

He leans over, stuffs my dick down his throat, and makes me see stars.

thirty-one

4 WEEKS AGO - NEW YEAR'S EVE

FINN

THE AIR IS COLD, biting my skin and I shiver, pulling Landon closer. Always wanting him close. God, to be in love with him. To always love him and never, ever have a chance to be more.

I glance over at him and he's staring at his phone screen, the blue hue lighting up his handsome, gorgeous face. The face I've memorized for years. The one I could draw in the dark.

"So, who are we gonna kiss when the clock strikes twelve?" he asks and his question makes me freeze in place.

Because he can kiss me. *Me.* But I'd never say it. I'd never utter that ridiculous, hopeful word.

Me.

"Who says a kiss is mandatory?" I ask softly.

He rolls his eyes, even though I can't see it, but I know him so well. I know exactly what he's doing.

"It's not a new year if we don't kiss someone, and my dad says it's bad luck not to," he tells me and my heart flutters painfully in my chest. A thousand bee stings to my sternum.

God. The hope.

"We'll kiss," he says, pulling away slightly. "You and me. My family has enough bad luck without throwing this into the mix."

"I don't think that's a good idea," I manage to mutter. Even though it is. It's such a good idea. My lips on his is my dream. But I can't handle it. Can't handle having it, only for it to be ripped away.

He cocks his head and I trace the lines of him with my eyes.

"Why not? Does it gross you out, thinking of your lips on mine?"

I run my hand over my mouth, pressing into my lips, holding my words back, but it slips out. It can't be held back.

"No."

He sounds smug, always convincing me to do things when I know it's not a good idea. It's a superpower of his. God, to bend to his will. No matter how often I tell him no, I do it anyway.

"Then we'll do it," he replies, and then he's silent.

For a long-drawn-out minute I can feel the seconds tick by as if they're physical manifestations. They burn me.

"How many more minutes?" I blurt out, desperate to

know. The waiting is withering my soul. So close. So fucking close.

His phone clicks on and I can see it, the time slowly fading away. Almost.

Almost.

"Seconds," he says softly.

And then he's counting down, each number closer to one setting my entire body on fire.

So close.

Closer.

Yes.

And without warning, his lips are on mine, those soft fucking lips, pressing against my mouth.

And I ignite and melt all at the same time.

I memorize it. The taste, the smell, the feel of him against me.

Good *god*.

"That wasn't so bad, was it?" he mutters, his words whisps floating away on the cold breeze. Those lips that were just on mine.

"No," I say on a shaky exhale.

Not at all. It was *everything*.

He is everything. It's always been him. Landon. Mine. The man I've dreamt of, yearned and ached for.

Doesn't he see? I will never look at another. From the moment my eyes landed on him, it's been him.

Always him.

epilogue

FINN

JESUS, he really did it. Basil Lewis showed up in his Robin Hood costume ready to shoot some arrows at the archery range, and he managed to convince everyone else to do it too.

Not that I mind. Landon looks fucking hot dressed as an elf. I want to lift that robe up around his waist, bend him over and slide right inside of him.

He'd probably let me too. Horny fucker. It's been two weeks since the night his memories came back and a week since we got the okay from his doctor for normal activity. He's been completely insatiable ever since. Fuck, I'm glad he remembered. Remembered me. *Us.*

"It's cool, right?" Basil asks, bouncing on his feet. "We look like real-life archers."

Logan snorts, leaning into Theo.

"You look ridiculous, Dad," he says.

Basil rolls his eyes. "Yes, well, so do you, and you looked even more silly crying in the escape room earlier!"

Theo lets out a choked laugh but bites it back when Logan glowers at him. That glower doesn't last long though because it almost immediately turns into a grin.

"Gah, laugh away. You look way too hot dressed up like this. I can't stay mad when I just want to kiss you."

Theo disappears inside his hood and Logan rolls his eyes.

But my gaze turns to Landon who is pressed up against me, his warm eyes meeting mine in a clash of hazel and flecks of gold.

"You okay?" I ask and he nuzzles into me.

God, the feel of him against me is something dreams are made of. I can't believe this is real, can't believe he's mine.

"I'm just having a lot of fun. This is the best twenty-first birthday I could hope for. You did good, Finn."

He leans up, brushing his lips with mine and I cup the back of his head gently, sliding my tongue into his mouth and kissing him long and slow.

When our lips finally pull apart, everyone is looking everywhere but at us, and Landon chuckles, his forehead pressed against my shoulder.

"Alright. Let's get shooting. You know Dad can't wait any longer," he says, hugging me to him tightly.

Basil pretends to be insulted, but he bustles past us to the range, pulling his quiver off, ready to fill it with arrows.

I don't even know if that's allowed, but whatever. Basil does his own thing. Always has, always will.

"You gonna show me how it's done?" Landon asks, picking up a bow and eyeing me.

I move up behind him and press my front to his back, letting my lips slide against his ear.

"And what would you like me to show you?" I ask lowly.

He shudders, pressing his ass back against me and I bite back a groan. This is so inappropriate, but then again, what did I expect with Landon?

He's absolutely filthy and ravenous.

And I couldn't love it more.

"I'd like you to show me what a good boy I am," he says softly, blinking up at me and I press my face into his neck and tighten my grip around his waist.

Because I'll show him.

I'll fucking show him who owns him.

And later that night, when he's slightly buzzed from all the wine he drank, he falls onto our bed, his legs spread wide.

"Force me, Finn," he says and I groan. "Make me your bitch."

I don't even hesitate. I just strip him down and enter him slowly. There's no force needed. He's loose and ready.

God, the feel of him surrounding me, tight and warm, the way he clutches onto me, how he takes me.

I'm so glad I waited. I'm so glad I waited for him. That he was my first. My only.

When we come, we come together, and then I pull him into me, breathing him in and just falling more and more in love. With each minute, with each day that passes, I love him more.

"I'm going to put a wedding ring on your cock," he says and chuckles. "A nice gold one with diamonds."

His mouth, his ridiculous mouth. I have loved it since the minute he said my name.

"I'm going to marry your penis." He squirms against it, and I groan, my cock oversensitive and tired. But still, it twitches, ready for more. I will never, ever have enough of this man. My man.

"Fine, marry my dick, Landon," I mutter and then shut him up with my tongue.

1 YEAR LATER

LANDON

OH GOD, my lungs burn. But fuck, there it is, the finish line. I can see it in the distance.

"You've got this," Finn says jogging next to me, looking much too sexy for someone who just ran thirteen miles.

I glance over at my man and manage a small smile.

We trained for this, for eight whole months. Ever since I was fitted for my new running prosthetic—a running blade—I've been running with Finn. We started at once a day and then moved to twice per day, running along the river near our apartment. It's been an exhilarating adventure, this past year—moving in together, graduating college, getting our first jobs.

And here we are, running our first half-marathon.

Together.

"You're going to carry me over the finish line," I wheeze, and Finn bites down on his bottom lip.

He doesn't even look out of breath. Fucker.

It's a good thing I love him so much or else I'd be a little irritated at how much weaker than him I still am.

But I'm getting there. I'm getting stronger each time I hit the pavement. Getting used to moving fluidly with this prosthetic was something I had to master, and it took weeks, but I did it.

I did it.

And here we are.

About to finish this shit.

People pass us as we approach the finish line and I come to a stop and throw my arms out.

And Finn doesn't even hesitate. He just sweeps me up in those arms I'm so obsessed with and brings me over the finish line.

My parents, Logan, and Theo are there, with signs of course, each looking ridiculously proud. My dad is sniffling, and Logan is swiping at his eyes.

I didn't expect anything less to be honest. The only one still composed is Theo, and even he has a small smile on his face.

"We did it. You and me. We did it," Finn says, not setting me down, just holding me as people move past us. My gaze moves to him, just basking in how wonderful he is, and how lucky I am that we found each other in this chaotic world. How we held on despite it all.

I reach up and cup the back of his head, tugging his mouth down to mine.

"I love you."

He lets out a shuttered breath as if hearing those words wrecks him every time, and when our lips meet, he mutters,

"I loved you first."

acknowledgments

First, I would like to thank my editor, Angela O'Connell, for all of your hard work on this book. You all don't realize how much she does to make this readable. I can get a little ridiculous.

Also, thank you to my alpha readers Corinne Rochelle and Lark Taylor for taking time out of your busy schedules to read this and offer suggestions.

Margaret Neal thank you for beta reading this and picking out the lingering mistakes we all missed. You are amazing.

And last, but not least, thank you to all the readers who reached out to me with words of encouragement. They mean everything and keep me writing.

Cora Rose loves any kind of romance and consumes way too many books each year. She currently lives in the U.S. and spends her days daydreaming about the characters inside her head.

You can reach her on her website or email her at Cora-RoseRomance@gmail.com